◇◇◇◇◇◇◇◇◇◇◇◇◇◇◇◇◇◇◇◇◇◇◇◇◇◇◇◇◇◇◇◇

MURDER on the First Day Of Christmas

A Chloe Carstairs Mystery

By

Billie Thomas

◇◇◇◇◇◇◇◇◇◇◇◇◇◇◇◇◇◇◇◇◇◇◇◇◇◇◇◇◇◇◇◇

To my sweet, funny mom.

Cover Art by Angel Nichols
nicholsangel86@yahoo.com
http://www.freewebs.com/angelnichols/resume.htm

To the reader:

The story, *Murder on the First Day of Christmas,* is a work of fiction. Any resemblance to real people or events is completely accidental. A few literary liberties may have been taken when it comes to some geographic locations in the interest of creating great literature.

CHAPTER 1

"Chloe, Lady Chablis has taken the Baby Jesus again."
Mom's voice crackled on my cell phone. "Get the Vaseline."

The annoyance in Mom's tone didn't bode well for Lady
Chablis or for me, and even the Baby Jesus would have probably
done well to tread lightly. Four weeks before Christmas, I did
not want to be the one causing chaos in Amanda Carstairs'
perfectly ordered world.

"Has the Baby Jesus been located?" I said into the phone as I
pulled my Austen Healy under the portico of Saul Taylor's
Birmingham mini-mansion, at which my mother and I were
supposed to spend the day decorating for Christmas. With only a
glance at my lipstick in the rearview mirror, I grabbed the
Vaseline jar from my tool kit and headed, not up Saul's front
steps, but across the street to the scene of the crime. We had
decorated Tom Madison's house the week before, complete with
a nativity scene on the front lawn.

"Still MIA, I'm afraid, and Lady Chablis's not talking." Mom
said.

No surprise there. Like most chocolate labs, Lady Chablis
wasn't known for his witty discourse. I couldn't fault him for his
sense of theater, though. Starting life as Lady Marmalade, the
discovery of an un-dropped testicle had resulted in one of the
few documented cases of canine sexual reassignment and his
name change to Lady Chablis, as in the drag queen from
Midnight in the Garden of Good and Evil.

Trust me, the name suited. His latest transgression? Faced
with all the statues in the life-sized nativity on the Madison's
front lawn, the ditsy dog invariably chose the Baby Jesus to
clamp his teeth into and go streaking though the neighborhood,
as if he knew that this would cause the biggest uproar.

Mom took this affront personally. She had commissioned the gorgeous hand-carved, hand-painted nativity scene for LC's owners, the Madisons, and considered every member of the fifteen-piece ensemble, from the kneeling shepherds to the solemn-eyed camel, to be a valuable work of art. A slightly chomped Baby Jesus or, even worse, a crèche with no Baby Jesus at all would seriously undermine said value. It would also compromise Mom's standing as one of the premier interior designers in Birmingham, maybe even her place in heaven.

But not if she had anything to say about it.

"For heaven's sakes, Chloe. What took you so long?" Mom abandoned her search of the Madisons' flowerbed as I walked up.

"I'm not that late." I clipped my phone to the waistband of my skirt. "Chill."

I'm not sure at what age a daughter stops being cowed by that scary Mom look, let's just say it isn't thirty. Apparently, when constant crises at one home you've decorated prevent you from finishing up at another home - this just three days before the first holiday party of the season - it's physically impossible to "chill" and physically risky to tell someone to do so. (I was still pretty new to the decorating game, and not yet hip to all the trade secrets.)

I did know enough, though, not to point out that my slim DKNY optic print skirt and sleeveless black turtleneck were hardly appropriate for a search and recovery mission. Mom would spare even less sympathy for my favorite strappy black wedges, shoes she said made me limp around like a flamingo with bricks strapped to its feet.

"Gold, frankincense, myrrh and Vaseline," Mom sighed. "Not exactly the greatest story ever told."

We fanned out, each keeping our eyes open for a glimpse of swaddling clothes under bushes, behind garages or on front porches. There were just six mini-mansions, the smallest seven-thousand-square feet, in Arbor Farms and Lady Chablis had complete access to all of them. He had taken the Baby Jesus before and seemed to favor dark, moist hiding places. The statue was only slightly worse for wear for being relegated to chew-toy status by the world's dumbest dog, but it was time to break the cycle of abuse, hence the Vaseline.

A skim coat, when mixed with cayenne pepper, is a sure-fire way to keep teeth marks off everything from Chippendale chair legs to Kate Spade sling backs. We had hoped we wouldn't have to subject the Baby Jesus to such undignified treatment, but Lady Chablis left us no choice. I, for one, did not envy the poor dog his fate, having years ago confused the Vaseline-and–cayenne concoction Mom meant for her miniature Schnauzer, Josie, with a cranberry glaze meant for the ham she had thawing in the sink. Torture. But just as I had learned to look before I licked, so too would Lady Chablis have to mend his cradle robbing ways.

After twenty minutes of fruitless searching, Mom and I met back in front of the Madisons', where Lady Chablis watched us from the front porch. I swear he was grinning at the sight of my limp curls and sweat mustache. November in Birmingham, and you're still only as good as your deodorant. True, this was an unseasonably warm year, but as usual, the only white we saw in Alabama at Christmas were streaks of un-rubbed-in sunscreen or someone gutsy enough to wear an ivory skirt suit this side of Labor Day.

"I'm going to kill that dog," Mom said. "And Tom Madison, too, for not having an invisible fence." She looked down at my feet. "What's that on your shoe?"

I rolled my eyes. "Wedge heels. They're very popular this season."

"Not that." She gestured. "That."

I looked down. "I'm going to kill that dog."

I limped over to the Madisons' curb for some serious scraping.

"Maybe if we just…" Mom broke off.

I followed her gaze to the Madisons' front porch. Lady Chablis was on the move, headed over to Saul Taylor's house, where we were supposed to be finishing up the Twelve Days of Christmas theme he had requested.

Christmas houses were the only projects that could lure Mom out of retirement, since she had closed the doors of Amanda C. Interiors two years before. Her clients spent $30,000 and up— way up—on their holiday décor, and Saul Taylor's house was one of her most lavish projects. I knew she was anxious to get back to it with my help, of course, and apprenticing under her was the perfect way to launch my own budding decorating career.

"We're not following you," I sang to LC, although we were.

Not that he was paying us any attention. He was on a mission, trotting across Saul's yard without a backward glance. Whining in the back of his throat, he let out a little yip.

Guilty conscience? I hoped so. Taking out the Baby Jesus and a pair of $200 shoes (after double markdowns) did not reflect well on his character.

The temperature dropped about twenty degrees as Mom and I rounded the back of Saul's house. The canopy of trees and wind off the man-made lake beyond them hinted at a winter we were weeks away from actually getting.

"What's wrong with him?" I whispered, because something was clearly amiss. The dog was whining and sniffing the air, his attention focused on something near the back door of Saul's house.

"We do not have time for this," Mom grumbled.

LC barked, and we both jumped. His anxiety was contagious. We couldn't see what was making him so edgy, but it was clear he was totally fixated on whatever he was looking at - moving first forward, then back, hackles raised.

"What is it, boy?" I said, my tone soothing. "What is it?"

Mom pulled me a little behind her, keeping her hand on my arm as we edged forward. Lady Chablis let out another bark, then another. Finally he was barking, full out - loud snarling barks, completely out of character for him. We were about three feet in front of the door before we fully understood why.

"Oh, Jesus God," Mom said. "Oh, my good Lord. Is that a...?"

It was.

On the stoop under Saul's back door was a hand. A man's hand, by the size of it, completely unattached to anything else and nestled into the "O" of the red-and-green Noel doormat.

Someone sounding a lot like me let out a scream, which made Lady Chablis bark louder. Mom was squeezing my arm painfully, but I didn't mind a bit. It was good to have an arm.

Two of them in fact, both with firmly attached perfectly working hands.

But, except for the Vaseline jar, my hands were empty. The hand on the stoop was not. Its stiff, fat fingers curled around an equally stiff, even fatter, very dead rat.

"Police." Mom's voice shook as she stumbled backward. "We need the police."

"Whose is it? How did it get there?" I looked around, but didn't see anything else out of place. No other body parts, no hand-less man shambling toward us, waving his bloody stump. There was only a dense, dark line of trees.

Mom started hustling me towards the side of the house. Lady Chablis barked on and on.

"God bless it! I'm going to kill that damn dog!" Saul Taylor tore open the back door. "I'm trying to work in here." He looked down. "Holy shit."

"We were just about to call the police," Mom assured him.

"Where in hell did that come from?" Saul looked to make sure all our appendages were present and accounted for.

"We just found it," I explained. "It was there when we got here."

"Get back, Lady! Get!" Saul shouted.

For the second time, Mom and I jumped, but Saul was talking to LC, who was still going crazy. The dog whimpered and slunk back down the driveway. The silence was creepy.

Saul hitched his pants and knelt down. He wasn't much taller than my five-foot-three-inches and had a body like a toothpaste tube, all his weight squeezed from the bottom to a bulging middle - not a figure that looks good in a squat.

He peered closely at the hand.

"Don't touch it!" I said, far more interested in keeping down this morning's cranberry muffin than in preserving evidence.

"That's my ring," Saul said. "The bastard's wearing my ring."

"What?" Mom craned in his direction, but didn't seem any more interested in going over there than I was. Cowardice is an inherited trait.

"Right there. My ruby pinkie ring."

My mother and I exchanged queasy looks. Men's pinkie rings have that effect on us.

"Look, we've got to call the police," Mom said. "We'll meet you around front."

Saul stood up and yelled toward the trees. "It's not going to work, you know. If you're trying to scare me, it's not going to work."

Well, it had worked on us.

Mom and I scurried around to the front of the house, where we encountered our second dismemberment of the day. Only Lady Chablis' version involved a very muddy, very valuable Baby Jesus.

CHAPTER 2

"I'm going to kill Saul!"

Both Mom and I took a step backwards. Given yesterday's ordeal with the hand, it was only natural for us to be on edge back at Saul's house, but Angela Jannings, Saul's research assistant, could give even the Dalai Lama a nervous twitch. If she wasn't sneaking right up on you - like she just had, she was saying creepy, off-the-wall things - like she just did.

Yesterday had been a nightmare - wailing sirens, endless questions and flashbulbs going off in every direction. Not exactly conducive to good decorating.

Our plan had been to install nine pipers piping in Saul's study, maybe even get started on the drummers drumming in the keeping room. Instead, we had told our story to the police again and again: Baby Jesus, Noel doormat, and pinkie ring. Constant repetition, even in real time, made the scene no less surreal.

When the police had finished with us, we had decorated the tree in the living room. Saul had thought it would make a nice backdrop for his interviews on today's network morning shows.

I suppose I should mention that Saul's a local celebrity - a true crime writer with fifteen titles to his name, the last of which had a quote on the cover from a nationally bestselling author, "A suspenseful read. Taylor knows his stuff!"

For some people, myself included, finding a severed hand at your back door would be an indescribable horror. Saul considered it an occupational hazard.

"A man like me makes enemies," he had told the interview show's producer during set up. "Hell, I'd wear a Kevlar vest to court if they would let me through the metal detector."

Not that we were any better. One thing Mom's drilled into me about decorating: you have to develop a narrow focus to get the job done. Post-traumatic stress has to wait.

Right now we were more concerned with what these delays had done to our schedule. Mom had been on the phone non-stop since yesterday replacing the Baby Jesus (at this point, it would have been easier to hire a live stand-in), while I hung ornaments and tied bows. Today, we were in catch-up mode, starting with the pipers in the study.

"Angela," Mom addressed the research assistant and simultaneously patted her own chest to make sure her heart was still beating without even pausing as she cleared off Saul's desk. After all, the clock was still ticking.

"What? He's driving me crazy." As usual, I was amazed to hear the petulant teenager tone Angela used with my mother. It was an uncharacteristic show of vulnerability that only my mother, it seemed, could elicit.

"Better not let the police hear you say that." I continued unpacking supplies from our plastic bins. "They're itching to hook someone up to a lie detector."

"He's so stupid." Angela ignored me completely, a trick she had perfected in high school. "He's turning this whole thing into a circus."

"You can't be surprised." Mom passed me some ribbon to tie around sconces that flanked the exterior French doors. She looked meaningfully at the stepladder. I should have known.

"Nothing surprises me anymore." Angela raked her fingers through red hair that would benefit from a leave-in conditioner. "Especially where Saul's concerned."

"The pipers are here." Cassie Winthrop slipped past Angela into the study.

Immediately the mood of the room lightened. Cassie worked as an assistant for Flower Fantasy, Mom's favorite vendor, and was here this morning to position flowers and greenery in the study and dining room. A total godsend, this girl, willing to work late into the night or show up at sunrise whenever Mom needed her. Right now, we needed her desperately.

Angela's piercing eyes raked over Cassie, dismissing her as superficial and insignificant or, worse yet, cute. Angela's version of natural selection rivaled that of the Serengeti, and Cassie's shining blue eyes and excited smile couldn't make the cut.

"Your bow's crooked," Angela said to me and stomped off. Mom sighed. "That child."

Cassie made a face and turned to me. "I know she's your friend and all, but she creeps me out."

"I never said she was my friend." I twisted my bow an inch to the right.

"Chloe," Mom said. "She is, too. Y'all used to be good friends."

"In eighth grade, when we had adjoining easels at art camp, but that was about it." I climbed off the stepladder.

"I thought y'all went to high school together." Cassie got on the stepladder and pushed the bow a quarter inch to the left.

"Yeah, but we barely spoke to each other. She was always reading books like *The Bell Jar* or trying to uncover malfeasance among the lunchroom ladies for the school newspaper. So dreary."

"Angela's mother died when she was in high school," Mom told Cassie.

Ok, there was that. And since Mom and Mrs. Jannings had been good friends, I didn't point out that Angela had been little miss gloom and doom long before then. My mother worked with guilt the way she worked with Venetian plaster, subtly and with a sure hand.

Even Cassie recognized that it was time to change the subject. "These guys are hot!" She snuggled up to one of the pipers, her blond head on his shoulder. "Do we make a cute couple?"

"Careful," I warned. "Mom'll set me up with one."

Cassie lifted her new friend's smock to check out his impressive backside. "You could do worse." She arched a brow.

"And has." Mom smacked Cassie's hand away from the front of the smock before she could check out the poor guy's other attributes.

The pipers were incredibly lifelike with molded rubber faces, sharp brown eyes and real hair beneath their black caps, but they were, alas, not anatomically correct. Definitely not son-in-law material. Mom wanted grandchildren, and so far, only my sister had obliged.

"So the cops don't have any clues about yesterday?" Cassie began unpacking her own supplies.

"Nothing. Dad said the medical examiner thinks the hand was removed postmortem and not that long ago," I said. The rat was fresh, too." My father is a lawyer, semi-retired, so he had filled us in on the gossip downtown. The rest we had gotten from a local newscast.

Cassie shuddered. "Gross. Though I've never seen Mr. Taylor so happy."

She was right about that one. During previous interviews, Saul had crowed about how dangerous his work was, how it took him to dangerous places, and how it attracted the attention of dangerous people. Then he had promised his next book would be his most explosive one yet, he said that about each one, and lurid threats wouldn't stop him from writing it.

The man, the myth, the legend - even more importantly, the client. Despite the uproar, Saul was determined to go ahead with his holiday party this Saturday, just two days away, and we were determined to have everything ready in time.

To the trained eye, things were shaping up beautifully. Where others saw chaos - lights yet to be strung, ribbons to be tied, pine needles everywhere - I glimpsed an installation that was progressing nicely. While a severed hand was certainly the most gruesome of our delays, it wasn't the most challenging. That came courtesy of Robin Woodall, Saul's girlfriend, who was "supervising" the installation.

Thanks to her, the Twelve Days of Christmas theme was easier said than done. Turns out there is no hard and fast rule about whether it's nine ladies dancing or nine pipers piping, whether the drummers drumming number ten or twelve, or whether you'll get to see ten or twelve lords-a-leaping. In fact, once you get past eight maids-a-milking there are as many versions to the Twelve Days of Christmas as there are ladies dancing. Which is to say, nine or eleven, depending on whom you ask.

We were going by the version depicted on the hand-painted china plates Mom had painstakingly collected over the last years, scrounging up five full sets from antique dealers, eBay and other sources she wouldn't reveal. This version, with nine ladies dancing, ten lords-a-leaping, eleven pipers piping and twelve drummers drumming, was by far the most common and widely accepted.

Robin, though, insisted we use the version of the song she had known all her life: nine pipers, ten drummers, eleven ladies and twelve lords. We could still use the plates, she had assured us sweetly, not realizing how this inconsistency tortured Mom, but for the room installations, she preferred that we did it "the right way."

We, of course, had agreed.

"Client appeasement," Mom had pointed out, "no matter how capricious their whims or silly their concerns, is always job one."

We had scrambled to readjust our cast of characters. The two extra pipers, both a head taller than I and decked out in velvet smocks, tights and boots, were stashed in Saul's garage. The two extra drummers were repainted, stripped of their uniforms, put into tights and leotards and made to perform painful scissor-kicks without so much as a stretch to warm-up. Two additional dancing ladies had been ordered.

Confusing enough? If Robin didn't stay out of the way so we could deck the halls, Mom would deck her.

"Did you find a replacement for the Baby Jesus?" Cassie asked.

I nodded. "Compared to the other pieces, he's a little big, because he's not really a newborn, but you would have to know what you were looking for to realize it." I didn't mention that his luminous sheen came from a thin glaze of Vaseline, rather than innate divinity.

"You never told us how your blind date went this past weekend," Cassie said. "What was the guy's name? Trevor?"

Mom had taken me at my word a couple of months ago when I halfheartedly mentioned getting back into the dating game, and she had wasted no time setting me up with sons of some of her friends. Big mistake.

"Well, let's see." I recounted. "Trev was not as bad as Simon, who showed up for our date wearing pants so snug I could guess his religion, but not as promising as David who, despite being so short he probably had to stand on a box to reach a conclusion, at least made me laugh." With David, I was all set to be won over by someone I didn't necessarily find physically attractive, but alas, the creep never called back. Ted was OK, but his upper lip didn't move when he talked and, after David, my standards were again high and my priorities shallow.

"So this Trevor won't be fathering my grandchildren, is that what you're saying?" Mom gestured for me to move Saul's mahogany partner's desk forward about six inches, so the pipers could stand in two rows between the desk and the doors.

"I wouldn't count on it." I accepted slack from the computer and phone cords as Cassie fed it to us. "He became a veterinarian because he prefers animals to people - actually came right out and said that. By the end of the salad course, the feeling was mutual."

"Darling," Mom paused in her work and addressed me. "I've always said a woman shouldn't compromise her standards when it comes to choosing her men, but really, you have to give people a chance."

"Tell that to Trevor. Besides, he's a mouth breather." I didn't elaborate on how this trait was made particularly endearing by a meal that included garlic toast and ranch dressing.

Again annoyed by my lack of compassion for the socially challenged, Mom changed the subject, thanking Cassie for the arrangement she had sent to Judge Bernard Stone's funeral for us.

"White lilies, white roses and green santini," Cassie said. "Works every time. I would've done a poinsettia, we had just gotten some beautiful white ones, but he got two of those while he was in the hospital."

"Judge Stone - the big death penalty guy?" I asked, recalling the judge was known for telling his law school classes that Yellow Mama, Alabama's electric chair, was 'the best seat in the house.'

"That's the one," Mom confirmed.

"He also had something of a nurse fetish," I added, "if his reaction to Bridget at Dad's 50th birthday party was any indication."

"I'm sure your sister can take care of herself," Mom pointed out. "Your father didn't exactly share the judge's politics, but he's going to miss old Bernard, cantankerous devil that he was. Speaking of white poinsettias, Cassie, I need two dozen for

Monica Dupree's house. That's two dozen in addition to the two dozen I've already ordered." Mom grimaced, afraid she was asking too much of Flower Fantasy's already overtaxed stock, as we were installing Christmas décor for four families in Arbor Farms: Saul Taylor, the Browleys, the Madisons and Monica Dupree. That's a lot of poinsettias.

"I already put extras aside for you," Cassie assured Mom. "Margie always says to give you first refusal."

"Ms. Dupree does keep it simple, doesn't she," I commented dryly.

"Deceptively so," Mom said, thinking, I was sure, how outrageously expensive Monica's dramatic all-white décor really was. What she spent on Swarovski crystals alone was astounding.

Some may find such extravagance at Christmas sinful, silly or the worst kind of self-indulgence, and, well, I wouldn't argue the point. I would, though, point out that Mom's clients pay for the pleasures life affords them, and she, in turn, gladly shares their wealth with her vendors, artists and craftsmen who count on such crass commercialization to see them through the off-season. Saul Taylor's seven swans-a-swimming punch bowl alone would put the son of our ice sculptor through a semester at Samford - books and lab fees included.

"I wonder what conditioner these guys use?" Cassie still pretended to swoon over the pipers as she attached holly boutonnieres to their smocks. "Something with chamomile, I'm thinking. Brings out their highlights."

"I like their boots. Would you say a size seven?" I measured one against my own shoe.

"A pathetic attempt to get your own hideous shoes noticed." Mom eyed my platform sandals, then turned to Cassie. "Chloe wants me to comment on them, so she can act like the long-suffering hipster oppressed by her oh-so-square mother. But really, dear, if you want to hobble around in those shoes, far be it from me to comment."

"Girls! This place looks amazing!" Robin Woodall stood in the doorway, looking about sixteen in her tennis whites and high ponytail.

Saul's girlfriend was in her mid-thirties, but weekly spa appointments, private Pilates lessons and tennis every other day kept her looking showroom new. Her appeal to fifty-something Saul Taylor was obvious: long legs, brilliant blue eyes and the dewy innocence that men slay dragons to protect.

More mystifying was what she saw in Saul who was loud, sly, bald and so out of shape he got winded jogging his memory. Money wasn't a factor. She had plenty of her own, and he refused to let her anywhere near his.

The two had met while Saul was researching a book on black widows, women who kill their mates for their money. Woodall was twice widowed herself, losing one husband to an allergic reaction and the other to insulin shock, both deaths long on speculation and innuendo, short on evidence to even indict Robin, much less convict her. After a few martinis, Saul often joked that they would never marry, because Robin might think he was worth more to her dead than alive. That kind of talk made for a stormy relationship.

Mom thanked Robin for her compliment. "It's really starting to take shape, isn't it?"

"All the loose greenery everywhere will be cleaned up, right?" Robin took her role as supervisor seriously.

"Of course," Mom assured her. "Most of it will be done today. We've got two more rooms tomorrow, and then finishing touches on Friday."

"And you'll be back on Saturday to help the caterer set up."

"Eloise." Mom smiled. "Yes, she's excellent. We've worked together often."

"And outside? You think we have enough lights?"

"More than enough."

Mom's outside guys, Carlos and Juan, had spent three days on ladders and the roof draping the three-story house in white lights. Saul's electricity meter would be whirling like a propeller.

"I know Saul wants a lot of lights to make a statement from the road."

"He'll make a statement from the moon," Mom promised.

"And the lights are on timers?"

Mom threw Robin a bone. "Naturally. Six o'clock on the dot."

"Six? You don't think five-thirty would be better? It starts getting dark around five-thirty."

"So it does. I'll take care of it." Mom matched Robin's satisfied smile with one of her own that said rookie.

Robin gave a nod - her work here was done. "Good. Well, I'll leave you to it then. Great job, Amanda. Really great. Have fun, you guys." And she was gone.

"Lovely girl," Mom said as the front door closed. "Just lovely."

Cassie and I exchanged looks. Mom's Southern good manners weren't fooling us for a second.

Over the next couple of hours, we finished the study and moved on to the dining room, where we threaded a red pepper berry garland into the Baccarat crystal chandelier.

We had just stepped away from the window to see if three small pepper-berry kissing balls looked better than one large one, when Saul's phone rang and the answering machine picked up. Since the large foyer was all that separated the dining room from the study, we could easily identify the caller - Bunny Beaumont.

What can one say about Bunny Beaumont that hasn't already been scrawled onto the bathroom walls of some of Birmingham's finest restaurants? You know the type. Skin always a little too tan, teeth a little too white, laugh a little too loud and bras just a little too ambitious, lifting and separating till her breasts looked like two semaphores positioned to say "Howdy, Sailor."

The effect wasn't cheap, necessarily, though it could have been and probably should have been. A lot of money had been spent to obliterate Bunny's backwater upbringing, and handlers on Louisiana's local pageant circuit had taught her to get the most bang out of every buck.

It was a near perfect façade. Her tendency to wear sequins in broad daylight and skinny dip with her friends' husbands at the country club Christmas party? Well, honey, that was just stuff that seeped occasionally around the edges.

On the Arts Council, Mom was president, and Bunny was vice president. In the Garden Club, it was vice versa. Despite these common interests, they weren't exactly what you would call friends.

"Saul, sweetie," Bunny said to his machine, using her slopping-sugar voice. "Where have you gotten off to? Gavin and I just this minute got back into town and were delighted to get your invitation. I wanted to let you know we'd love to come to your party, wouldn't miss it for the world. Word on the street is you've had Amanda there for weeks doing up the place. I always get such a kick out of her cute little designs."

Cassie and I checked Mom's reaction, but she didn't seem fazed. Guess it wasn't Bunny's best work.

Mom signaled for me to hold up the smaller kissing balls as Bunny continued.

"You tell that Robin I plan on cornering her Saturday night about joining the Arts Council and Garden Club."

Mom motioned me out of the way and sent Cassie in with the big ball.

"Amanda probably hasn't mentioned it," Bunny blathered on, "but I think we're desperate for some new blood, new blue blood anyway, and I think Robin would be a terrific addition. It'd be great to bring some more youth to the Council. I get lonely hanging out with those old gals."

Mom cut her eyes at me. Forty-eight-and-a-half is what Bunny told people. Forty-nine-and-seven-sixths would be more accurate.

"I mean seriously, sugar, some of those girls on the Council aren't so much 'art' as they are 'artifact,' if you know what I mean."

"Says the woman who puts the 'hor' in 'horticulture,'" Mom murmured, again eyeing the smaller kissing balls.

Cassie and I laughed, and I knew that if Bunny had heard Mom she would have laughed, too. Bunny accepted catty remarks and scandalized double-takes as her due. We were meant to be jealous, shocked, outraged and intimidated - anything less would've been a waste of good collagen.

"Well, gotta run, hon. Saturday night. We'll be there with silver bells on." She gave her fake tinkling little laugh, classic Bunny, and rang off.

"Lovely woman." Mom smiled. "Just lovely."

"I bet she knew you might hear," I fumed.

"Bunny performs for the audience whether she has one or not," Mom said absently. "I'm thinking two and one. One big kissing ball flanked by two smaller ones."

"Oh, Amanda, I do love your cute little designs," I gushed - a perfect imitation of Bunny.

Mom rolled her eyes - a perfect imitation of me.

We spent some time tidying up and readying the house for tomorrow's last big push. The outside lights snapped on as they always had at five-thirty p.m. on the dot, and we pulled away in the '56 Austin Healey that Dad had restored as a thirtieth birthday present for me.

I was exhausted, but in a good way. The day had been a productive one, and when you're decorating other people's houses during the holidays, that's the most you can ask for.

Mom looked tired, too. Leaning her head back onto the black leather seat, she closed her eyes. "Now Chloe. About those shoes."

CHAPTER 3

"Well, well. You certainly went all out," my mother greeted me, giving my ivory Nanette Lepore skirt suit the once over.

"I'm a single woman these days. Thought I'd look the part." I accepted champagne from a passing waiter.

Saul's party was in full swing, and despite my dateless status, I was determined to eat, drink and make merry if it killed me.

"Where did you get the outfit?"

"Saks. You like?" I stepped back to give her the full effect.

"Gorgeous. And the accessories?" Mom nodded to my chest, which was making quite a showing beneath the deep V-neckline.

I feigned shock. "Are you implying I look enhanced?" Everyone knows I'm slightly obsessed with breasts in general and my lack thereof specifically. When your nicknamed Niblet in high school, you tend to develop an unnatural preoccupation with these things.

"I'm just saying it takes a village to raise that kind of cleavage."

"Speaking of villages, looks like this one's lost its idiot." I gestured across Saul's crowded living room to where Trevor, the veterinarian from my last disastrous blind date, was chatting up Kendra Daniels. One look at Kendra's glowing face, which resembled that of a slightly bewildered Pekingese, and I knew I'd be purchasing a gravy boat for the happy couple within six months.

"Daniels rhymes with spaniels." Mom sighed and toasted my champagne flute with hers. "You never stood a chance."

I consoled myself by taking in the beauty of Mom's handiwork.

The foyer, where a black velvet partridge nestled in the scarlet and purple leaves of a silk Bradford pear tree, was a stunning introduction to the theme. Two blown glass turtledoves cuddled in a nest of sticks and straw that draped the foyer table, while three French hens peeked from the greenery that adorned the stair rails.

In the great room beyond the stairs, four calling birds, a.k.a starlings, lined the mantle, over which hung five giant gilded wreaths. Six silk geese made their nests on the hearth, and for the bar, seven ice swans swam in a giant ice bowl of champagne punch.

Our eight Waterford crystal maids-a-milking sparkled by candlelight on Saul's exquisite Biedermeier pedestal table in the dining room. The pipers stood guard in the study. Drummers drummed, ladies danced and lords leapt in the keeping room, kitchen and sun porch, respectively.

"Mrs. Carstairs, you outdid yourself on this one." Cassie had beamed that afternoon after doing her final walk-through before Margie Vaughn, owner of Flower Fantasy, had come to approve her work.

"I couldn't have done it without you girls," Mom had said fervently. "Or you either, Marco. Stunning. Some of your best work ever."

Marco Bruno, the brawny ice sculptor, and his son had just dropped off the seven swans punch bowl, a true work of art. (As was the equally brawny Marco Jr., I might add.)

Now, just six hours later, I found myself wishing Cassie, Marco and the others could be there to see how enthusiastically people were responding to their hard work. Ol' Scrooge himself couldn't have resisted getting his holiday groove on in this place.

In the basement game room, a Dixieland Jazz band scorched through every up-tempo Christmas carol they could think of, while braver guests burned up the dance floor. Music and laughter drifted upstairs where people were swooning over Eloise's lobster puffs and wasabi-dressed asparagus, while making plans they had no intention of keeping for the upcoming year.

Since those plans would include fitness related-resolutions and I was working part-time as a personal trainer, I expected my bookings to pick up at the same rate the tiny Gruyere quiches were disappearing.

God, I love Christmas!

"Twelve days was my idea," Saul crowed as he accepted a drink from his neighbor, Oscar Browley, and the two of them moved toward us. "Amanda just wanted to do twinkle lights and ribbon, but I said, 'No, this year I'm going all out.'"

What Saul lacked in height he made up for in volume, with a voice that made you wince when it boomed. "Amanda! Did I call it, or did I call it?"

"You called it." Mom glued on a smile.

Robin, looking starlet-sexy in a black sequined Ungaro gown, chimed in. "Actually, if I remember correctly, I'm the one who came up with the theme. You wanted Christmas Nightmares like that movie."

"I still think that would've worked." Saul shook his head. "You people just don't have my vision."

"I would've liked to have seen you pull that one off, Amanda." Oscar gave my mother an enthusiastic one-armed hug, almost spilling her champagne. She looked around for Dad to rescue her, but he was off foraging for lobster puffs.

"If anyone could, it would be Amanda," Saul shouted, raising his glass. "To Amanda, a beautiful, talented decorator, and to Robin, my lovely idea girl. You always know just how to keep me in check, doncha baby." He pulled the latter down, so he could give her a somewhat sloppy kiss on the cheek as we toasted.

"Why haven't I made an honest woman of you, sweetheart?" he then asked in mock seriousness. "Oh, yeah. I want to live a long life!"

Robin's face fell, but she quickly recovered and swatted at Saul with an "oh, you" wave of her hand.

I checked to see if she was saving up her outrage to lash out in private later, but she seemed more hurt than angry to me. The rest of us shifted a little uncomfortably, pretending Saul was more drunk than he was and, therefore, should be ignored.

The only person who seemed unperturbed was Saul's assistant, Angela. I couldn't tell whether my old classmate was just inured to Saul's blustering, didn't like Robin, or was merely lost in her own thoughts. Whatever it was, I could tell that her lipstick would have matched my dress perfectly and made a note to ask her what its name was before the end of the party.

"How 'bout those interviews, huh?" Saul basked in his amped-up celebrity status, aware that people had been discussing the severed hand all evening, unable to drop the subject their host was only too happy to bring right back up for them. "Does the camera love me or what?"

"I can't believe they still don't know where that thing came from," Robin interjected. "I mean fingerprints, DNA, something."

"No fingerprints on record." Saul shrugged. "I think the message was pretty clear, though."

"Has anyone talked to Ellie Stone?" Nancy Browley, Oscar's short, plump wife, eagerly changed the subject. "I meant to call her today."

Mom seemed only too happy to leave the subject of the hand, even if it meant bringing up Judge Stone's widow. "I went by to see her yesterday. The kids are still in town, so her family's around her."

"So sad," Nancy said. "He was just in for a pacemaker - a routine procedure."

"He got off easy if you ask me, dying in his sleep like that," Oscar commented. "The man thought the four food groups were fried, smothered, buttered and Alfredo. We should all be so lucky."

"Did I tell you people they got what's-his-name for the movie version of *Slave For Love*. Not bad, huh?" Saul repeated a general announcement he had made earlier, having mentioned it twice already to us during the decorating of his house.

"That's the Bonnie and Clyde one, right?" I figured what the hell. Throw the guy a bone. "About that couple in Georgia?"

"Yes, yes. One of my favorites. You know they never found that girl's head. Most likely, some hunting dog will dig it up one day."

Mom caught my eye. We knew just the dog for the job.

"So, is this a feature film? Independent? What?" Nancy couldn't have sounded less interested. To hear Saul tell it, crime in the Southeast was only committed to provide his books with plot points and story lines. Some people got into it. Others didn't.

"Made for television."

"Oh." Nancy's well-timed sip of wine didn't quite hide the upward turn of her lips.

"When is someone going to option your bestseller about the black widows, that's what I want to know," Oscar said. "That one was my favorite. Robin, you're so pretty, I bet they would ask you to play yourself in it."

Robin didn't flinch. "There are far better actresses out there than I."

Thick skin and good grammar. This girl was clearly no pushover.

Nancy again felt the need for a subject change. "Amanda's doing our house next. I'm not going to tell you what she's planning, so don't ask. Just prepare to be dazzled."

"Hate to break it to you, Nance, but after tonight's little shindig, this town's going to be partied out." Saul beamed, knowing this was the second year in a row he had planned his holiday party right before the Browleys' and it drove Nancy crazy.

She hid her annoyance with a litany of tiny gestures, running a soft white hand over her complicated blonde updo to check for stray hairs (none), touching the diamond pendant at her throat (straight) and flashing Saul a tight little smile (cold).

Saul remained oblivious. "You doing your Santa Claus bit?" he asked Oscar.

"You know it."

A former prosecutor, now living it up in private practice, Oscar put his excess weight and love of pipe tobacco to good use by crashing his yearly party as Santa Claus, handing out trinkets to guests he thought had been good and wicked little "lumps of coal" to those who had been naughty. All in good fun, of course, but then, old habits die hard.

There was a bit of a commotion in the entry hall, causing a subtle change in the party's happy tenor. A tall, powerfully built man, who I guessed was in his mid-fifties, drew our attention. Even from across the room, I could tell that his eyes were a rich topaz color that contrasted nicely with his dark skin and hair.

Oscar Browley glared at Saul, who responded with a poor imitation of a "What? What'd I do?" look. Oscar wasn't buying

Saul's act and abruptly moved off into the crowd, headed for the game room. Nancy, in placatory mode, followed.

Without a word to us, Saul went to greet his new guest, and Robin followed him.

"Typical." Angela's eyes were hard and shrewd as she took in the scene at the door, then turned and headed toward the kitchen.

"Was it something we said?" I asked Mom, the rest of our little circle having deserted us.

"Wait till your Dad sees who just walked in." Mom's voice was grim.

"You know that guy?"

Before she could answer, though, in walked Bunny Beaumont, barely dressed in silver lamé and fox fur. Since the crowd's attention was already focused on the door, Bunny got her grand entrance, oblivious to the man who had entered before her.

"We can start this party now!" She threw her silver fur to squat, creepy little Gavin Beaumont, her husband-slash-gynecologist (I kid you not), who had entered after her. The videographer, who had been circling the party all night, made a great show of capturing the whole thing on tape, much to Bunny's delight.

"Let's find Alex," Mom said.

Turns out Dad had been looking for us, too. We met in the butler's pantry between the kitchen and the dining room.

"Guess who…"

"Did you see who…"

"Would somebody tell me who… Now, please." I demanded.

Mom and Dad could communicate without completing their sentences, but my question still hadn't been answered.

"Tony Trianos," Mom whispered.

Ah…

CHAPTER 4

The grainy pictures on the front of the Birmingham News hadn't done the man justice. Tony Trianos was the closest thing our town had to a gangster, just a man trying to run a legitimate business while staying ahead of all those pesky racketeering charges the DA kept trying to pin on him.

No wonder Oscar Browley, the former prosecutor, had been peeved. He had made Trianos a pet project, but could never make anything stick.

As a true-crime writer, Saul prided himself on having friends on both sides of the law. Browley was a great source, listed in the acknowledgements of several of Saul's books. But Trianos, now there was a real get. The inside scoop on Trianos's world must have been too tempting for Saul to resist, even if it did upset his good friend.

"Has Oscar seen him?" Dad asked.

"As soon as he walked in," Mom confirmed. "Less than pleased."

But the arrival of one shady character was just a momentary distraction, guests returning quickly to their crab cakes and champagne. I followed my mother to the bar. She ordered a flute of champagne for me, and a sparkling water for herself.

"It was the ring I bought myself when I sold my first manuscript," Saul was enlightening a couple of aging debutants, both of whom had indulged in a lethal cocktail of Botox and bronzer for the evening.

"You mutha been so scared," one of the desperate debbies lisped.

"Heard anything from Jacob?" Mom asked me.

Jacob West (cute architect, soccer player calves) was the reason I was decidedly single.

"No."

"So, you're seeing other people exclusively?" Mom sipped on her drink.

"Yet another negotiating tactic in the world of modern romance." I shrugged.

"I don't understand his fear of commitment."

"He's got baggage," I repeated for the umpteenth time.

"There's baggage and there's baggage. This guy owns a Louis Vuitton matched set, from hatbox to steamer trunk. I say send him packing."

"Why do we come to this thing every year?" I glanced around. "It isn't as if you and Saul are big buddies. Or Dad and Saul. Or Saul and anybody for that matter."

Mom's look said she had identified my pathetic attempt to change the subject for what it was, but would take the hint. "I think it has something to do with the fact that what's-his-name has been cast in *Slave For Love*."

"Really? I hadn't heard."

Another hour of dancing and eating. The next time I spotted Mom, she was in conversation with Nancy Browley and the Beaumonts. Tony Trianos and Robin were having a cozy tete-a-tete nearby. Dad was across the room getting an earful from Oscar Browley, while another tall, good-looking man listened gravely.

"Is your dad negotiating your dowry?" My friend Dana Wilson appeared beside me

"I should be so lucky." I gave her a hug. "Where's Dan?"

Dana's fiancé labored as a construction foreman by day and played as singer in a band by night. The ten-year-old relationship was volatile, as in making you realize there are worse things than being single around the holidays.

She and I had lived in the same college dorm our freshman year, both enduring roommates from hell. Mine had turned her first taste of freedom into a sexual revolution, returned home and married her high school sweetheart before giving birth six months later to a nine-pound "preemie."

Dana didn't transfer to my room officially, but she had camped out there all the time. We amused ourselves by replacing her roommate's chocolate Slim-Fast powder with an 1800 calorie plus weight gainer supplement, then sharing the poor girl's dismay as she gained weight on a strict diet. Such experiences solidify a friendship.

Now my dorm room BFF was a serious young lawyer making a name for herself as a public defender. Dan, who had turned the feedback whine of bad equipment and poor acoustics into an anthem for teenage angst, was always one month away from signing a huge recording contract.

Dana was terrified he would never succeed in the music world (his tortured artist routine was wearing thin), but equally terrified that he would. Groupies were already a problem. What would happen when he had more than free drinks and the shorter lines of a backstage bathroom to offer them? One wondered. I was slated to be a bridesmaid in their January wedding.

"He's got a gig tonight at two, so he needed a disco nap. Where did you get those?" She admired my chest.

"They came with the suit. So who's Mr. Six Feet of Sex Appeal?" I nodded at the guy talking to my dad.

"Jack Lassiter, the new darling of the DA's office. He and Oscar Browley must be having a fit over Trianos being here."

"Saul Taylor's playing with fire, don't you think?"

Dana shrugged. "It's his party. He can fry if he wants to."

"So, this Jack Lassiter? Single? Sane? Straight?"

"Hard to say."

"Really. What's the story?"

Dana's unerring instinct about men was a funny thing. If she gave Jack the red light, I'd take her word for it. Unfortunately, she was like those fifties superheroes, unable to use her powers for her own benefit.

"I think he's single, he seems to be sane, and he's definitely straight."

I raised an eyebrow. "And you know this how?"

She did her Scarlett O'Hara voice. "He looks as if he knows what I look like without my 'shimmey'".

This I could understand. Men always looked at tall, whippet-thin Dana like they were X-raying her clothing. "I'm not seeing a downside," I commented.

"Well, there's one somewhere. Girls throw themselves at him, literally tripping and falling into his arms on a regular basis. The guy gets propositioned more than a plumber in a porn movie, all to no avail."

"Maybe he doesn't date gals from work."

"Three girls have already quit, thinking that very thing."

"Interesting." I sighed, not really meaning it. Jacob was too much of a challenge already. I needed a sure thing.

"Want to shake your moneymaker?" Feeling sorry for me, Dana pointed toward the floor, where the band thumped under our feet.

"I think my mother needs rescuing." I smiled brightly, proving that, beneath my power push-up bra, beat the heart of a survivor.

I found Mom talking to the Beaumonts and Nancy.

"How people can lavish so much time and money on Christmas trees, I'll never understand," Bunny said. "I, for one, would rather decorate something more worthwhile like me." She bent forward and gave us a cleavage shot usually reserved for pay-per-view. "Don't I need something dramatic around my neck?"

Mom's eyes met mine as she telegraphed, "Like a noose?"

Standing nearby listening to something Robin was murmuring to him, Tony Trianos caught the look. Amused, his topaz eyes raked over Mom in a way that was less than wholesome.

"Speaking of more worthwhile," Bunny said to Nancy, her tone slightly suggestive. "Still taking Pilates?"

Nancy's round face lit up, "Three times a week, and I can tell such a difference."

"I should say so." Bunny laughed. "Each session is one big hour-long Kegel exercise, right Gavin?"

Undaunted by a mouthful of stuffed mushrooms, Bunny's husband agreed, "Yes, indeedie."

I couldn't tell if he was offering a personal or professional opinion.

Nancy's creamy skin turned a light pink, "I wouldn't know about that."

"Girl, that's not what I've been told," Bunny teased. "Maybe I should sign up for a few sessions with Lance. I hear he really knows how to work out the kinks."

"Oh, you should." Robin leaned into our conversation for a sec. "I've been going myself. It's great for flexibility and toning. So important as we age." Her eyes moved over Bunny, lingering on the places that proved why silver lame is so hard to pull off.

Naturally, this didn't faze Ms. Beaumont. Anything you've done, she's done faster, better, more often and in higher heels. Even the spectacularly decked out Robin wasn't much competition.

Saul pushed his way into our circle, stumbling against Nancy. "You owe me a dance," he told Robin, glancing at Tony standing close to her. "Having a good time, Trianos?" Saul slurred his words. "Help yourself to anything you want. Well, not anything."

"Thank you, I will."

I detected no accent in Trianos's voice. Rather, he had a quiet, silky way of speaking that commanded the attention of his listeners - a sexy voice.

"Did Angela fix my drink?" Saul switched his attention to Robin.

"Doesn't she always?"

"Be back as soon as I call Meagan." He headed off to speak with his daughter, Trianos watching him thoughtfully.

"Why's the study off-limits?" Nancy asked me.

Following her gaze, we could both see Saul toss back his nightly Scotch through the French doors as he dialed up Meagan, a perpetual student working on her third doctorate.

"You know Saul," I said lightly. "Always scared someone's going to rip off his plot ideas. He made a big deal of locking his files when we were setting up, but if he wanted everything on one floor, he didn't have a choice but to let us in there. Even so, he only agreed to have the door unlocked while he was greeting guests in the foyer."

I turned to find Trianos's eyes on me, but glanced quickly away.

"I'm surprised Saul let you in there at all." Nancy eyed the buffet. "But then, he's one to talk about snooping." She headed toward the food.

Saul was frowning as he rejoined our group, and I wondered if Meagan Taylor had had something better to do on a Saturday night than talk to her dad. Announcing loudly that he was ready for that dance, he took Robin's hand as his mood brightened.

"They're playing our song, idea girl!" he all but shouted, as the band downstairs launched into a jazzy version of the *Twelve Days of Christmas*, the dance-floor guests joining in.

"I'm taking off." Trianos clapped Saul on the shoulder. "We'll talk next week."

I couldn't tell if he meant the comment for Saul or Robin, who seemed disappointed to see him leave.

"Hear you're a personal trainer now." Gavin Beaumont cornered me as he mouthed another lobster puff. "Think you could whip me into shape?"

"Absolutely, I love a challenge."

"Maybe we could trade services. You get me back into fighting shape, and I'll give you free Pap smears for life."

I watched him lick lobster puff from his fat little fingers. Somehow, my usual line, "Let me check if I have any openings," didn't seem quite appropriate.

All this and single, too? God, I hate the holidays.

By midnight the party had wound down. Saul was stationed at the door as another wave of guests got ready to depart. Thankfully, we were part of that group.

"Got something for you, Amanda!" Saul's liquored voice boomed into the silence that followed the band's departure, as he handed her a CD and then snagged a lobster puff off Gavin Beaumont's plate as he passed by. "You gotta hear Rosemary Clooney's version of the *Twelve Days of Christmas*." He roared. "She does it better."

Before Mom could ask, "Better than whom?" Saul punctuated his comment with a playful pat on her bottom.

Mistake. Big mistake.

My father's look of amusement mirrored my own. Saul shouldn't have done that. We knew it. Everyone in the foyer knew it. Only our host seemed oblivious to the fact that taking liberties with Amanda Carstairs could severely shorten one's life expectancy.

Before Mom could get Saul's attention with a glare that would decimate the little man with laser-like precision, though, his girlfriend stepped forward.

"Your medicine." Robin held out a pill.

"I already took it." He waved dismissively.

We'd seen this routine played out more than once. Saul was notoriously forgetful about taking the digitalis he needed twice a day to control his irregular heartbeat.

"No, you didn't." Robin pressed the pill into his hand.

"You're not in the will, so give it up." He laughed at his own joke, seemed surprised when no one else did, then caught sight of Mom's poisonous stare. "Fine. But you'll all miss me when I'm gone." He swallowed the pill with the last of his champagne - not what the doctor ordered. "Happy?" he demanded of Robin.

"Ecstatic."

Bunny Beaumont slinked up to our group and squeezed Dad's arm against her chest. "Y'all aren't going home yet, are you? It's early," she pouted. "I've still got some mileage left on this dress."

Unable to formulate an appropriate response, my father barely managed to extract his arm from Bunny's grasp. A lesser man would have crumbled.

"We're just getting started, right, Gavin?" Bunny didn't even look at her chubby little husband.

"You're the boss, Buns."

The only thing Mom likes less than being touched without permission is seeing her husband pawed by an over-sexed predator like Bunny "Buns" Beaumont, but before Mom could school Bunny on her bad manners, Saul grabbed his stomach.

"Let's go." Dad pressed forward, having a low tolerance for drama, but it quickly became clear that Saul wasn't joking.

"I don't feel so good." Our host doubled over, clutching his stomach. He stumbled left, then right, and finally grabbed the potted Bradford pear tree to get his balance.

"I told you not to drink so much when you're taking your meds." Robin sounded disgusted, but looked worried.

We all did.

"Oscar..." Saul gasped as another spasm of pain seemed to rip through him, then he fell to the floor, taking the tree and its partridge with him.

Before the ambulance could arrive, before the last scream split the cool night air, before Robin's first tear even fell, Saul Taylor's agonized writhing stopped.

He was dead.

CHAPTER 5

For the second time that week, the police were called to Saul's house.

I guess they had to be, but as to whether they would just take a few notes or launch a full-scale investigation when they arrived, that's where the situation got tricky.

Oscar Browley's thoughts on the matter were immediately clear. "We need to lock down the crime scene," he told Assistant District Attorney Jack Lassiter.

"Crime scene?" Jack and Robin exclaimed in unison.

Oscar wouldn't meet Robin's eyes. "Till we determine cause of death, we must do this by the book."

"He had a bad heart," Robin protested. "He was on medication. Ask Dr…" She trailed off.

Saul's cardiologist would be of no help. "'s the didgy-tal-s," he had slurred over the body a few minutes earlier. "Getcha evertime." His twenty-three-year-old girlfriend had giggled and led him into the dining room, where his mortified twenty-five-year-old daughter waited with coffee.

"We'll need everyone to stay put," Oscar announced. "Please have a seat in the living room. The police will get your names in case we need to contact you further."

The shocked crowd, which had thinned considerably, moved toward the fireplace.

"You don't understand," Robin cried.

"Ms. Woodall, please. We're just trying to make sure." Oscar addressed his comments to a point just over Robin's shoulder, a fact that wasn't lost on her.

"Ms. Woodall? Oscar, you know Saul adored me." She panicked. "You can't think I'd hurt him."

Oscar realized we were dragging our feet and gave us a dark look. We got moving.

Around us, the other partygoers were murmuring.

"Alex," Browley called to my father. "Let's you, Jack and I check the entrances and exits around this place."

I could see that Lassiter clearly resented the way Oscar had taken charge.

Robin stumbled over to us, her eyes wide, her voice childlike. "Amanda, you've got to help me."

My response would have been "duh," but Mom chose a more soothing, "Everything's going to be fine, dear," accompanied by a reassuring hand squeeze.

Dad rejoined our group a few minutes later. "Everything was all locked up," he said quietly. "All the doors were locked from the inside, except for the kitchen door being used by Eloise's catering crew and the front door, where the coat check girl was taking invitations and coats."

By now the police had arrived and were getting to work.

Oscar introduced a tall, intense looking man standing by his side to the group, "Detective McGowan here has a few questions. Be sure to give him your names and addresses in case we need to contact you over the next few days. If, however, you saw anything out of the ordinary tonight, you need to tell us now."

Jack Lassiter was getting more and more impatient with every "we" and "us" out of Oscar's mouth.

"I mean, anything - no matter how small or seemingly insignificant," Oscar continued. "Particularly if you saw Tony Trianos give Saul anything to eat or drink."

The words caused an immediate reaction among several of us.

My first thought was, "Leading the witnesses."

Beside me, I felt an almost imperceptible relaxing of Robin's shoulders.

Jack Lassiter's face lit up at the thought of seeing his name in the headlines.

"Trianos," Angela murmured to herself, knowing better than anyone what dealings the writer and the notorious Trianos had had.

A look of satisfaction crossed Nancy Browley's face. Even Bunny perked up as she always did at the mention of a good-looking man.

After Gavin and Bunny spent a few moments with the detective, my mother and I took our turn, while Dad spoke with Browley and Lassiter.

"Max McGowan." He shook our hands with that hard, alpha-male grip that makes you want to massage your own fingers afterward. Then he flipped through his notes as if looking for a few salient points from our permanent record. "So, you're the decorators. Oscar tells me you gals found the hand on the back porch a couple of days ago."

His tone was pleasant enough, his warm brown eyes friendly and curious. I couldn't stand him on sight.

This was probably what Mom meant about giving people a chance, but my instincts told me all I needed to know about Detective McGowan - overgrown frat boy, charmer, women in his life would always play second fiddle to his dog, his muscle car and the post-game recaps at the local sports bar.

"We found it quite by accident," Mom said.

"Dog led you to it, right?" He sounded like this was hard to believe.

"I'm sure it's all in the report." Mom's eyes flicked across the living room to where Dad was talking to Jack Lassiter.

"You know, opportunity is a big part of an investigation. If this turns out to be murder, we'll have to ask ourselves who knew where Saul kept his medicine? Who could've stolen his ring?"

"Do we look like the kind of people who could get hold of a severed hand?" I pointed out. "Or who steal ruby pinkie rings?"

Mom's tight smile said my sarcasm wasn't helping matters. "Before you start looking for motive, opportunity and means," she said to McGowan, "don't you think you should establish that this is a murder?"

Angela, her voice flat and unemotional seemed to answer for him. "They're gone," she said from the doorway of Saul's study. "Saul's discs - the ones with the notes for his new book. They're gone."

CHAPTER 6

We spent Sunday trying to process what had happened to Saul, without much luck. In addition to our shock, Mom was also worried about Angela.

While Sunday had been calm and quiet, Monday was anything but. The day began with a call from Nancy Browley, which Mom graciously put on speakerphone while we calligraphied place cards for a museum fundraiser.

"Amanda, I can't cope. The invitations are out, everybody's RSVP'd, but how can I have a party Saturday after what happened to Saul?" she wailed.

"Have you…" Mom began, only to be cut off.

"Oscar is beside himself," Nancy continued. "He and Saul were so close, but I can't help thinking a party, well more like a gathering, could help everybody get back to normal, give us all a little comfort during this very, very sad time. What do you think?"

"Well…"

"Not that I want it to be morbid, mind you. I still want it to be fun. It's a holiday party for gosh sakes, but it would have to be in good taste. I just don't know."

"I don't…"

"I guess if we knew what really happened, it would be different, but with all these questions swirling around, it might be unseemly to have a party if it was…you know."

"Murder?" I supplied, proud to have gotten in a complete sentence, even if it contained only a single word.

Nancy gasped. "So you think it was?"

"I have no idea," I admitted.

"I heard the police are taking a very hard look at Robin. If you know what I mean." Our caller stage whispered into the phone.

We waited for her to rush on, not even attempting to jump in. "Amanda. Chloe. Are you still there?"

"Yes..." We tried simultaneously.

"I know. I'm at a loss, too. On the one hand, I can't believe Robin could so coldly poison Saul right there in front of us. I thought she really loved the guy, and they were adorable together when he wasn't being such an ass. On the other hand, men don't enjoy long life spans around her. I heard that her last husband was loaded and she got everything. On the other hand, Saul's heart was bad, and he didn't take care of himself. What do you think, Amanda? I really want to know."

"About what, exactly?" Mom asked, still reeling from all Nancy's vacillations. Just how many "other hands" did the woman have?

"Robin. The party. Anything." Our caller couldn't hide her impatience.

"I have no idea what happened to Saul," Mom said carefully. "Till the autopsy comes back nobody does. As for your party..."

"You know what galls me most about the damn party," Nancy barged on, her voice turning vicious. "Everything was a competition with Saul. His party always had to be first, to be biggest or the best. It was like he was jealous of me and Oscar. Like he was in competition with me for Oscar's affection or something. And he would do anything to win - anything. I knew he'd find some way to ruin my party."

"By dying?" I said incredulously. "I don't think that's something you can take personally."

"Not that, Chloe. Let's just say you didn't know him like I did. Sometimes, I thought he was out to get me. He liked hurting people. Whoever left that rat on his doorstep got it right."

"Nancy, listen to me..." Mom tried again.

But our caller wouldn't. Instead, she said she needed to work out some things and that for now the party was on hold, which meant any decorating we were doing would have to wait. Her goodbye was brusque, and she hung up with a sharp click.

Well...

Before we could begin to assimilate what had just happened, the phone rang again. Bunny Beaumont - compelling case for Caller ID.

This time, I let Mom do all the talking.

"How may I help you, Bunny?"

"Spill it, Amanda." Bunny was breathless.

"Spill what?" Mom looked a little dazed. After all, she hadn't finished her first cup of coffee yet. I brought over the pot and topped off her cup.

"Girlfriend, I know you know what's going on. That husband of yours must have told you something."

"Could you please be more specific, Girlfriend?" Nobody got under my mother's skin like Bunny.

"Do I really have to spell it out for you? Was Saul murdered right there in front of us? Do the police think Robin or that hunk, Tony Trianos, did it?"

"I have absolutely no idea, Bunny. Why would you think I'd know?"

"You're married to a lawyer, aren't you? Alex must have his ear to the ground."

Mom said nothing, but Bunny was undeterred by the silence.

"I think they suspect foul play," she continued. "I mean why else would Oscar make the police start an investigation?"

Desperate for the clarity that only caffeine can bring, Mom clutched at her coffee cup as Bunny prattled on.

"I mean they collected all those food and drink samples. Checked all the doors and windows. Why do that if they weren't suspicious? What did they find out?"

This we did know. Food and drink samples had been taken, and Saul's medication plus any glasses he had touched had been bagged and labeled. Oscar had used his still considerable influence to get the samples tested immediately.

Mom wasn't about to share this information with Bunny, but Dad had heard that preliminary tests showed none of the food and drinks had been tampered with. Saul's champagne glass and the scotch glass he had used in the study were also clean.

Bunny was dying to dish, but Mom wasn't about to get sucked into idle speculation. After receiving only perfunctory responses, Bunny got the hint, said the dress Mom had worn that night was "cute" and hung up, probably to gather gossip elsewhere.

Unbelievable!

The rest of the day was four more phone calls, two drop-ins ("I was just driving by and thought I'd poke my head in and say hi."), and countless questions about what we had heard, what we thought, and what we suspected ("I mean, you found the hand. You were right there."). The whole town was buzzing about Saul's death, and there hadn't even been an autopsy.

As for the news coverage, Saul would've been disappointed. Two mega-stars had filed for divorce with rumors of infidelity swirling. Because the infidelity involved the wife and the couple's manny or male nanny, Saul's death in little ol' Birmingham, Alabama rated only one short blurb crawling across the bottom of the screen on national news and a couple of brief mentions.

Things were a little calmer Tuesday. I actually got some bills paid and some invoices out. I worked with two of my personal training clients, did a little Christmas window-shopping and didn't call Jacob - a small triumph.

On Wednesday everything switched back into high gear when Nancy Browley popped in unannounced at my mother's house, while we were working on plans for another party we were doing in Arbor Farms.

"The party is on, definitely on, unless you think it's too soon," she announced to Mom.

"No, I..." Mom began, only to be cut off. Would she never learn?

"I knew you would agree!" Nancy gushed. "Oscar is sure that if there was any foul play, it was at the hand of that Trianos character. I mean, they say the majority of all crimes are committed by criminals, so it just stands to reason."

Mom cut her eyes at me. We didn't even try to argue with that logic, not that we were given the chance.

"And since Trianos is definitely not invited to our party, I see no reason to postpone. Moping around isn't going to bring Saul back. Do you agree?"

"Mmm."

"Exactly. Thanks for being so supportive, Amanda. Come over anytime to get started." And then, she was gone.

My mind reeled as I recognized what this did to our schedule. We were two full days behind on finishing Nancy's décor - two full days and starting on a third.

Mom wasn't a bit flustered. She could roll with anything and ran upstairs to her office to get the three-ring binder that held everything we needed to know about finishing the Browley house.

The downstairs phone rang, and almost against my will, I answered it.

It was Dad. "Thought you two would want to know that they finished the autopsy."

He thought wrong about my wanting to know, but I listened anyway. An overdose of digitalis, Saul's heart medication, was determined to be the COD or cause of death, for those of you who don't watch cop shows. My mom and I do, so terms like GSR (gun shot residue) or ALS (alternative light source) just roll off our tongue.

"So they're saying it's murder?" I asked.

"They're starting an investigation - a quiet one. It could still be a bizarre accident, but given the whole thing with the hand and the rat, nobody's taking any bets on it."

As much as I wanted to speculate about Saul's death now that we had some real information, we just didn't have the time to spare. Nancy's 8,500-square foot house had to be decorated, top to bottom, in just over two days. It was get-busy time.

Miss a client deadline? Over my DB!

CHAPTER 7

"Want to know what I think?" Cassie spoke around the straight pins she was holding in her teeth. "I think, in your heart, you're not really single. You're looking at this as a forced, but temporary exile till Jacob comes to his senses."

This was her take on why I left Saul's party with my parents rather than some sexy stranger.

"Well, there was that little matter of a dead body in the foyer," I protested, feeding her more ribbon to be pinned to the mantle's evergreen swag.

"Excuses, excuses."

Across the room my mother shot us a dark look, the reason behind it hard to read. Was she irritated that we were being flip about Saul's death? Were we gabbing too much and working too little? Did I sound like I was on the prowl, trying to pick up men at parties? Or did she think Cassie should know better than to talk with pins in her mouth? Whatever the reason, Mom had been in a mood all morning.

Yes, we had tons of work in front of us. And yes, we were behind schedule. But every job brings with it some kind of challenge (severed hand, anyone?), and Mom always manages to pull them off. I didn't think the Browley's house would be any different, even if Nancy Browley had asked for a blanket of fake snow on her front yard. Mom hates fake snow.

The theme for the Browleys' house was simple enough - Santa Claus. Since Oscar dressed up like the jolly old fat man every year, it was a natural. And in typical Amanda Carstairs fashion, the décor would be over the top and fabulous.

Scattered throughout the house were three thousand Santas of all shapes and sizes, from the fur draped Old World Santas, to nesting dolls painted like Russia's Ded Moroz or Grandfather Frost to France's Papa Noel. And that wasn't even counting the life-sized version in an antique sleigh on the front lawn. The faux-snow covered front lawn.

Of course, Mom could've over-ruled the idea. Her name doesn't go on any design unless she's completely happy with it. But Nancy had pleaded and had seemed so stressed that Mom had relented. A good designer knows how to work with a client's vision.

Cassie took the last pin out of her mouth and smiled. "Not that I'm one to talk. I can't remember the last time I had a boyfriend around Christmas. Too bad Jacob can't set me up with one of his architect buddies. My dad would love that. Being an architect was his dream job growing up."

Jacob was not a subject I wanted to discuss. Our breakup was going a little too well for my taste.

"Women are going to seem very dull to Jacob after me," I had complained to Mom when we had first decided to see other people. "Bigger breasted, sure, but very dull."

"Well, for Heaven's sake, don't tell him that," she had said. "You'll only strengthen his resolve."

Trouble was, I thought Jacob was a keeper. What else could you call a man who grows his own basil, makes his own pesto and freezes single-serving portions in ice cube trays?

"Gay?" suggested my mother, ever helpful.

"Not gay," I had insisted. And this had been confirmed by my friend Reggie, who had pronounced Jacob hopelessly heterosexual. Said it kind of snotty, too, like my man wasn't cool enough to join such an exclusive club. "He's a nice guy, Mom. A down-to-earth nice guy like Dad."

I wasn't ready to give up on Jacob. As his workout partner, I had given him abs of steel. As his decorator, I had glazed two rooms in his house and tiled a bathroom. I had gotten him into his first pair of flat-front khakis, increased his sense of humor by 25% and broken him of his embarrassing habit of going "Woo-hoo!" every time he saw cleavage. A significant investment had been made in the man, and if any woman was going to reap the rewards, it was going to be me.

Now if I could just get him on board, I'd be all set. I glanced in the mirror over the Browley's fireplace. Perhaps if I went half a shade blonder with my highlights.

"Who has time for romance this time of year anyway?" I asked Cassie, more to distract myself than anything else. "There's too much to do. Christmas is like three weeks away, and I've barely started my shopping."

"Shocking," Mom said as she arranged antique papier-mâché Santas on a mahogany coffee table.

"Oh, and I suppose yours has been done for months," I retorted.

"Not months." She smiled. "Month, as in one."

I looked to Cassie for support.

"Sorry. I finished mine last weekend."

"What's the fun in that?" I demanded. "Where's the stress? The last-minute panic? The impulse buys? That's what Christmas is all about."

"Says the girl who has given personal training gift certificates the last two years in a row," Mom countered.

"People love those." I said. "And we could all stand to get healthier. Besides, I've gotten Dad's gift."

We always went in together on Dad's gift, and Mom had already gotten it. She wasn't impressed.

"I'm all for procrastination," Cassie said, "but Dad's in Louisiana, so it's easier to do my shopping here before I head down."

"What does your father do, dear?" Mom asked absently.

Given her mood, I wasn't about to tease her, but she did sound an awful lot like her own mother: "Now tell me, dear, who are your people?"

"He's the manager of a savings and loan, but in a good way."

"There's a bad way?" I asked.

"Well, you know, all those scandals and bankruptcies. Nothing like that ever happened in New Bedford. Typical small southern town."

"It's nice that you can make it home for the holidays." Mom unwrapped more Santas.

"I wouldn't miss it for anything. Seems like the whole town comes over to celebrate with Dad. He still lives in the big old house I grew up in. Mom, too, of course."

Mom arched her eyebrow at me.

"We sing carols and open gifts on Christmas Eve. That way, on Christmas Day, we can just enjoy each other's company and pig out."

"Sounds lovely, dear," I said, taking the words right out of Mom's mouth. She was so not ready to be teased this morning.

"It's great." Cassie sighed. "Simple, you know?"

I thought of the work ahead of us and all the money the Browleys were lavishing on their Christmas. Simple sounded heavenly.

My mother's thoughts seemed to be running along the same lines. "I know."

We broke for lunch around noon, and Cassie left to make other floral deliveries. Over sandwiches at a local deli, I broached the subject of Saul's death to see if that's what was bugging Mom.

"So, the police don't think it was an accident?"

"Your father says they're starting an investigation, but aren't sure it will lead anywhere. It could have been an accident. Then again, if Robin gave him an overdose, he took it willingly, so is that murder?"

I thought about it. "You mean if he had taken his medicine earlier in the evening and then consciously took another pill, even with Robin's encouragement, it's not a crime?"

Having forgotten to tell the waitress no chips with my sandwich, I was now confronted with a huge pile. I just wouldn't eat them.

"I don't know," Mom said. "Saul wasn't mentally handicapped. He should have known whether or not he had taken a pill earlier that evening, and if he did, who is to say Robin knew it? We both saw the two of them go round and round about his medicine last week. I think her lawyers could put up a pretty good defense that it was an accident. He took a pill without her knowing it and then willingly took the one she gave him, as a roomful of witnesses can attest."

"But two other men she's been involved with have had similar 'accidents'" I pointed out.

Mom swallowed a dainty bite of her pasta salad. "Nothing's ever been proven."

"Still."

We sat in silence.

"And the discs," I said. "Who could've taken the discs? Angela was right. Saul was careful about those."

"Compulsively so, although Angela should keep some things to herself."

"You don't think the police really suspect her?"

"I just don't want her drawing attention to herself. She's always so desperate to prove how clever she is. People might take that the wrong way."

"And she's got serial killer eyes," I added.

"She does not." Mom took a sip of tea. "Though she does stare, doesn't she. It can be disconcerting. Maybe I should talk to her. Tell her to let the police handle this."

"You know she's going to want to solve it before they do. She's very competitive."

"The poor thing. Without a mother's guidance, a young girl is so lost."

No comment from this side of the table. Uh-uh.

"What about Tony Trianos?" I asked.

"What about him?"

"Oscar Browley thought he might have had something to do with it. Whatever 'it' is."

"As Nancy says, most crimes are done by criminals. If you've got a person with Trianos' background near a crime scene, you take a look at him."

"A chopped-off hand sounds like a mob thing, and the dead rat feels like a warning."

"Maybe."

"If anyone could get a chopped-off hand, it would be Trianos. And if anyone could get away with a crime, it would be Trianos. That is, if a crime were committed."

My sandwich was gone, and I was trying not to eat all the chips on my plate. They were hard to resist.

"If a crime was committed," Mom echoed.

"Do you think there was?"

She shrugged, and two more of my chips disappeared in quick succession, while she gathered her thoughts.

"I don't know what to think," she said finally. "Do I think Trianos left a severed hand on Saul's doorstep? I can't imagine why he would. Do I believe Robin stood there and cold-bloodedly passed a murder weapon from her hands to Saul's? I can't fathom it. Do I think someone slipped Saul something earlier so that when he took his pill, he overdosed? I don't know who could or why."

Mom's mention of "why" reminded me to tell her about Nancy's assertion at the party that Saul had been a snoop.

"Interesting." Mom sat back to let the waitress refill her tea glass. When we were alone again, she continued. "So Nancy thought Saul wanted to hurt her."

I swallowed a chip. "But how could he?"

"Perhaps, Saul didn't confine his prying to the books he was researching. Maybe he had discovered something about Nancy she would've preferred that he hadn't." She paused. "You say Trianos overheard your conversation?"

I nodded, licking salt from my fingers. Enough with the chips already. I wanted the waitress to take my plate, but she was across the room, obviously in cahoots with the cellulite fairy.

I tried to recall the moment when Nancy and I had been talking. "Was Trianos purposely eavesdropping? I couldn't say. He was definitely hip to what we were discussing, but then, he doesn't seem like a guy who misses much."

Mom nodded.

"For instance, he didn't miss how hot you looked in that red dress," I said casually.

"Don't be ridiculous."

I could tell by her blush that she, too, had noticed his appreciative assessment of her.

"You know," she changed the subject abruptly, " Robin really had no motive to kill Saul. He said it himself, she wasn't in the will."

I chewed thoughtfully. "But maybe she was sick of his being so cruel to her. He was pretty awful."

"It would have been easier for her to break up with him than to poison him, don't you think?"

"Not if you already have two homicides to your credit. Maybe it's easier to knock off your boyfriend than to divvy up your CD collection and give him back his key."

"You sound like the idea has some appeal."

"We're not broken up. We're seeing other people."

"Ah."

I consoled myself with another chip. "When you think about it, no one had a real reason to kill Saul. Unless it was someone related either to a book he had written or one he was writing. Maybe someone from his past snuck in."

"All the doors and windows were locked," Mom pointed out. "And everyone there had an invitation. If a crime was even committed, it has to have been an inside job."

"If a crime was even committed," I seconded. "So when is the snow falling on Birmingham?"

She sighed, but I could tell she had perked up a little. "Tomorrow, I guess. God, I hate fake snow."

"But the Santas are nice."

"The Santas are very nice. Thanks for all your help."

"No problem. It keeps me off the streets."

Mom still worried about my unconventional career path. In her mind, three part-time jobs did not add up to one stable profession. I wasn't a degreed designer like my mother, but I had a good eye, years of experience helping Mom and a love of spending other people's money. My clients got a little of the Carstairs cachet at a much more affordable price. Throw in my personal training gigs and the Christmas houses, and I was making pretty good money. Even had a little savings and an IRA. Knowing that my lack of steady employment bugged my mother? Even better.

"Can I get this out of your way," our waitress asked, reaching for my plate - finally.

Looking longingly at the last chip, I handed the plate to her decisively.

Mom smiled. "Remarkable restraint, dear."

CHAPTER 8

Despite Nancy's best efforts to infuse the event with gaiety, her party got off to a rocky start. True, her décor was totally different from Saul's, though no less smashing. And, yes, the food was far more exotic, if the duck quesadillas the waiters served were any indication. Still, it was a holiday party, and at our last holiday party together, just a week ago if you could believe it, someone had died.

Naturally, Saul's death was the talk of the evening. Bunny Beaumont skipped her usual fashionably late entrance in order to gather information with the fervor of an embedded journalist broadcasting live from the front. And speaking of fronts, two strips of double-sided tape were all that was keeping hers from being on full display beneath a ruby red halter dress.

"Bev's House of Harlots must be having a sale," Mom murmured as we watched Bunny try to pump my father for information.

Wisely, Dad excused himself to sneak a peek at the buffet that the caterer was laying out on Nancy's George II serpentine mahogany sideboard. Bunny's eyes met Mom's. Mom smiled. Bunny smiled. The temperature in the room dropped fifteen degrees.

I was surprised to see Angela perched on the edge of a seat in the keeping room, since her only connection to these people had been Saul. She looked uncomfortable, which I knew had nothing to do with the chair she had chosen - leather and walnut, French 1940's.

Even more than uncomfortable, Angela appeared to be poised for flight, which, of course, made Mom want to put her at ease. That's kind of Mom's thing, but when she got waylaid by Nancy and gave me her Mom look, it became my thing.

"So, Angela, whatcha doing way over here? You're missing out on the quesadillas." Forced. Fake. Awkward. The usual.

She stood and smiled faintly, knowing I was on a pity mission prompted by my mother. "What does it look like I'm doing? I'm hiding out from that bitch." She nodded toward Bunny. "And her nasty little husband."

"Yeah, good plan. Gavin's harmless, though, just a little socially awkward, and Bunny will back off once she realizes you don't have any dirt to dish."

"I get paid to gather and disseminate information. I don't give it away for free."

Hearing an edge in her voice, I gave her a second look and wasn't thrilled with what I saw. Wearing an unbecoming beige dress that did nothing to complement her fair skin and red hair, there was a new and unattractive hardness about her, a false bravado that made her face look pinched as her small, dark eyes scanned the room searching for someone.

"How did your interview with the police go?" I asked.

"Same as yours, I guess. They're clueless."

"No suspects at all?"

She shrugged. "They're looking for leads in all the wrong places."

"Such as?"

"Me for one. Like I needed to steal Saul's research."

"You think they suspect you?"

Another shrug. "They don't know what they're doing."

"What about Robin?" I asked.

"What about her?"

"How's she holding up?"

Her smile this time held genuine amusement. "Robin isn't crying on my shoulder, if that's what you're asking. She's scared of me."

"Why?" I was losing patience with her sly tone and sneaky innuendoes.

"Let's just say I'm a pretty good investigator in my own right. Saul's name sold books, but my research gave them their juice. I know everything he knew and more. A lot of people are probably asking themselves how I plan to use that information."

"And just how is that?"

Her face brightened. "With all the information I've gathered, a book deal isn't out of the question. I could tell you something about everybody in this room. Things they would kill to keep secret, or at least pay big bucks to squelch."

I stared at her. "You do know blackmail is a crime."

"Who said anything about blackmail? I'm a journalist. I have integrity, which is something Saul knew nothing about."

"Then why did you work for him for eight years?"

Her brashness fell away, and for a moment, I glimpsed genuine sadness, maybe even something else. "Saul was good to me. We were a good team." She took a deep, steadying breath. "But now, I'm on my own."

Uh-oh. True confession time. When I'd told Cassie that Angela and I weren't friends in high school that hadn't exactly been the whole story.

Yes, Angela had been riddled with teenage angst, which was totally annoying to those of us who never wanted life to get any deeper than a movie plot. What I hadn't realized at the time, though, was that beneath all that black eyeliner and unwashed hair beat the heart of a vulnerable girl seething with unbridled passions you usually find only in erotica.

So when my friends and I accidentally found her journal in eleventh grade (hidden in her gym locker under two books, her tennis shoes and her Sony Walkman), we were shocked to learn that some of those passions had found a very complicated, intense outlet - her forty-year-old journalism teacher, Mr. Kramer. Reading the juicier sections out loud, it was clear that most of their relationship had only taken place in her mind. The rest had occurred in the darkroom after sixth period journalism class.

All hell had broken loose after we found out. We hadn't planned on telling anyone, but Ms. Watkins, the girls' volleyball coach, had overheard Sonya snort-laughing the words "throbbing maleness" and confiscated what she thought was pornographic reading material. Turns out she was right.

Kramer lost his teaching license and went to jail. Angela got a twice-a-week standing appointment with a therapist, not to mention an even bigger chip on her shoulder, and I got the wrath of my mother. Even worse, Angela's mom died a year later - not good.

Angela had been sent to live with her dad's brother and finished out her senior year at another school. She and my mother had maintained the uneasy closeness of an unstoppable force sending college care packages to an immovable object.

They had never confirmed or denied it, but I got the feeling my parents had paid for Angela's journalism education. She shared our Thanksgiving dinners, had a picture on our mantle, and had hugged my mother with genuine affection eight years before when Mom announced she had gotten Angela an interview for a research assistant position with one of Mom's most famous clients - Saul Taylor.

So when I heard Angela talking about Saul with such naked emotion, naturally I suspected the same kind of thing she had written about in that journal - infatuation with an older man. Respect for a mentor that had turned physical. Throbbing maleness.

I wanted to touch her arm, but something stopped me from offering that small gesture of comfort. I was the last person from whom she would want sympathy.

"When's Oscar supposed to get here?" Angela's eyes again scanned the room.

I shrugged and looked around. "He makes a grand entrance every year dressed like Santa Claus."

"And passes out little surprises for those who've been naughty or nice? Oh, if he only knew."

Again, I was distinctly chilled by her insinuating tone. "Angela..."

She cut me off. "There's Jack Lassiter. See ya."

Thirty minutes later, I was desperately trying to get Dana to give me the scoop on the bridesmaid dress I'd be wearing in her wedding, but she wouldn't divulge even a ruffle.

"Just a hint. Just the color?"

"You'll like it. I chose them with you in mind," Dana said as Mom joined us at the buffet. "Easy there on the mashed potatoes, though. If your stomach's going to be on display in front of three hundred people, you'll want it to be flat."

Dana laughed. I didn't.

"Where's Dan tonight?" Mom asked, innocently.

Sore subject.

"He wouldn't come unless he could wear the same outfit he was going to wear to his 'gig' tonight." Dana made little quote marks with her fingers as if the disdain in her voice wasn't enough. "Combat boots, black leather pants, no shirt. I know, so I said wear whatever you want. I mean, put on a shirt obviously, but come on. It's a party, and we haven't been to a party together in so long, at least one that didn't get busted up by the cops."

Why did you have to ask about Dan, I telegraphed to my mother, as if she wasn't already asking herself the same question. Catch Dana in the middle of one of her rants about Dan, and she goes from polished and pulled together to girl uninterrupted with alarming ease.

"But then he gets all huffy and says that if I'm going to be that way about it, maybe I should just go alone. And I'm like 'what way?' and he's all like, 'Oh so I never take you to any parties, I never take you anywhere nice.' And I'm like, as a matter of fact…"

"Oooh, prawns!" I tried to move off down the buffet, but Mom blocked my escape.

Dana didn't seem to notice we had lost interest. In fact, she seemed fully prepared to recount the fight in real time for Mom's benefit, lest there be any doubt as to how unreasonable her fiancé was and what a saint she was to put up with him. And remember, this girl is a lawyer. Arguing her point is what she does for a living. God help us.

"I mean we're not even married, and it's like the romance is already dead. Well, not dead, but on life support. And he's like, you're such a princess, you're such a yuppie, which is his idea of, like, the worst insult ever."

It was then that I had a feeling of déjà vu, a sense of talking at a party when something strange happened. Oddly, a silence had rippled its way across the laughter and chatter of what had been a lively party. I thought people were reacting to Dana's tirade that had grown steadily louder.

"So I'm like, oh yeah? Well, guess what? You're…"

But the silence wasn't around us and moving outward. It had started at the door and moved toward us, until finally Dana was the only one speaking.

"...such an asshole!" Dana covered her mouth.

"That's telling him." Mom quickly put down her plate. "Excuse me dear." She made her way to the Browley's soaring foyer. There, looking both nervous and defiant, stood Robin Woodall.

Rustling in peacock blue taffeta, Nancy reached Robin at the same time as Mom.

"Robin, you came!" The consummate hostess, Nancy made it sound like a good thing, not the utter surprise it obviously was.

"I just wanted to get out of the house tonight." Robin's tone was almost apologetic.

"I'm glad you did," Nancy stated firmly, though a tightness around her mouth told a different story.

"And you look lovely," Mom added.

True. Her jade gown - Narciso Rodriguez, if I wasn't mistaken - was a little over the top for woman in mourning, but it did set off her green eyes quite nicely.

"Come look at all the good things on the buffet." Mom took her arm. "Nancy's put out quite a spread."

"I am a little hungry," Robin said gratefully.

They headed for the dining room, and the crowd noise picked up, although it carried an anxious, whispering tone with it. I didn't even have to guess at the topic of conversation.

Instinctively, my eyes searched the crowd for Angela as I, too, headed for the buffet. She wasn't talking to Jack Lassiter anymore. He was staring intently at Robin, while Dad waited patiently for him to resume their conversation.

Mom smiled at Dad, and he smiled back, a hundred things communicated in their exchange, not the least of which was we've got to get some new friends.

Finally, I spotted Angela back in her chair in the keeping room. Her smile was mocking, and I turned away. That chick needed a life.

Robin said she hadn't eaten much in the past week, but filled her plate, the brave girl, and smiled at Mom sweetly.

"You're always nice to me, Amanda."

"I'm so sorry about Saul," Mom said.

"Me too." I added.

"It's just awful."

"Have the police told you anything?" Mom's tone was gentle.

Robin shook her head. "They're investigating. They think I'm some kind of black widow."

Even Mom didn't know how to respond.

"Are you sure Saul hadn't taken his medicine earlier?" I met Robin's gaze.

Mom gave me a look that indicated I had been less than subtle.

Robin chewed on a sesame-studded prawn, eyes closed as if she were trying to relive the day. "I kept only necessities over at Saul's, so I went back to my house to get ready for the evening, needing the heavy duty stuff for the party."

It made sense. The strapless bra, the body shimmer, and hair jewelry she had for special occasions would stay at her house. I was with her so far.

"All I did when I got to Saul's was slip into my dress. He could've taken his medicine while I was gone, or even while I was there, without my knowing it. But he never did that. You saw him. He had to be hounded to take it."

It felt like she was going over it with us so we could get our stories straight.

"I don't think the police would even be pushing this if Oscar hadn't caused such a fuss. Where is our host, anyway?"

My heart sank as I pictured Oscar ho-ho-hoing his way into the party and catching sight of Robin. Would there be one of his naughty little gifts for her in his bag?

Bunny came over with Nancy hot on her heels, probably intent on making sure Bunny kept her wicked tongue firmly in check. As if a barrier had been broken, Dad and Jack Lassiter joined our little group in the dining room. Angela hovered nearby, staring at us as if she were writing the scene in her head.

Everyone extended awkward condolences to Robin, which she accepted graciously. The spotlight suited her, and I couldn't help thinking that she knew it.

The only person who seemed uninteresting in the little drama unfolding around us was Gavin Beaumont. He called to us from the keeping room, "Nice touch, Amanda, putting a Santa Claus by the pool."

I did the math. Three thousand Santas, front yard in a sleigh and on every conceivable flat surface inside, but out back by the pool? That one wasn't ours.

Ah...

"I didn't put a Santa by the pool," Mom announced, gladly helping Oscar pull off his little joke.

The crowd caught the import of her words, and with much laughter, all fifty of us headed onto the deck, down the stamped concrete steps to the patio and over to the pool. In the moonlight, we could see the cheerful bulk of a red-suited Santa waiting patiently.

Dad, Mom, Robin and I were at the back of the crowd. For some reason, we felt protective of Robin, sincerely hoping Oscar wouldn't cause a scene in his sanctimonious way.

"Oscar, you scamp, we wondered where you were." Bunny rushed to be the first to sit on Santa's lap, then stopped short, causing a traffic jam of bodies behind her. "Fake!" She pointed dramatically. "Fake! I can spot it in diamonds, and I can spot it in a Santa."

Sure enough, the Santa was a fake - a realistic, life-sized fake, but a fake nonetheless.

The crowd turned on Mom as if she had misled them. "That's the Santa from the sleigh out front," she said.

"No, we saw that Santa when we came in," Gavin protested.

Apparently when we came to the party, we had all walked past Oscar in his sleigh and been none the wiser.

The crowd divided in two. Half went around the house toward the front, while the rest of us made our way back inside and out the front door.

On the front lawn, Bunny tramped (and I use this word deliberately) through the fake snow to where Oscar waited.

"He's real alright!" Bunny hiked her gown up to mid-thigh and climbed into the sleigh on top of Oscar. "Alright big boy, give me my present."

But Oscar had been given a present all his own. One of our clear Lucite icicles, having once hung artfully from the eaves of the Browleys' house, was now plunged deeply into his back.

Bunny's screams went on and on, as she scrambled out of the sleigh and fell face first into the faux snow.

CHAPTER 9

It was a testament to Bunny Beaumont's resilience (and to the strength of double-stick tape) that she pulled herself together so quickly. I mean, had I hopped into the lap of a dead man, I'm not sure I would have recovered as well.

But Bunny picked herself right up, checked that her boobs were where she had left them and stalked past the stunned crowd back into the house, not even giving the devastated widow a second glance.

Mom stopped Nancy from rushing toward her husband, who was obviously past the point of resuscitation. It was a clear, brisk night with just enough moonlight to see how grey Oscar's face was and how lifeless his eyes looked. The blood had long since dried to a muddy brown down his back. Nancy, sobbing uncontrollably, let herself be led back into the house, while Jack Lassiter (how had Oscar Browley put it last week?) locked down the scene.

More police. More questions.

With Nancy resting upstairs under her doctor's care, the rest of us gathered in the living room as the investigation got under way. Detective McGowan seemed particularly interested in which guests had been present at both parties. The list was a short one: my family, Nancy, Robin, Jack Lassiter, Angela Jannings, Gavin and Bunny Beaumont, my friend Dana and a handful of other people I didn't know. A few members of Eloise's catering crew had also worked both nights.

"I'm not sure it matters," Dad said quietly. "Anyone could have killed Oscar tonight. With Saul, it had to be someone in the house, but anyone could've come by and killed Oscar while he was sitting there."

"So," Mom finished, "if Saul's death was murder…"

"It wasn't!" Robin insisted.

"But if it was," Mom pressed forward gently, "and if both men were killed by the same person, it had to be someone at Saul's party, whether or not they were here tonight."

"Like Tony Trianos," Jack Lassiter said grimly.

"I think it's obvious now that Saul was murdered," Angela said from her place at the edge of our group.

"Obvious?" Robin protested. "I don't see how!"

Angela flashed a superior smile. "Two men, two friends, die one right after the other at holiday parties. It's a little too much of a coincidence, don't you think?"

"Oh, I don't know," Gavin Beaumont commented. "The holidays can be a rough time of year. People drink too much, eat too much. Emotions run high. Lot of suicides."

"I hardly think Oscar stabbed himself in the back," Angela scoffed.

"And Saul didn't kill himself either. It was an accident," Robin insisted.

Angela made a derisive noise. Robin glared at her.

Gavin wanted to finish his point, even if he looked less comfortable with all eyes upon him. "I'm just saying that Saul's death could have been an accident." Robin looked triumphantly at Angela. "Or it could have been murder." Angela nodded with satisfaction. "But a murder completely unrelated to what happened tonight. The holidays can bring out the best and the worst in people. They can be happy, or they can be tragic. I think they're hard for more people than we'd like to admit."

I wondered if he spoke from experience.

"Are you saying murder's contagious?" Angela was intrigued. "That whoever killed Oscar got the idea from Saul's murder?"

Gavin shrugged. "They say suicide is contagious. Why not murder?"

An uncomfortable silence settled over our group, as we watched the police do their thing on the front lawn.

Finally, Bunny Beaumont spoke up, clearly cheered by a thought that had just occurred to her, "Amanda, sweetie, you poor thing."

Mom took a deep breath as if she knew what was coming. "I think Nancy's the one who deserves our sympathy tonight," she said quietly.

"But, darling, two murders in houses you decorated can't be good for your business."

The police didn't think so either.

At first, Detective McGowan seemed satisfied when we explained our connection to Oscar, but then his questions became more pointed.

"Remember what I was telling you two about opportunity? Once again, you're both near the top of a short list of people with opportunity. We have to ask ourselves who was standing right there when Saul found that hand? Who was standing right there when Saul collapsed? Who knew Oscar would be in the sleigh?"

"We didn't know Oscar would be in the sleigh," I pointed out.

McGowan shrugged. "You knew about the sleigh and the icicle. You knew both men's routines."

"Is there an accusation in there?" Mom asked.

"Not at all. Just trying to go over the facts. Fact is, no one saw how that hand got on Saul's back step. No one even knew it was there, till you two found it."

"That's right. We found it there," Mom said. "We didn't put it there."

"Any idea who did?"

"None."

"Know of anybody who had a reason to kill either Saul or Oscar?"

"No."

McGowan looked at me.

"No." I seconded. "On both counts."

McGowan stared at us for a long moment. I don't much care for blond hair on guys, and he had a head full of it. He looked older than me and in good shape. I wondered what gym he belonged to. Strictly out of professional curiosity, I assured myself.

"Tell me about Saul's girlfriend." He consulted his notes. "Robin."

"What about her?" Mom was reacting to McGowan the same way I was, if the edge in her voice was an indication.

"Got quite a past."

"We don't know her well," Mom said. "She was the girlfriend of a client."

"But you do know Angela Jannings, that right?"

"Since she was a child."

"You two friends?" He asked that question of me again.

"We grew up together, but we weren't really close."

"What's her connection to these people?"

"She worked for Saul." Mom's voice had a 'whole truth, but absolutely nothing but the truth' tone to it, so help me God.

"But Saul's dead. Why was she here? His cook wasn't here. His agent wasn't here."

"She had been invited." Mom was irritated now. "She knew we would be here, and I was glad to see her."

"Now there's a girl with opportunity - her and Robin both."

"Angela wouldn't hurt anyone. She and Saul were very close."

You don't know the half of it, I thought, recalling what I'd suspected about Angela earlier in the evening.

"One of the guests I questioned said that you didn't care for Saul, Mrs. Carstairs. Said you thought he was crass."

"I don't know why someone would tell you that," Mom said, though I suspected she knew exactly why and whom. "Saul was more a client than a friend, that's true, but I didn't dislike him."

"You two ever have a personal relationship?"

"Certainly not!"

"The way I hear it, he was a little free with his hands at the party last week. Gave you a little love tap."

"An unwelcome gesture."

"Made you mad?"

Mom's expression said it all.

"He ever threaten you?"

"What?"

"I was told he might've suspected you of overcharging him on some things, maybe double billing him on purpose."

I've never seen my mother so furious, and I missed a lot of curfews growing up.

"We had a couple of discussions about billing. Some things were changed at the last minute, and I billed accordingly. Saul was surprised, but I had documentation showing that his girlfriend.."

"Robin?"

"Yes. She had okayed the overages, and Saul was satisfied."

McGowan just stared at her.

"Look," I said, fearing for the dumb guy's safety. "My mother's retired. She doesn't have to work. She does the Christmas houses because she likes to. If Bunny Beaumont's telling you otherwise, she's full of it."

McGowan shrugged. "Like I said, there are people a lot higher on the list than you two. Still, I'd like copies of all the invoices you've sent to both Mr. Taylor and Mr. Browley."

"I dealt with Mrs. Browley, but that's fine. I have nothing to hide. Two murders over high-priced Polonaise ornaments, Detective McGowan? A severed hand because of double billing? I hope you're a lot better at this than you seem to be."

"Yeah," I seconded again.

After being interrogated by McGowan, I was longing for a shower and bed, but Mom wanted to stay till Angela had been questioned. McGowan called Robin first, and we all figured that would take a while.

"Don't let him intimidate you, dear. He's making all kinds of accusations to see what reaction he gets." Mom patted Angela's arm.

"I've interviewed murderers. I can handle a cop."

I could see Mom keeping her temper in check. "This isn't the time for false bravado. This is serious."

"Oh I'm serious, Mrs. Carstairs. Deadly serious. I'm going to figure this out, and write all about it."

"Oh my God," I said, "she's lost it."

"Angela…" Mom headed me off.

"I know what I'm doing. This is my shot, and I'm going to take it."

"Detective McGowan pretty much said you were one of his top two suspects," I informed her.

"What does he know? That bitch in there had more motive than I do." She jerked her head at the closed office door, where McGowan was questioning Robin.

I had none of my mother's patience or tact. "Look, if you go in there begging for a fight, McGowan's going to give you one. It's hard to investigate behind bars."

She turned on me. "What do you care?"

"I don't."

"Girls, stop it. We need to…"

But whatever Mom thought we needed to do had to wait. Robin came out of the study looking relaxed and radiant. Her hair was down, curling softly around her shoulders. She carried her shoes in one hand and paused at the door to slip them back on. Behind her, McGowan looked shell-shocked.

Angela," he said. "Whenever you're ready."

CHAPTER 10

"That girl." Mom sighed the next day.

Four hours sleep, an hour of Mass and brunch at my older sister, Bridget's house in Homewood with her granddaughter, Lily, had done nothing to lessen my mother's irritation.

"That man." I was still annoyed at McGowan's accusations, and at the way he had caved in the face of Robin's obvious charms. Why are men so utterly predictable?

"What man? Detective McGowan?" Mom raised a brow.

"He practically accused you of murder."

"Dear, he was just doing his job. It isn't really his fault that he has been so misled."

"By Bunny Beaumont," Bridget added. "What does Dr. Beaumont see in her?"

Bridget, a nurse at St. Vincent's, only has good things to say about Gavin, though she admits that his bedside manner could use a little work. I was glad people who were scared about being in the hospital had Bridget there to comfort them. She had a way of putting people at ease. Stand behind her in line at the grocery store and you'd probably get her life story before you unloaded your cart. Get her as your nurse when your baby's blood pressure dropped and you'd still be sending her Christmas cards two years later.

Mom had already gotten calls from concerned friends. Bunny had been burning up the phone lines, dishing the latest dirt on the party, and we could all guess exactly what spin she was putting on the murder.

"I can just hear Bunny now," Mom grumbled, after Dad had taken Lily upstairs to play a computer game. "'Of course, Amanda's designs are darling, but are they worth dying for?'"

"Well, you have made a killing over the years." I helped myself to more of Bridget's three-pepper frittata.

"And I've always said your décor was dead on," Bridget added, spreading blackberry conserve onto an English muffin. "Think how many people are dying to get on your waiting list."

"Maybe I'll go get my design degree after all. Think I should take a stab at it?" Leave it to me to take things too far.

"Enough!" Mom said, in a way that made us get very interested in the food left on our plates. "The person we really need to be focusing on here is Angela."

"That girl," I sighed, a perfect imitation of Mom.

Bridget smirked. Mom did not.

"That girl has no idea how much trouble she's in." Mom was probably thinking about the raised voices we had heard from the study the previous night.

"I'll ask the questions here," McGowan had shouted at one point.

"It was my research. Why would I need to steal them?" Angela had yelled at another.

After that, we only heard McGowan's rapid-fire questions and Angela's increasingly querulous replies. When Angela had come out of the study, she was visibly shaken and had brushed right past us, headed straight for the front door, and slammed it behind her.

"We warned her that being confrontational was the wrong tact to take with Detective McGowan." Mom pushed her plate away. "But she's never been overly burdened by common sense. One way or another, I'm going to get to the bottom of this, and you're going to help me."

"Me?" I squeaked. "Why me?"

"Bridget's got work, and Lily can't be running all over town."

My sister smiled her Number One daughter smile. I flicked frittata at her.

"So, we're going to start chasing down clues like a couple of amateur detectives? Is that seriously what you're thinking? The two of us uncovering clues, following leads?"

"Banana Republic has the most darling trench coats on sale," Bridget interjected. "Y'all could get matching ones."

"Why not?" Mom asked.

"That's what I say." Bridget nodded. "Waterproof and fifty-percent off - that's a steal."

"Not the coats, dear," Mom said patiently. "I mean, why shouldn't we look into the murders to help Angela?"

"I'll tell you why not." Bridget stirred her coffee. "It's too dangerous for you two to go poking around when there's a killer on the loose."

"Besides," I said, "I'm boycotting Banana Republic. One of the sales guys was snotty to me last time I was there."

"We're perfectly capable of asking a few discreet questions," Mom continued. "I'm not talking B&E or stakeouts."

"Did you complain to the manager?" Bridget asked me. "I would have, or at least given that guy a piece of my ass."

I snickered at another of her tangled clichés, "Yeah that would have shown him."

"Girls!" Mom used her Mom voice. "We're not talking about trench coats. We're not talking about specialty stores or salespeople. We're talking about helping Angela. The topic is investigation."

"What does Dad say about all this?" Bridget asked.

"He's not too keen on the idea," Mom admitted.

"What did he say?" I asked.

"Nothing specific. It's just a feeling I got."

"Because you didn't tell him anything specific, did you?" Bridget proved herself to be better versed in nuance than I am. Must be a mom thing.

"I hinted at the subject, met with resistance and thought it best to bring it up another time. We'll just be asking questions. Your Dad will warm up to the idea after I ease him into it. So, are you in?"

"Explain to me why this is so important to you. You weren't really even friends with those people."

"You know why. Marissa Jannings was my best friend," Mom said. "If anything had happened to me, she would've looked after my daughters, and I'm going to look after hers."

"But Angela isn't in trouble - not really." I put my fork down. "She's just being stupid and immature."

"Sound familiar?"

With two simple words Mom had conjured back up the sick guilt I had felt years ago sitting in the Jannings' living room, listening to my mother in the kitchen comforting a sobbing

Marissa Jannings. Angela had long since disappeared upstairs, slamming the door behind her.

"I can't reach her. Nothing I say, nothing I do, has any effect," Ms. Jannings had said.

"She's almost seventeen, Mari. She thinks she knows everything.

Unable to be alone with my shame any longer, I had crept up the stairs to Angela's room, where I had ignored the "keep out" sign on the door and tried the knob. It had turned.

"Angela?"

Face buried in her pillow, she had told me to get out in a way that had let me know that she meant it.

"I just wanted to say I'm sorry. Really."

"Really?"

I had nodded, not quite able to meet her mascara-smeared eyes.

"Really sorry?"

"Really, really sorry."

At this point, she had pushed herself off the bed and come over to me. "Bitch," She had slapped me across the face.

Before I could even react, she had shoved me out of the room, slammed the door and locked it.

I remained in the hall for a while, heart pounding, hand to my face, until I identified the emotion churning inside me - relief.

But now, thirteen years later, I wondered if that slap had let me off the hook the way I had thought it had. Maybe it had just bought me a little time until I was more emotionally equipped to atone for hurting Angela.

That I still felt guilty about the situation surprised me. Maybe the holidays, my break-up with Jacob, seeing two people die right in front of me and my mother's stare had left me feeling more raw and vulnerable than I realized.

So, what the hell. I would make a cute P.I. I had my Austen Healey, and even if our streets were tree-lined and safe enough for dog walkers and bike riders, I could be sly and sophisticated. Plus, I could finally set things right with Angela, regaining some karma points where she was concerned.

"I'm in," I agreed.

CHAPTER 11

Like everyone else in our family, Mom drove one of the restored cars Dad loved so much and cared for so compulsively. I had barely made it from the bed to the settee Monday morning when I saw Mom's British racing green MG convertible whip into a parking place on the street below.

Straight up nine a.m., you could bet on it. The only thing less likely than my running early was for Mom to indulge my habit of running late. I watched her feed the meter, trying to gauge the weather from her outfit: a coral twin set, chocolate skirt. Pearls probable or at least implied. No coat. Looked like another a typical Birmingham December day, mild and breezy, the first real cold snap still weeks away.

As soon as Mom walked in, I eyed the shopping bag she hoisted onto my counter with grave disappointment - nothing edible or wearable inside. "What, no bagels?"

"What, no shower?" she countered.

I chose to ignore her remark, shuffled to the pantry and scrounged for food.

My loft isn't the cool, sleek urban dwelling you sometimes see on television. More like glorified office space - eleven hundred square feet with hardwood floors and one wall of exposed brick, another of floor-to-ceiling windows. I love the open, airy feel and the lack of structure. Plus, I can keep the loft as office space after I get married, God willing.

Dad built two interior walls, ten-feet-tall banks of sleek mahogany cabinets placed at a right angle to delineate my bedroom and give me some storage. Or really, a place to shove my clothes piles when Mom came over.

I'm into Seventies chic, so the place is decorated in what Bridget calls "Early Brady Bunch." Unlike my sister and mother, who are obsessed with cleanliness, order and the way the toilet paper should face on the roll (new sheet forward, pull from the front), I'm not much of a housekeeper. I seek only peaceful coexistence with the dust bunnies. And though my bathroom is clean, I have a feeling Mom fights the urge to paper the toilet seat before using it.

There's only one other loft in the building, since a pet grooming shop and a health food store reside below. Dad describes the foot traffic on my street as the "hippies and yippies."

Mom walked around checking out my Christmas décor, which included a large Fraser Fir decorated only with colored balls, my snowman collection lining the console table in front of the window, and lots and lots of candles.

"Nice job," she said.

I hadn't even realized I had been holding my breath.

While Mom got comfortable on a boxy sofa with the same coloring and cushioning as a Granny Smith apple, I munched Frosted Mini Wheats out of the box and fired up my MacBook.

"So we're really going to do this?" I asked.

"We're really going to do this."

I hid a smile. Who would've thought my straight-laced little mother would want to get involved in something so harebrained. I mean, Amanda Carstairs Girl detective? Amateur sleuth? Shameless shamus? Or worst yet - busybody? Get outta here.

"This isn't a midlife crisis, is it?" I asked. "You're not going to run off with a cabana boy, are you?"

"Chloe Elizabeth, the things you say sometimes."

"It happens. People think this retirement thing is going to be great - a chance to do all the traveling you've put off, spoil the grandchildren, remodel the house. Then boredom sets in."

"I assure you, my life is very full as is your mouth, dear. Please swallow before you spew any more talk show psychology at me."

"Just know that I'm here for you."

"I appreciate that, and if I come across any cute cabana boys, I'll send them your way."

I laughed and pulled the MacBook onto my lap. This could be fun, or it could be a complete disaster.

Mom and I had never shared the easy camaraderie she and Bridget enjoyed. They're both levelheaded, direct, disciplined, maternal - things I've never been. Our night-and-day personalities caused conflict between Mom and me from the beginning.

On the other hand, when introduced to a tidier, more efficient alternative to diapers, Bridget had potty trained herself. While Bridget never missed a curfew, I had had trouble mastering the concept. Bridget had known from childhood she would be a nurse. I had changed college majors three times and my career twice. With this decorating thing, Mom and I had finally discovered a somewhat shaky common ground.

"Perhaps you've finally outgrown the phase when tantrums, slammed doors and rejecting everything your mother stands for are knee-jerk reactions," she had told me, when I announced my plan to go into the business full-time. "Since that phase has lasted roughly twenty-nine years, you can see why I'm be grateful for the respite."

Mom emptied her shopping bag on the coffee table. "I brought over Saul's books that he gave us as Christmas and birthday presents."

"Have you read them?"

"Are you kidding? Saul quizzed you on them and pouted if you hadn't done your homework."

I flipped through a couple. "Are they any good?"

"They're not really my thing."

"Pictures?"

She nodded. "Most of them have some in the center. They range from the lurid." Mom flipped open *Kill or Be Killed* and showed me a crime scene photo. The grainy, black and white pixilation did nothing to lessen the horror of a smashed skull. "To the melodramatic. Caption: 'Shearer, 36, is led off to death row as his mother holds a crying Sandy, age five.' That's from *We, the Jury*, his first book."

"Right. Saul was on that jury, wasn't he? That's what started his fascination with true crime?"

"And fifteen books followed. Like *Lady Killers*, which he dedicated to Robin."

"He did not!"

"'Fraid so."

I took the book from her and read the dedication. "'To Robin. Your secrets are safe with me.' That's sick."

"That's amoré."

"You think his death could be connected somehow to one of his books?" I asked.

Mom shrugged. "It's hard to say, but they'll help us get to know him better. Oscar, too, since he provided source material."

"These books are so old, though. *We, the Jury* was published twenty years ago."

"But *Lady Killers* was published within the last five.

"What about the book Angela said he was working on when he died? That's the one we should be examining."

"My thoughts exactly, especially if it involves Tony Trianos."

"Think about how paranoid Saul was about his files," I pointed out.

"I have been."

Saul had been paranoid, but in light of what had happened, had he also been justified?

Having seen one gruesome picture too many, I closed the book I was skimming with a snap. "Ok, let's do Oscar. Why would someone kill him?"

"He's a former prosecutor. Lots of enemies there."

"And he was pushing the investigation of Saul's death pretty hard. Maybe that made someone nervous."

Mom nodded. "And he really had it in for Tony Trianos. A dangerous pastime if ever there was one."

I frowned. "What about Gavin Beaumont's theory? That the murders may not be connected at all."

"I'm not buying it. It's incredible enough that there's one murderer running around Arbor Farms. Two unrelated ones? Hard to believe."

I picked up another of the true crime books, *Deadly People. Deadly Passions*, and flipped to the center. "Gross."

"Another skull?"

"Worse. Hot-roller hair."

Mom opened her notebook. "So. Where should we start?"

"Who knows? It sounds pretty overwhelming."

"We just need to start poking around and see what we learn by talking to people."

I pushed the books and my laptop aside and got a folder from my desk. "This morning, while decent people were showering, I googled everyone we're interested in, thinking that might be a good place to start." I passed over a small stack of handouts I'd printed out the previous night.

"And I thought cyber-stalking your ex-boyfriends was a waste of time." She flipped through the papers. "You've honed your skills."

"Nice to be using them for good instead of evil."

"Is Leo still doing personal injury law?" she asked, referring to an ex-boyfriend.

"In a storefront office right down from the Dollar Tree. And, yes, I take great satisfaction in that, no matter if it seems small and petty. It's who I am."

"Jacob better watch his step."

"Why? I'm watching it for him."

"So, what's in all this?" She indicated the stack. "Anything interesting."

"No smoking guns. Nancy is listed in the minutes of about thirty clubs. Gavin Beaumont has published a couple of articles in peer review journals about a new form of birth control. Angela once signed an online petition requesting a new vampire slayer."

Mom raised a questioning eyebrow.

"Robin's condo was featured in a local magazine last year," I continued. "Saul's books got reasonably favorable online reviews, except from one guy who called them schlock. He also had a web site that's a shrine to himself."

Mom flipped through the stack till she found printouts of the site. "I see what you mean. His author's photo is hilarious. He looks a foot taller and thirty pounds lighter."

"I know. That must be a Matchbox version of his Maserati. He's towering over it."

"Look at this one. He didn't even own a dog."

"He references Angela, although it took seven clicks to find it."

"Is this her in the picture?" She showed me a tiny shot of Saul with an even tinier woman in the background. The caption identified Saul and his research assistant.

I took a deep breath. "There's something I didn't tell you at the party. Something about Angela."

Mom met my gaze.

"I think she and Saul might've been involved."

"Oh, God."

"I mean, she didn't say it right out. But the way she talked about him sounded, well, familiar."

"Oh, God."

"It was Mr. Kramer all over again."

"Chloe, I get it. This is worse than I thought. Detective McGowan might read more into that than there really is."

"What if he's right?"

My mother's eyes narrowed. "You can't possibly believe Angela would hurt someone, especially someone she cared about."

"But if she cared too much? Or if he rejected her? Or if she thought he was using her?"

"Whose side are you on Chloe? We've known Angela since she was a child." Mom was well into irritated. "Even if a crime of passion were a possibility, which it isn't, she wouldn't have cold-bloodedly poisoned Saul or killed Oscar, and how does that hand fit into your little theory?"

"Ok, chill." I was startled by her mama lion vehemence. A major change of subject was definitely in order, and I grabbed the printouts. "I also found a bunch of stuff about Bunny and Garrison."

Garrison Moseley, a lawyer at one of the big downtown firms, had been Bunny's first husband. Mom didn't need to look at the articles to remember the scandal. Her friend Shelley Henderson had been right in the thick of it.

"I didn't read all the articles, but they're juicy," I finished.

"That's one word for it." Mom leaned forward. "Remember my friend Shelley who handled media relations for Garrison's firm and for Garrison himself, when he made a bid for mayor?"

I nodded. "A dream come true for Bunny."

"The campaign was going well until his barely legal lover threatened to expose their affair if he didn't buy her a car for her birthday. She needed more reliable transportation on the nights when she closed at the fast food restaurant where she worked. Call it sticker shock, but the Moseleys felt the girl, who had once been content with gifts of stuffed animals and Victoria's Secret sleepwear, was getting too big for her britches."

"Bunny knew about the affair?" I couldn't believe she had tolerated not being the center of any man's attention.

"Not till the blackmail started. Garrison was such a dolt that he turned to his wife for help with his girlfriend."

"Idiot."

"Once Bunny was on board, her life's mission became damage control, and if that meant squashing the girl like a bug under her four-inch Ferragamo heels, so much the better. To hear Shelley tell it, there were twice-daily come-to-Jesus meetings and almost hourly phone calls with the Moseleys. Talk about Lady Macbeth."

"I shudder to think what Bunny would have trouble washing off her hands."

Mom gave me a disapproving look tinged with a smile. I was easing back into her good graces.

"Shelley advised Garrison to 'fess up to the affair before the girl dropped her bombshell," she continued. "Do the whole 'I have sinned' routine and throw himself on the mercy of public opinion, but he and Bunny refused. Garrison insisted the girl had no proof, and it was her word against his."

"But there's always something."

"Shelley tried to tell them that. Hotel receipts? Love letters? Eyewitnesses? Garrison denied they existed."

"Video tape, audio tape, naughty text messages?" I asked.

"Garrison claimed he had been careful. Maybe he had been, I don't know, but Shelley wasn't about to help them advance a lie. So, when the girl went public, the Moseleys set up their own interviews in their living room of that big house in Mountain Brook, the one with the fountain."

I nodded that I remembered.

"They expressed their dismay that this girl could tell such a terrible lie, posed on their gazebo and begged the press to respect their privacy. They even walked down the front steps of their church and told reporters they had prayed for the poor misguided child. I have to hand it to them, it made a credible story. The girl had no proof."

"Like I said, there's always something."

"In this case, it wasn't what the girl had, it was what Garrison didn't as in self-control. He never actually broke off the affair."

"No."

"Yes. So, when a Jefferson County deputy ran he and Missy in for committing lewd acts in her car near the old cannon on Altamont road, it pretty much ended that run for mayor. He'll have to wait six or seven years to get elected now, this being Birmingham and all. We never forgive, but we always forget."

"But Bunny wasn't that magnanimous."

"To say the least. She divorced Garrison faster than you can say 'extreme emotional distress' and took him for a bundle. Before the papers were even filed, she met Gavin Beaumont at a fundraiser and was lounging naked on his examining table three days later."

"Love in the stirrups. That's our Bunny."

We shook our heads, good moods restored.

"Oscar was all over the Net," I said. "Mostly articles about cases he prosecuted and now clients he's defending. Lots of overlap with Saul, especially about black widow stuff. When Saul did his book tour for that one, he gave Oscar a lot of press. And then, when he started dating Robin, the two guys appeared on all the major talk shows."

"Instant publicity."

"For Saul's book and for Oscar's new private practice - not that he needed it, really."

I chewed my pencil thoughtfully, in what Mom would see as a complete disregard for all the money she and Dad had spent on my orthodontia. "You think Saul could've been a blackmailer? Knowing all that he did about people gave him a lot of power. Angela said as much."

"But why? He had plenty of money."

"Maybe he lived beyond his means. Maybe he gambled."

"His checks cashed," Mom pointed out.

Good thing too. Nothing would have incurred her wrath faster than getting stiffed on four French hens and five golden rings.

"Maybe he wasn't in it for the money," I suggested. "Maybe he held things over people's head as an ego thing. He had one." I held up the Maserati picture. "Exhibit A."

"It's definitely a line of inquiry, and whoever killed him might've thought he had told Oscar what he knew."

"Exit Oscar."

"So, who among our suspects has something to hide?" I kept chewing my pencil knowing Mom was restraining the urge to yank it out of my hand. "My money is on Nancy. She's big on appearances, and she was way too interested in Saul's locked study door."

"Ok," Mom agreed. "Write her down. The funeral is tomorrow, but I could probably talk to her Wednesday. I was planning to check on her anyway."

"Tomorrow? That's fast isn't it? What's going on with Saul?"

"I haven't heard anything about Saul's arrangements, but Nancy wanted Oscar's service over with as soon as possible. She's nothing if not efficient."

"I can talk to Robin. She works out at my gym. Maybe her trainer would let me take their next session."

"Stairmaster confessions? I like it."

"Yeah, nothing like a little oxygen deprivation to coax the truth out of a person."

Mom grimaced. "I guess we have to talk to the Beaumonts?"

"Not that anyone would blackmail Bunny. Her life's an open blouse anyway."

Mom suppressed a smile, "No stone unturned."

"We could talk to Jack Lassiter. Get the inside scoop on the investigation."

"I see you've already googled him."

"Just trying to be thorough. There's a lot of overlap with Oscar, and he's on the design review committee for his neighborhood. I can question him since he and Dana work together." I said it casually, but I could feel Mom's eyes on me.

"That leaves Angela, and the Beaumonts," she said. "I've been calling Angela all morning. She's not answering."

"Let's see how it goes with Nancy and Robin and Jack."
Again, I used the breezy tone.

"And Jack." Mom stood and stretched. "There were other people at Saul's party, and your father is right, they didn't have to be at Oscar's party to have killed him. But somehow, I think we should start with the people that were most connected with our victims."

"Agreed. I feel good about this. We have an in the police don't have, which gives us the edge."

"It's not a game, Chloe."

Maybe not, but I still like to win.

CHAPTER 12

My printouts had given us a lot of background on our first round of suspects. Facts, dates and places. The on-the-record stuff. All necessary, but Mom never underestimates the value of rumor, hearsay and innuendo, so she treated us to manicures and a little gossip at Nails and Tales, her friend Charlotte's salon being famous for both.

Charlotte Marshall's husband was a successful plastic surgeon, so she didn't need to work. In fact, she claimed she earned two dollars less per hour than her housekeeper and one dollar less than her pool man. Still, she wasn't the sit-at-home kind, so after her fifth child headed off to college, she had opened up shop.

"I love doing nails and feet, love visiting with the girls, so why the hell not?" she often said to anyone who would listen.

And we all listened and talked, which is why you always headed for Charlotte's for the best scoop. Rub somebody's feet the way Charlotte does, and they'll tell you anything. Plus, Charlotte was always willing to share what she had learned.

"Robin Woodall?" Charlotte blew blond bangs off her forehead, naming the color when Mom complimented her new 'do' – a woman with no secrets.

"She used to be in here twice a week - Sushi Surprise on the nails, Mango Coulis on her feet - a combination that looked better than it would've tasted, I assure you. Then she started going someplace else. Not sure why. She had hands to die for. Long, slim. Perfect for the piano."

Her eyes widened, "Speaking of hands. What was the deal with that one you found at Saul's house? Way I hear it, you girls walked right up on it."

"Not quite, but close enough," I said, as Shana, Charlotte's assistant, worked on my feet with disconcerting vigor. In the winter, I'm a little lax with foot care.

"So what happened?"

Mom gave Charlotte the abbreviated version.

"A rat, huh? Sounds like someone who knew Saul, alright."

"You didn't like him?" I asked.

"Did anybody? If it wasn't for those awful books of his, you think anyone would've put up with him?"

"I don't guess so," Mom agreed.

Charlotte worked on Mom's cuticles, while Shana razored my heels. I tried not to look at the dead skin piling up, thinking if I'd gone another week without a pedi, I might've grown a hoof.

"Why do you want to know about Robin?" Charlotte asked.

"We're looking for new blood on the Arts Council," Mom gave her the line we'd thought up in the car. "Not too late for you to sign up, you know."

Charlotte snorted, something only she could make look cute, and massaged cream into Mom's hands, tugging on each finger in turn. "Me? What do I know about art? My kids' drawings on the refrigerator was the only art I've ever appreciated."

This, of course, wasn't entirely true. The woman had an antique collection Mom would have traded her own kids for.

"The only thing about Robin," I interjected, keeping us on course, "is that with Saul's death, she's developed a certain reputation."

"Developed? Honey, that woman's a black widow if ever I saw one. It's just a matter of time before the police catch up to her and then, you watch, men will still be sending her marriage proposals in the big house."

"The big house?" Mom laughed. "Why would they want a want a woman in the big house?"

"Her kind of charm prison only enhances. Chained heat," Charlotte said knowingly, although from where she had gotten that knowledge I didn't ask.

"I'm still thinking about asking her," Mom said. "Unless there might be a conflict of interest with Nancy Browley."

"Why? Because Oscar thought Robin was sin in a sundress? Mmmhmm. Could be touchy, but Oscar should have been guarding his own henhouse, way I hear it."

"Really? Do tell."

Charlotte shrugged and buffed, glancing my way, as if to ask, "In front of the children?"

Mom gave an almost imperceptible nod.

"I don't know the whole story, but I heard Nancy has a wandering eye."

"No."

"Yes. You know she's real big on playing Lady of the Manor. Well, apparently she keeps a firm hand on the hired help."

"Sweet little Nancy Browley?" I was aghast.

"One and the same."

"And this is common knowledge?" Mom asked.

"Well, I wouldn't say common. My clientele's exclusive with one or two notable exceptions."

We followed her gaze to the front door where Bunny Beaumont was making one of her signature breathless entrances.

"Amanda, honey! I thought that was your car," the newcomer trilled, probably having done a U-turn on two wheels once she had spotted it.

Ms. B plopped down in the chair beside me, "So what ya girls up to today?"

"Amanda's recruiting me for the Arts Council." Charlotte began painting Mom's nails with base coat like a true artist. "Me and Robin Woodall."

An open book, our Charlotte.

"Robin?" Bunny's eyes gleamed, not missing a trick. "Interesting."

"Why?" Mom blew on her nails, now painted a soft mauve. You could mark the seasons by the subtle lightening and darkening of my mother's manicures.

Bunny got up and chose a blue-red shade from the counter that was named Lust…of course. "She's not the typical menopause maven you usually recruit for the Council, not that I mind. I'd like having someone closer to my age on board."

Charlotte's eyes met Mom's. Uh-huh.

"Amanda needs to know if there would be a conflict of interest to have Nancy on the Council with Robin, what with Oscar trying to convince everyone she's a murderer and all," Charlotte supplied.

So much for working under the radar.

"Your small town roots are showing, girl - among others." Bunny peered at mom's hair, still a good two weeks away from needing a touch up, I assure you. "Conflict is good for the Council. Stirs the pot."

"We count on you to do that for us," Mom countered.

"And I never let you down, do I?"

Mom had to laugh. "Not so far."

CHAPTER 13

Getting Robin's trainer to switch sessions with me was a cinch. Randy Falcone was a total gym junkie and leapt at the opportunity to squeeze in a few extra sets on the squat rack. I wondered what kind of girls he attracted with all those bulging muscles, crisscrossed veins and a neck the size of a pony keg. But watching him flirt with an equally buff girl on the treadmill, I figured he did okay.

All trainers keep a notebook on their clients - recording their measurements, their workouts, sometimes even before-and-after pictures. Randy had kept meticulous notes about Robin, and I was impressed.

She was a cardio queen, with spin classes and tennis being her favorite aerobic workouts. But she was no slouch on the weights either, lifting pretty impressive amounts for a girl with her slim build. Randy had her weight at 120, which had remained pretty consistent in the two years he'd worked with her. I found her height (5'8") and her body fat (18%). Bitch.

I tried scanning Randy's handwritten notes, but couldn't make out his less-than-literate scrawl, so I headed to the back weight room where the serious hard bodies worked out. Sure enough, Randy was doing squats, pumping close to four hundred pounds and grunting as if in great pain - not attractive.

"Quick question," I said apologetically, knowing he was in the zone and wouldn't want to be disturbed.

"Shoot."

"I couldn't quite make out your notes and wanted…"

"Smoke her," he wheezed.

"Smoke her?" I ran through my gym vernacular and came up empty.

"Smoke." I didn't think he had another rep in him, but he was going for it. "Her," he said on the exhale.

"Got it." I backed away, not wanting to be there when he expelled a kidney or something.

Really, what was the point of working out that hard when there was so much good TV to watch? As for his advice that I "smoke" Robin, I could only assume he meant to work her out really hard.

I'm not usually the no-pain-no-gain type of trainer, working my gals just hard enough to keep the dimples on the back of their legs from reading like a blind man's diary. But, as with decorating, you give clients what they want.

I looked over Robin's last workouts and saw she was due to move up on the weights. A challenging interval workout seemed to be in order - weights with cardio mixed in. That should do it.

Robin appeared on time and ready to work. I had expected a cute little spandex outfit and lots of lip-gloss, but she had kept it low key - ponytail, no makeup, shorts and a pretty tank. Dynamite figure, not a tablespoon of cellulite. Hard not to hate the girl.

I fibbed that Randy had asked me to take his session.

"Trying to get in a few extra workouts before the competition, is he?" She sounded amused.

"You know Randy." I dimly recalled that he competed in body building competitions from time to time, as good an excuse as any.

"So he told you how I like it?"

"His exact words were 'smoke her.'"

"Show me what you got."

This was a new side of Robin, who I'd always seen as a girly girl - kind of fragile, kind of glamorous. But here she was challenging me to challenge her. Gladly.

We started on the treadmill. Just a warm-up, nothing too strenuous. I decided to get some questions in while she still had her breath.

"So how you doing?" I asked. Again, just a warm-up.

"Same."

"My mom said to tell you she was thinking about you. We're all here if you need anything."

"Right now, I just need a killer workout."

A subtle hint to forestall further questions? I ignored her remark.

"Mom asked me to find out about the funeral." I put on a suitably sober look.

"Not going to be one. Saul donated his body to the University of Tennessee's Forensic Anthropology Facility."

"The Body Farm?"

"A true-crime god right to the end."

Had her tone been a little derisive? I couldn't tell.

Warm up complete, we moved over to do some legwork. Walking lunges with...

I checked the book and saw that Randy had her using two twenty-pound dumbbells. I handed her the twenty-fives. She didn't bat an eyelash.

I trailed after Robin as she went down and up, down and up, along the back hall, making my tone confiding. "You know, until Oscar died, I was with you. I mean, Saul's death looked like some kind of weird accident, but now I don't know. There's got to be a connection."

I noticed with satisfaction that her breath had become a bit jagged. Lunges are hell.

"I know what you mean," she admitted to my surprise. "At first, I was stunned that anyone would even suggest Saul was murdered. I mean, I know how it looks."

She reached the end of the hall and dropped the weights, sinking into a stretch to catch her breath. "But if I were some kind of black widow, someone who had gotten away with two murders, I'd be crazy to kill again, right?"

"Maybe killing your husbands means that you're crazy." I chuckled, keeping it light.

She laughed and picked up the weights. "There's the problem. Saul wasn't my husband, and I'm not entitled to any of his money. What's the point?"

I let her lunge back down the hall in silence. Again she stretched, and then we headed over for some squats.

"So who else had a motive?" I asked.

"Take your pick. My money's on dear, devoted Angela. Did you see that dress she had on at the Browleys? Talk about death warmed over."

"Angela? No way. Much too mousey." I checked her form. The girl knew what she was doing.

"Don't be fooled by her bland exterior. Inside, that chick's pure piranha. Saul knew it, too. Said it made her invaluable as a researcher."

"But she's kind of goody-goody, don't you think? A crusader for justice?" I didn't let on what I knew about Angela and her seething passions.

"Professionally, yeah, she's got it together," Robin admitted, stretching while I set her up to do chest presses. "But in her personal life, a real whack job. Completely in love with Saul, pathetically so. Real smug about it, too, like the two of them shared something I couldn't understand."

"Did Saul return her affections?"

Robin settled in on the weight bench. "Saul kept her where he wanted her - on his payroll, in his shadow. It didn't take much, I assure you."

"So their relationship wasn't physical?" I wondered if Angela had learned her lesson or lost her touch.

"Hardly. That's where Saul was so brilliant. He got to her heart through her head. Had her thinking they were like Sartre and de Beauvoir, their love flowing onto the page, pouring into the work. Angela saw love letters where everyone else saw stories of child molesters and love triangles gone wrong. See what I mean? Whack job."

Was that good or bad? The spurned lover or the spurned wanna-be lover – either way cops called it motive. I let Robin see I was unconvinced. "But why kill Saul if she loved him, and why kill Oscar?"

She sat up. "Her ambitions. Saul was never going to help her get published on her own. Why should he? She realized what an idiot she had been and snapped. Maybe Oscar figured it out, and she had to silence him."

She slid onto the leg extension machine. "Did I hear you're doing some decorating these days? I'm thinking about redoing my guest bedroom."

I couldn't help being pleased. "Yeah, I've been at it for several months now. I could show you my portfolio."

"Is it weird following in your mom's footsteps like that?"

"Not really. She has her own style, I have mine. She's been great about helping me."

"Y'all do get along pretty well."

Nothing like the holidays and homicide to bring people together.

"What about the hand?" I asked, back on task.

"What about it?"

"Did Saul have any theories about who left it for him?"

"Not that he shared. He loved it, though. Wanted to know if he could have it back when the cops finished their investigation."

"Nice."

"What about that Detective McGowan? Slightly dishy in a blue-collar kind of way, don't you think?"

I kept making notations on her chart.

"Maybe he'll ask you out." She stretched again.

"I'll pass, thanks."

"You never know."

We continued alternating upper and lower body, occasionally mixing in cardio. I was impressed at how hard she worked, how good she looked drenched in sweat and how willing she was to gossip.

On the treadmill again, I confided about Nancy's interest in Saul's locked study door.

"No surprise there," she gasped, trying to keep up with the pace and incline. "And she was right to be worried."

"How so?"

Robin shook her head indicating conversation wasn't possible, and I waited patiently till her interval was up.

"You're good," she gasped. "Just what I needed."

I smiled. "Flattery won't get you out of another set of lunges."

"Wouldn't dream of it."

In the back hallway, I asked again why Nancy should be worried.

"Affair. With Lance. Pilates guy. Saul knew all about it."

"And Nancy knew he knew?"

"He told her. To her face."

We both grimaced at how immature the male of the species can be.

She dropped her weights at the end of the hall and leaned against the wall to catch her breath.

"How did Saul find out? Angela?"

She dabbed off sweat with a towel. "I told him, although Nancy hasn't put it together. I was just making idle gossip. I didn't know Saul would hold it over her head like that. He was kind of a jerk that way, you know?"

I noticed Robin had attracted the attention of several men working out nearby. Tank-Top-Boy murmured something to Oversized-Shorts-Guy, and they nodded appreciatively in her direction.

Robin bent one leg behind her in a deep quad stretch and they were even more impressed. She picked up her enormous weights to do more walking lunges, and they were humbled. Good for her.

Which brought up an interesting point. Robin was independently wealthy, twice widowed and unemployed. How did she fill her days?

"Travel, shopping, working out," she answered, "and movies. I'm really big on movies."

"Me, too." I laughed, surprised we had that in common. "If I don't see at least one flick a week, I get all out of sorts."

"And don't even get me started on movie popcorn."

"More addictive than heroin."

"You can go alone, right?" She turned serious. "I can't respect a woman who can't go to the movies by herself."

"Are you kidding? Sometimes, I actually prefer it."

"I'll see anything, too. Schlep across town for the art flicks. Hit the mall for something with no nutritional value."

"And the chick flicks?"

"Good mindless entertainment. We should go together sometime."

Back to business – ab work. I questioned Robin about Trianos. She didn't know anything about the book Saul was working on, if it was about Trianos or if Trianos was just a source.

"I got the feeling you two knew each other, seeing y'all talk at the party," I ventured.

She shook her head, not easy when you're in the crunch position. "Just through Saul."

"He looked quite taken with you."

"Sequins have that effect on men. Ask your mom. Trianos looked taken with her, too." She sent me a wicked little smile.

Just for that, I made her do an extra set of bicycle crunches before sending her to convalesce.

As I completed her session notes, I realized I had a new respect level for Robin. On the one hand, I felt pretty smug about how hard I had worked her out. On the other hand, though, she had taken everything I had thrown at her without uttering a single complaint.

Her motivation shamed me into seeking a killer workout of my own before heading home. Checking the schedule, I noted that there was an advanced step class starting in ten minutes - just enough time for me to find Lance, the Pilates guy, and see what he could tell me about Nancy Browley.

CHAPTER 14

Lance Martin was strutting in from the pool like an over-tanned god in his tiny Stars-and-Stripes Speedo. Apparently, he was the only one who hadn't noticed that the unheated water had him flying at half-mast. Ignoring two girls giggling by the smoothie machine, I approached him, my eyes fixed squarely on his.

"Hey, Chloe-Jo. Whattaya know?" He gave a satisfied nod, as if he had known this moment would come and I was right on schedule.

"Not much. Just wanted to ask you a couple of quick questions."

He smiled indulgently. Questions. Yeah, that's what they all say.

"It's about Nancy Browley. One of your clients?"

He nodded, fixing me with an intense look that probably made dozens of bored housewives slide the passenger seat of their SUV's into the recline position. "I hear you," the look said, "and I think what you're saying is important."

Trying not to be completely grossed out as Lance toweled off his sinewy muscles in a suggestive manner, I pushed on. "It's just that some people are saying you and she have more than a client-trainer relationship."

His intense gaze never wavered as he nodded thoughtfully.

"I mean, I don't care if it's true. I'm certainly not some big stickler for the rules. I was just wondering if, you know, it was." He was really weirding me out with that stare.

"Was what?" he asked finally.

"Was true."

"What's true?"

"That you and Nancy have a relationship."

"Nancy who?"

I managed to hide my frustration, but really. That Speedo must've been tighter than it looked.

"Nancy Browley. Are you guys…um…dating?"

He smiled broadly, his towel now covered in the bronzer that enhanced his golden tan. God, I hate being single.

"I'm not seeing anyone exclusively, if that's what you're asking," he volunteered.

"It's not. I'm asking if you're seeing Nancy."

"Because there's a little room on my social calendar, if you'd like me to squeeze you in."

"I'm good, thanks." I quickly adopted his oily tone. "But if I flipped through that big ol' social calendar of yours, would I find Nancy's name penciled in?"

"You'd find lots of names. I'm a busy boy."

"That's what I hear." I winked. "Any chance you've been getting busy with Nancy lately?"

"There's always a chance."

Grrr. I was about ready to rip out his professionally highlighted hair. Instead, I kept the smarmy note in my voice. "Because, Nancy's quite a handful, right?"

"Right on the money." He winked.

"Likes to be in control."

"Likes to call all the shots," he agreed.

"Bet she even made the first move."

"And the second and the third. The woman's a tiger."

Almost confirmation, but not quite. I tried again. "Is quite the contortionist, from what I hear."

"That's yoga," he said seriously. "Yoga's very different."

I raised an eyebrow, which got him right back on track. "She likes it every which way, let me tell you."

I dropped the bantering tone. "That's all I wanted to know."

"Don't run off. Maybe you'd like a free session or two. Help you loosen up a little."

"Can't. Gotta run." I sailed off without a backward glance. First a workout, then a shower - a long, cleansing shower.

In the aerobics room, I was glad to see Ted Markris was teaching. The man has a gift. Instead of making up routines, he calls out rapid-fire combos that require complete concentration in order not to fall on your face – the perfect antidote for those of us with murder on our minds.

I set my bench in the middle of four guys, so I could watch myself in the mirror and pretend I had backup dancers. It's a little thing I do, and it worked. With Ted yelling and my heart pounding, my mind completely emptied of suspicion, infidelity and murder. At least, until I saw Robin in the back row, completely focused on her workout as if this was the first exercise she had done all day. So much for smoking her.

In the locker room, I wrestled out of a wet sports bra, amused by all the Save the Whales and Preserve the Rainforest T-shirts that had suddenly appeared ever since a gorgeous guy, known as Stairmaster-Dude had begun workouts.

He had granola-guy bumper stickers on his Jeep, and several women apparently thought like-minded T-shirts would attract his attention. Not that I'm above such behavior, but I had it on good authority that Stairmaster-Dude preferred the scenery in his own locker room to that of women's.

As I undressed, I also thought about everything I had learned from Robin and Lance. Nothing that could help Angela.

If anything, Robin had made a pretty convincing case that Angela's ambitions had gotten the better of her, and you only had to spend a minute or two with Angela to corroborate the theory. It gave her a pretty strong motive for killing Saul, but right now her only motive for killing Oscar was the one Robin had suggested - he might have suspected her in the first murder.

I didn't see how, though. Oscar had been fixated on Robin and Tony Trianos.

And what about Robin, I wondered as I headed toward the sauna. She was a mystery unto herself.

Really, you have to admire women who feel confident in a locker room without swaddling themselves in towels and darting from locker to towel rack (take the shape of the towel rack), from towel rack to upright scale (take the shape of the upright scale) before finally slipping into the vapor folds of the steam room.

In the sauna I coated my hair with deep conditioner, let the steam work its magic and thought about Robin and her somewhat ingenuous claim that she hadn't expected Saul to use his knowledge of the affair against Nancy. Really?

Given the way Saul had treated Robin or the way he had treated Angela for that matter, it had been obvious the man liked to hold things over people's heads. Had Robin been deflecting some of his mind games away from herself and onto someone else? Couldn't blame her for that.

And what about Saul, knowing his best friend was being cuckolded, to use the *Canterbury Tales* term for it? Did he tell his best buddy Oscar? No. He taunts Oscar's wife with his knowledge - not a nice man.

My skin was pinking and puckering like a finely done roaster. Heaven. Just then, who should walk in but Robin herself, wrapped only in a towel round her hair. Walking slowly enough for me to see that every inch of her was waxed, buffed, plucked and polished to perfection, she joined me on the cedar steps, one tier up.

I was a little surprised that she sat so close. There were just the two of us in the room. And yet, there were Robin's long bare legs, curving right next to my head. Her intent wasn't sexual, but rather one of intimidation, someone who knew how to use her body as a weapon.

She clasped her bent knees and rested her cheek on her hands so that her mouth was near my ear. I scooted over a little, but that's not a good idea on a soft wood like cedar. To get up would have been to admit that I was unsettled, and for some reason, I didn't want her to know that.

"Now I want to ask you a question," she said softly.

I waited, marveling at this sudden shift in her personality. From trophy girlfriend to uber athlete to dangerous adversary, all within the space of a couple of hours.

"What's your family's interest in all this?" She used that same soft, confidential tone. "First your mom, grilling me at the Browley's. Now you at the gym. What gives?"

I shrugged with more nonchalance than I felt. "Guess we're just nosy like that."

"You two wouldn't be playing girl detectives, would you? Spicing up your dull routines."

"Hardly. My mom's life is full."

"Because, as either of my former husbands could tell you if they were in a condition to do any talking, I'm not someone you cross."

I pretended to play a piano in minor key, "Da, da, da DUM. Come on, Robin. Naked threats? Very Movie of the Week."

She sighed and sat back. "Why do people continue to underestimate me? Is it the ponytail? The boobs?"

"I don't underestimate you. I just don't intimidate easily." Lie. Lie.

"Is that what you think I'm doing? I thought I was letting you in on a little secret."

"That you killed Saul?"

"Not even close. I've got a lot of sins on my soul, but that isn't one of them."

"How about your husbands?" I countered.

"Let's just say I find widowhood to be a very satisfying lifestyle and pursued it."

"With insulin and an empty Epi-pen?"

"One sometimes does what one must."

"So you're admitting you killed them?" I wanted to be clear on this.

"I'm telling you that I didn't kill Saul or Oscar. I hope my being candid on other subjects will convince you of my truthfulness."

"So by admitting you killed your husbands, you think I'll believe you when you say you didn't kill Saul or Oscar."

"No stranger to nuance, are you?" she said dryly. "I admit nothing. I merely point out that if I killed before, there was something in it for me. Saul's death and Oscar's? Not much benefit for Robin."

"That we know of."

She stood up, towering over me. "I'd like it if you believed me, but it's not crucial. Just stay out of my business. Because if I am a killer, I'm a good one. I'd think about that if I were you."

I wanted to do the whole minor key piano thing again, but didn't trust my voice to come through. I watched her go in silence, the back view even better than the front.

When I was sure she had had enough time to clean up, I left the steam room and did my walk of shame toward the showers.

Stopping for gas on the way home, I felt tired and a little depressed. After my talks with Robin and Lance, I needed an infusion of Christmas spirit and fast.

I wondered if any of the classic claymation shows would be on TV that night. The previous year Jacob and I had gone to the Alabama Theater, where we had sung Christmas carols with other theatergoers to the Mighty Wurlitzer while lyrics flashed on-screen. But there was little chance of our doing that this year.

Chilled in my light warm-up jacket, I got back in the car while the gas pumped and watched a girl and two guys who were hanging out by the back of an old Chevy Blazer. Their stories were immediately clear.

She was pretty enough, dark hair and smooth skin, but the baggy jeans and too-big cotton cardigan she wore to conceal her weight accentuated her self-consciousness. The skinny guy who was flirting with her looked to be about thirty, although he had the build, mischievous grin and animated hand gestures of an eleven-year old. His tawdry charm and her low self-esteem promised a long and rocky relationship. The third man - smoking and saying nothing - was bigger, older and harder, and he watched his little friend close the deal as he had many times before.

The younger man opened the Blazer's tailgate, which was crammed with luggage, boxes and a dog carrier holding a yappy dog. Skinny wiggled his fingers into the carrier, and he and the woman laughed as the yapping cranked up a notch. He then dug in the Blazer's way-back and pulled out a gift for the woman, a piece of corrugated metal cut out to look like a fish and painted the Alabama state flag colors. She was touched and would sleep with him the first time he asked.

He reached back into the depths of the Blazer and pulled out a tin of store-bought cookies. She hugged the tin to her and would soon let him store his things at her apartment, trusting him with the pin number of her ATM card.

The dog barked sharply, and Skinny slammed a fist against the door of the carrier, probably the same way he would react in six months when she complained of the charges he'd run up on her cell phone bill.

I replaced the nozzle back into the pump and screwed on my gas cap. What was Jacob doing right now?

CHAPTER 15

"The hardest part is waking up in the morning." Nancy stared into her glass.

We were in her back sunroom overlooking the pool. Neither she nor Mom had touched the bagels I had contributed to this little party. I'd eaten mine with a speed and enthusiasm Mom obviously found alarming. Luckily, our hostess provided plenty of distraction.

Eleven-thirty on a Wednesday morning and here was Nancy, still in a matching nightgown and peignoir, sipping mimosas like it was Sunday brunch. The Pekingese pup at her feet regarded me warily.

"I thought getting to sleep would be the worst, tossing and turning, but it's that moment when I realize for the first time each day that he's gone, that it wasn't a dream."

I felt my eyes tearing up. Mom reached over and touched Nancy's hand.

"Our marriage wasn't a great one. What marriage is?" Nancy spoke with great concentration, her high-heeled slipper going still on the soft cork floor, stained a rich mahogany.

Mom's eyes met mine as we both thought of one.

"But now that he's gone..." Nancy gulped some mimosa. "I always thought he would be around to take care of me. There's never been a time when someone wasn't taking care of me."

"We're all here for you," Mom said. "You have many friends who are here for you."

Platitudes - all we had for her. It felt even more wretched.

"We hadn't made love in fifteen years, you know."

Okey-dokey, then.

At this little tidbit both Mom and I reached for our own drinks, and seeing our discomfort, Nancy giggled and sloshed juice on the table. I suspected this wasn't her first cocktail of the morning. Maybe not even her first pitcher.

"I'm being horrible, but it's true. Good thing I didn't have to identify the body. I don't think I would've been able to." Here her laugh ended in an unbecoming snort. Not exactly the picture of a grieving widow.

The previous day's funeral should have been our first clue that Nancy wouldn't be observing an extended mourning period. It was a small private ceremony, the family and a few of Oscar's friends. The main goal had been to repay Nancy's social debts and to throw another elegant party. The Christmas theme at this one had been garish and unseemly. The only genuine emotion the grieving widow had displayed was when her hairdresser asked delicately if she would need to cancel her standing Friday appointment.

"No! Of course not. Whatever for?" Nancy had removed the thought from consideration.

Standing appointments at Tress Chic were hard to come by, and it had taken several minutes and half a Xanax to calm her down. So now, I was a little curious about how far Mom would push her.

"You two always seemed so happy," Mom ventured. "I know he cared for you deeply."

"And I cared about him. Of course, I did, but.." She looked out over her beautifully maintained pool and exquisitely manicured backyard. "It was a partnership more than a marriage. A joint venture without passion. Remember passion, Amanda?"

I looked away, not really wanting to know the answer to that one.

"Marriages evolve over the years," Mom said. "You do what you have to in order to keep them strong."

"I think he had girlfriends," Nancy confided. "I never asked, and he never said. He was very careful."

We weren't about to touch that one. Her dog sank into a weary heap at her feet, obviously having heard it all before.

"Women always turn a blind eye, don't we?" Mom sympathized.

I hid a smirk. Yeah, like Amanda Carstairs would ever live like that.

Nancy chuckled. "I come by it honestly – a mother who put up with anything to keep the peace and a father who thought of himself as a patron of the arts. Put a lot of strippers through Ole Miss one dollar at a time, my daddy. Class of '76 had an unusually high concentration of fake boobs and press-on nails, thanks to our family's money."

Mom smiled, knowing Nancy was taking her measure, trying to determine if we were shocked by her alcohol-induced honesty.

"Some men don't have a lick of sense," Mom commiserated. "Sometimes it works in our favor, sometimes it doesn't."

A nice, neutral response. Empathetic. Just one of the girls.

Nancy refilled my glass and her own, then topped off Mom's from which only two sips had been taken. We were in.

"Fifteen years, you say? That's like forever," I prompted.

"I guess he thought I'd be content to dry up and wither away."

Detective stuff is not for the squeamish.

"You're still a vibrant woman," I pointed out.

And she was, really, with the well-maintained look of a woman of a certain age - hair still a honey blond with enough highlights to look luminous, enough lowlights to look natural. Plumpness worked in her favor, the effect girlish and pretty. Her skin was smooth and clear, only its structural underpinnings - the telltale softness about the chin and hollowness around the eyes - giving any hint of her age. Maintenance had become a full time job.

I glanced at my mother, whose face was so familiar, but I couldn't look at it as objectively. Still, she looked damned good.

Nancy remained on the subject of her husband's indifference. "What did he think I was doing for the last decade and a half? Crossing my legs and waiting for death? Hardly."

Too much. I grabbed the empty pitcher. "Are we ready for another?"

Without waiting for an answer, I headed for the kitchen. The Peke flashed me a look on the way that said, "Coward."

Nancy's huge, Spanish-style kitchen gleamed with mahogany cabinetry, limestone counters and more stained cork floors. Over an old porcelain farm sink, a gorgeous leaded glass window turned the blue of the pool and the green of the grass into a watery fresco.

We had offered to break down her Christmas décor. One the services Mom offered with her designs was the packing away of ornaments and trim in neatly labeled boxes, so they would all be within easy reach next year, but Nancy had said the trappings of Christmas gave her comfort.

As a result, thousands of Santas smiled at us from every surface. Now I don't know about you, but if my husband had been zipped into a body bag wearing a red flannel Santa suit, I wouldn't want reminders of the fact staring me in the face. Call me crazy.

But back on the subject of infidelity.

Through the screen door, I could hear Mom taking advantage of my absence to get to the good stuff. I hid a shudder as I mixed another batch of mimosas in the Waterford pitcher. From where I was standing, I had a clear view of the action.

"What woman can live without passion?" Mom asked.

Not that Nancy needed much prompting. "Not this woman. Oscar wasn't the only one who got a little on the side among other places."

She took a gulp from her glass and looked disapprovingly at Mom's full one. Mom took another sip.

"How did you manage it?" Mom morphed into the picture of innocence. "I would've been terrified of getting caught."

"It's not so hard." Nancy laughed and took an extra-large sip of her drink.

"Not so easy, either. You would have to keep your wits about you. Any close calls?"

Nancy remained quiet, clinking the ice in her glass. They sat for a moment, listening to the pool pump out back, a far-off lawn mower and the Peke worrying wetly at an itch on his back leg.

Damn. Just like that, we'd lost her. One moment it's sentimental musings, the next inappropriate sharing and now moody silence. I was having a hard time keeping up.

Mom sent me a questioning look through the screen door. I could only think of one way to get Nancy moving again and tilted an imaginary glass up to my lips. All the way up.

The Peke's glance said this was not my best work. Mom made a face, but I gave her a stern look. She took a deep breath and drained her glass.

"Any more where that came from?" Mom asked, meaning information as much as alcohol. I took that as my cue and headed back out.

Mom gave Nancy a 'not in front of the children' look, for which I was grateful, so after refilling their glasses I made a big show of clearing away the bagels and returned to the kitchen.

"What were we talking about?" Mom wondered aloud. "Oh, yes, trying not to get caught."

"As a matter of fact, I wasn't as careful as I should have been." Nancy was back in dish-the-dirt mode.

"Oscar caught on?"

From where I was standing, I could see that the Santa we had found by the pool the night of the murder was gone. Had the police taken him? Was he in an evidence locker at the police station? Weird.

"Are you kidding?" Nancy said. "I'm still walking around. Oscar was king of the double standard."

"Let me guess, someone else got wind of it and couldn't wait to lord it over you." Mom met my eyes over the rim of her glass.

"You got that right."

"Probably one of those catty wenches at the club, I bet."

"I wish."

"Who then? Not your…gentleman friend."

I rolled my eyes. Did she have to sound like such a goody-goody?

"Don't be silly. I chose them carefully. No, this was one of our friends. One of Oscar's friends, really, a college buddy with too much time on his hands." She stopped short of admitting it was Saul.

Liar, liar pants on fire, I wanted to sing. But didn't.

"Did he try to get in on the action?"

"Certainly not." Nancy grimaced. "He just wanted to taunt me with what he knew. He didn't care about Oscar. He wasn't looking out for his best friend. He liked secrets."

"Sounds like our dearly departed friend, Saul Taylor."

Up went Nancy's defenses. "I didn't know Saul all that well. I couldn't say."

"You weren't missing much," Mom said. "To know him was to dislike him."

"I thought y'all were friends." Nancy again took Mom's measure.

"Let's just say I knew him well enough to be careful around him."

Nancy glared out over the pool. "If you knew him at all, you knew that. Sneaking around with his notebooks and his innuendoes and making threats. My marriage wasn't perfect, but I sure as hell didn't want it to end." Her slip of admitting Saul was making threats didn't even seem to register.

"I wouldn't be surprised if someone found a way to silence those innuendoes for good," Mom coaxed.

"I wouldn't be surprised or upset."

"Do you know of anyone else Saul was holding something over?"

"I'd sure like to get a hold of his computer discs to find out."

Now this was good, and Mom must've thought so, too. "You think he kept more on those discs than book research?" she pressed on.

"Oscar thought he did. To tell you the truth, I wouldn't be surprised if Oscar had them, and they're now gone for good."

"Why Oscar?" Mom sounded as incredulous as I was.

"He didn't seem stressed that they were missing, and he would have been if he ad thought he could find something out about Tony Trianos from those discs."

"He really had it in for Trianos, didn't he?"

"It was tearing him up inside."

"And when Saul started hanging around him?"

"Oscar was furious, but Saul liked his little games." Nancy's tone was bitter, her glass empty.

"Did Saul say why he was spending so much time with Trianos?"

"A book, of course, the subject of which he only hinted at. Whether the book was about Trianos or he was just a source, I couldn't tell you."

"If Oscar did have the discs, wouldn't he at least have told Jack Lassiter?"

Ooh, good one, Mom.

"Probably not. Oscar thought Jack was a mama's boy."

I pictured the tall, broad shouldered Jack Lassiter. A mama's boy? Say it ain't so.

"You must have been going crazy, thinking Oscar had the discs." Mom plodded along like the trooper she is.

Nancy sent her a slow catlike smile. "Depends on how he got them in the first place."

"You're losing me."

"If Oscar wasn't supposed to have the discs, he couldn't admit what he knew except about Trianos, which he wouldn't be able to sit on because it was his life's mission to bring that man down. If he revealed something about me, then I'd know he had the discs, which would've given me leverage. At the very least, Oscar would've tampered with evidence. At worst, he had murdered Saul."

"You really think he would've done something to Saul?"

Shocker.

"Not really, but who knows? Not that any of it matters at this point." Nancy's tone had become philosophical.

"Meaning?"

"Saul was trying to hurt me with his little games. I lived in fear of my husband finding out about my…hobbies. Now Oscar's gone, and it all seems so meaningless. No one can hurt me any more than they already have."

I had to wonder if she had personally seen to that.

CHAPTER 16

Late afternoon found me finishing up sketches for our next large project in Arbor Falls - Monica Dupree's all-white installation. Mom was letting me take the lead on this one and I was determined to dazzle her. After all, this job was perfect for me.

Monica appreciated understated drama, pristine white with bold shots of color, gleaming silver and glittering beadwork. Her outrageous budget let me be completely indulgent mixing fabrics and textures, and I had snapped up bolts of burnt-out velvets and cascades of the softest silks. This was our last house of the year, and I couldn't wait to see it completed.

Truth be told, I couldn't wait to put this entire season behind me. It's hard to keep the Christmas spirit and work so hard around the holidays, especially with bodies turning up in houses you're decorating. I know I sound like a brat, but really. I can't work like this, people.

I was just completing another fruitless eBay search for Mom's Waterford Hope for Healing ornament, when she came by my loft to check on my questioning of Jack Lassiter. My friend Dana had set up a lunch for the three of us - on the sly, of course, so he wouldn't know we were trying to pump him for information.

"That's not what you wore?" Mom asked without even a hello as she gave my chocolate brown cords, striped tee and clogs a worried glance. "Cute, but hardly appropriate for sleuthing."

"Uh, no." My eye roll implied, but not executed.

Like I don't know any better. We're a pale people, we Carstairs women, and must rely on every artifice we can get our hands on to reach our cuteness potential. I would never go near Jack Lassiter in clogs.

My mother must've known she was overplaying the Mom card, because she didn't point out that the lenses of my glasses were so smudged they looked like I'd fallen face-first into a plate of mashed potatoes. For some reason this drives her crazy. And for some reason, that makes me happy. Typical mother-daughter stuff.

I fixed us some tea - hot for her, iced for me, and we headed to the settee. Two weeks before Christmas and still open window weather. You had to love Birmingham.

"Dana's still being cagey about the bridesmaid dress she expects me to wear, which does not bode well," I started conversation flowing.

"You still haven't seen it? I thought the wedding was next month."

I nodded. "She's got my measurements. I go for a fitting in a few days. As for lunch, I barely spoke to Lassiter. He was going to eat with us, but got a last minute call he had to take."

She wrinkled her nose. "Too bad. Now it'll be twice as hard to arrange a 'convenient' meeting."

"Not so hard," I smirked. "We're going out tomorrow night."

"You're kidding." She was impressed. "How did you manage that? Green dress?"

"Green dress." I laughed, remembering the way Jack had given me the slow up-and-down. "Never fails."

I don't know what it is, but my bottle green Tahari tank dress makes me irresistible to the opposite sex. When I get married (God willing), I'm having it bronzed.

She frowned. "Are you sure it's a good idea to go out with him?"

I grinned. "How else can I get close enough to find out information."

"How close are we talking?"

"Don't worry." I dismissed her concerns with a wave of my hand. "Dana's chaperoning. I will say though, Jack's really very attractive if you're into perfectly chiseled all-American types." I smiled to show her that I did.

"Just keep your wits about you," she said pointedly.

"Always," I replied, just as pointedly. "We're going Thai for dinner, then maybe UltraViolet for drinks."

"Jacob's favorite bar. Interesting."

"Is it?"

She let me off the hook and turned the subject onto what we'd learned from Nancy Browley. "Oscar taking the discs? The plot thickens."

"We should check with Angela on that one," I pointed out. "See if she thinks he could've pull that one off. Unless we find out someone else could've managed it, she and Robin are still our best suspects. They both had access that other suspects didn't."

"Angela still isn't returning my calls."

This time I did roll my eyes. Why were we running around trying to help someone who obviously didn't appreciate it? Oh, yeah, because guilt's a bitch.

"Nancy was pretty candid about her flings," I put us back on track.

"Disturbingly so."

"And Robin all but admitted she knocked off her husbands. Are we really good at this detective stuff, or are our suspects just not threatened by us?"

It was Mom's turn to roll her eyes. "I think the entire lot of them are crazy. Cheating spouses, black widows, Saul and his investigations, Oscar and his Santa suit doling out gifts - sickening."

"You forgot the ambitions of our little Angela and the Beaumonts.

Mom made a face. "Who could forget the Beaumonts?"

"We need to finish questioning all our suspects," I continued, "while at the same time looking for those discs, because whatever's on..."

"Good Lord, Chloe, how can you see out of those glasses?" Mom couldn't stand it any longer. Ten minutes she had waited. A personal best.

I cleaned them on my T-shirt and continued, "Because whatever's on them might give us new motives we don't even know about."

"What better motives do we need?" Mom counted off on her fingers. "Saul might have had proof of Robin's crimes. He knew about Nancy's affair. He was taking advantage of Angela. He was doing something with Tony Trianos, and Oscar was dying to know what."

"And the motives for killing Oscar?"

"All of the above. If Oscar had Saul's discs, he knew what Saul knew, and he also might've known who killed Saul."

I rattled the ice in my glass. "So motives we have, but we still need the discs to know which one was worth killing for."

CHAPTER 17

Thursday morning was uncommonly productive for me. I trained Martie Hollister in her spectacular home gym, paid bills, and did sketches for Marla Finster's vintage-inspired baby nursery, all before the morning talk shows ended. Then I hit a couple of shops in search of the antique broaches I planned on giving Mom, Bridget and my grandmothers for Christmas.

Procrastination? Not this year.

I already had a beautiful onyx Art Deco pin for Mom's mom and a funky, jeweled dragonfly for my sister. Two down and two to go, but no luck on this particular outing.

Exhausted before ten o'clock, I consoled myself with a Chai Latte, feeling virtuous for resisting a cranberry muffin. All in all, this was way harder than I usually work, but it couldn't be helped. Fitting detective stuff and holiday shopping into my already haphazard schedule was a challenge.

Today, I was supposed to meet Mom at Margie's flower shop to pick up supplies for Monica Dupree's house. Then, if we got the chance, we would head over to Saul's to see if Angela was around. All of which didn't leave much time for extensive grooming required before my night out with Jack Lassiter.

Before I could do any of that, though, I had to drop Mom's files off at the police station, our having stalled as long as she dared. According to Dad, who made a point of running into the detective at the courthouse, McGowan didn't seriously consider Mom as a suspect. Still, looking over the files was an unchecked box on his to-do list, and McGowan prided himself on being thorough.

So did Mom. She had pulled the invoices, highlighted the overages in three different ink colors, attached corresponding approvals and photocopies of the deposited checks, and then outlined everything in a typed cover letter. My acting as her messenger was her brand of passive resistance.

When I arrived at the police station, Detective McGowan was taking a call. He took in my grey BCBG pencil skirt, layered tanks and clacky sandals as if he were going to identify me in a lineup.

We were on the final countdown before Christmas, and yes, I was in short sleeves, no jacket. The thermometer read mid-sixties, but the day was pure '80's, as in 1985 or 1986. Chances of a white Christmas? Slim to none.

"The files you asked for." I plopped them on his desk when McGowan hung up.

"Thought I was going to have to get a court order. Your mom thinking about claiming client-decorator privilege?"

He waved at me to sit. I perched.

"She was giving you every chance to come to your senses."

"It's been known to happen. Coffee? It's fresh."

I shook my head.

"It's Starbucks. Made it myself. That swill you read about cops drinking in detective novels is pure fiction."

"I don't drink coffee."

"Don't tell me. Herbal tea? Squeeze of lemon, when you're feeling sassy?"

"Diet Coke." I hoped he couldn't smell Chai Latte on my breath.

"Be right back."

While he was gone, I leaned over to see if I could find anything of interest on his desk. Autopsy report. Suspect list. Anything along that line.

Instead, I saw a framed picture of a Golden Retriever. A girl's arm was draped over the dog's neck, but her part of the picture had been folded to the back. Just as I had suspected - the dog came first.

"I get a kick out of you Southerners and your soda at breakfast. Don't see a lot of that in Boston." McGowan popped open my can (presumptuous of him) and handed it to me.

If there are two words I loathe hearing together, it's "you" and "Southerners." Ranks right up there with sneeze guard and sanitary napkin. And it's usually followed by pithy observations like "I can't believe you Southerners have paved roads" or "I didn't know you Southerners had access to dental care." But at least now I had a reason for my ambivalence - the man was a Yankee.

"So, did you need anything else?" I asked.

"Signed confession?"

"'Fraid not."

"Anything you want to tell me about Angela's relationship with Saul?"

"She worked for him."

"And that's all?"

"That's all." Or so I hoped. It was time I spelled a few things out for him.

"Look, Angela sometimes rubs people the wrong way. The whole hyper-intense reporter thing, it's her passion. But it's also her way of keeping people at a distance, so she can relate to them in a way she's comfortable with."

"All of which means what to my investigation?"

"That she shouldn't be a suspect just because she's standoffish or because Saul was her mentor and seemed closer to her than most. Underneath her hard exterior and sketchy social skills is a kind of naïve girl." I was surprised to discover I believed what I was saying - a good sign. I might have an easier time proving Angela's innocence if I were convinced of it myself.

McGowan smiled his indulgence. "Angela's not a suspect because she isn't a social butterfly. She and Robin are suspects because they have the strongest motives for stealing Saul's discs and killing him."

"What motive could Angela have?" Feigned ignorance really doesn't become me.

McGowan's version of events played out like Robin's. No surprise there. My trying to refute his arguments only made him defend them more strongly, so I tried another tack.

"But Robin's a better suspect, right? I mean, men who hang around her do have a way of dropping dead." Sorry, Robin, desperate times and all that.

McGowan wasn't impressed. "She's definitely a suspect. I'd say they're neck and neck. On the other hand, the discs and the icicle? Robin's an ice princess, too cool for that foolishness."

"Whereas Angela, right up her alley?"

"I think you had it right. There's a lot going on under the surface there."

Great work, Chloe. At this rate I'd have them convening a grand jury.

I tried the old stand-by - best defense is a good offence. "What you're really saying is that you don't know anything. You suspect a lot of things and have a few theories, but as for cold, hard facts, you've got nothing."

McGowan's face hardened. "We know quite a few things actually."

"For instance?"

"For instance, I know where you can find a guy whose left hand doesn't know what his right hand is doing."

I couldn't hide my shock. "You found the one-hand man?"

"In the flesh. What's left of it."

I gaped at him. "Spill it. Who is he? What's his connection to Saul? How the hell did his hand get cut off?"

McGowan laughed at how I was salivating for information. If we hadn't been discussing severed body parts, I might've wondered if he was flirting with me.

"Vice arrested a guy on an unrelated case and he coughed up some information he thought might earn him some points with the DA. As in the location of a dismembered body, buried behind a warehouse in a not-so-nice section of Birmingham."

"Who is he? Was he?"

"Charles Moriarty. No criminal record, no connection we can find to Saul or Oscar. But according to our informant, Moriarty had a gambling problem that he couldn't stay ahead of. Stole some money from the wrong folks and got himself killed."

"Gambling?" I repeated.

"Illegal gambling, most likely. The kind someone with a problem usually gets mixed up in. And sooner or later, their problem becomes our problem." He twirled his pencil. "Every time we shut down one of these operations, another one springs up within a week."

I sat back in my chair. "But Moriarty couldn't have killed Saul or Oscar..."

"Not single-handedly."

"And if he wasn't connected to them, how does he fit in?"

"We'll figure it out. We always do."

I grabbed my purse. "Good luck with that."

I started to make my exit, but McGowan had some questions of his own.

"So, why wasn't your boyfriend at those parties?"

"What makes you think I have a boyfriend?"

"If you didn't have a boyfriend, you would've had a date. Going alone says one of two things to me - steady boyfriend who works odd hours or a military guy overseas. Or maybe you have an unsteady boyfriend, and you two are on a time out. Maybe he's one of those guys who picks a fight around the holidays, so he doesn't have to get you a gift."

"Is this part of your official investigation?"

He flashed a smile. "Just curious."

"I think you'll find those files thorough and complete. You've got a lot of work ahead of you."

"I better get on that then, hadn't I?"

"Thanks for the Coke."

"Anytime." He chuckled. "Another thing I like? The way you Southerners call soda Coke, no matter what flavor it is."

"Nice dog." I gestured toward the framed picture. And with him reeling from that deathblow, I left.

CHAPTER 18

When I got to Flower Fantasy, Mom's new Escalade, The Tank, was already parked out front. Though she loved her MG and all the other cars Dad had restored for her, Mom had insisted on at least one vehicle from this century.

"I need cargo space, Alex. I need amenities," she had made her point. "Women need cup-holders."

Dad, who loved all motorized things, had grudgingly agreed and taken the Escalade (not exactly the small, understated SUV Mom would've chosen for herself) in trade from a car-dealer client.

And funny? Lord, we laughed watching four-foot-ten-inch Amanda Carstairs climb in and out of the massive vehicle, using a maneuver banned in Olympic gymnastic competitions for being too dangerous. Of course, nobody laughed when they caught sight of her in their rear view mirror barreling down the Red Mountain Expressway or glimpsed her (gasp) parallel parking the thing.

Mom used the Caddy's newfound power for all it was worth. From our perspective, she needn't have bothered. My mother is plenty intimidating standing in her own size four pumps, as any ticket-writing cop or back-talking daughter could tell you.

As for Dad, once he had gotten over his disdain for a pre-fab vehicle that stayed in perfect working order (Mom refused to let him make custom "improvements"), he enjoyed all the car's luxuries.

"The bun warmer may just be the greatest automotive advance of our time," he had conceded.

Lily was our other big Caddy fan, having made friends with an OnStar operator a few months previously when we were loading the vehicle for a camping trip to Mt. Cheaha. The fact that she was being unusually quiet and cooperative as we lugged backpacks, coolers and camp stoves from the house should have been our first clue that she was up to no good. Make that quiet, cooperative and content to play in the front seat, chatting with her "imaginary" friend Miss Shelby, who could be summoned with the push of that little red button with a white cross.

Of course, the police had come - three of them. Thankfully, we were able to explain the situation before a SWAT team repelled from helicopters onto my parent's front lawn.

Margie's workshop always dropped my blood pressure at least ten points. Delicate floral scents and tangy citrus mingled with the darker undertones of lush greenery and moist soil. The air was cool, damp and still, as if no loud noise or sudden movement could exist produced there.

Inside the shop, Cassie was already giving Mom the rundown on arrangements she and Margie had put together for Monica's installation. There were dozens of white poinsettias, their soft white leaves tinged with pale green that would march up Monica's curving front staircase and sit in clusters around the three downstairs fireplaces. Sweetly scented nosegays of white roses, Oriental lilies, lisianthus, stock and greenery would serve as accents on side tables, tucked into niches and peeking coyly from Monica's Royal Copenhagen white open-lace teapot. The largest arrangements featured velvety white roses, snowy cushion pompoms and sprigs of fragrant jasmine nestled around spectacular Longiflorum lilies.

"Madagascar jasmine?" Mom stroked a white waxy flower with a pungent scent, looking especially tiny next to the huge arrangement that would soon grace Monica's antique Chinese entry table.

Cassie nodded. "Stephanotis floribunda. Cultivated specially for the Christmas market, since it usually flowers in summer. The Christmas rose, here and here, is white hellebore, known for its white or pinkish-green flowers. Legend has it that an Angel gave one to a shepherdess who had no present for the baby Jesus."

"Another last-minute shopper." I joined them behind the counter.

"It's also known as the semen of Helios," Cassie added with a mischievous smile.

"Mom arched an eyebrow. "We won't mention that to Monica."

"She the shy type?" Cassie asked.

"Definitely not, and we don't want to encourage her."

Cassie was in for a treat since she hadn't met Monica Dupree. Artist. Sculptor. Painter. Photographer. Above all, eccentric, as you might imagine of someone whose favorite subject matter is erotica.

Monica had a knack for depicting objects usually viewed as hard, slick and sordid in a delicate, loving way. Consequently, subject matter once banished to shrink-wrapped magazines sold behind convenience store counters was now being deconstructed by Mountain Brook blue hairs sipping dry martinis.

Cassie took Mom through the rest of the lineup, mostly hyacinths, another kind of jasmine (Jasminum officianale) and narcissus.

"She can plant these outdoors if she has a sheltered garden or keep them in pots to flower next Christmas."

"Tell Margie this all looks terrific."

"You can tell her yourself. I think I hear her pulling up out back. Speak up though."

The crunch of Margie's tires on the back parking pad ground to a stop.

"Still not wearing her hearing aids? They make her feel old," Mom sympathized."

"Well, being half-deaf makes her cranky."

"What was that, Cassie?" Margie carried a large takeout coffee, a folded newspaper, and a purse the size of a small valise through the back door.

Favoring a dogwood, she wore a black, white and charcoal grey caftan that flowed beneath a head encircled by whisper thin curls that might fly away in the slightest wind. She was younger that my mother but looked older, wiser and preternaturally serene.

"I said drinking half-decaf makes me crazy," Cassie enunciated with exaggerated care.

"Wouldn't touch the stuff myself. A little steamed milk starts my day." Margie presented her oversized cup as Exhibit A.

"Well, girls, what do you think? Do the arrangements suit, or should we turn them into mulch?"

"They're gorgeous. Perfect," Mom gushed.

"And the lilies are breathtaking," I added.

"Breakfast? No, you girls go ahead. I already ate." Margie tucked her purse under the counter and didn't see Cassie's rolled eyes.

"We're taking a few of the smaller arrangements to Monica's now," Mom said. "The others will be delivered when?"

Margie nodded. "Should be there in about half an hour. You can take some of the smaller arrangements now if you're heading over."

Oh, brother.

"See what I mean?" Cassie said, as we stowed the nosegays in the back of the Caddy. "It's like that all day."

"And she won't even try the hearing aids?" Mom asked.

"For a day or two, but she's into high-fiber health foods and says chewing with her hearing aids makes her crazy. Sounds like quarters in the dryer or something."

"They have volume controls, don't they?" I asked.

"That's what I said. To which she replied, 'So do you dear, speak up!'"

"This is the last of them," Margie spoke suddenly right behind us, then smiled when we all started. "See, all that caffeine makes y'all jumpy."

Cassie closed the tailgate. "I'll be over to help you guys set up in about twenty minutes along with the truck."

"Sounds good," Mom spoke very clearly. "Thanks again, Margie. You never disappoint."

So how did the investigating go after that? Let's just say it didn't.

I filled Mom in about Charles Moriarty and the illegal gambling ring on our way over. Then our big plan for checking in with Angela had to be scrapped as we explored every variation on the white theme Monica and my mom could dream up.

My sketches and ideas were well received, but became a jumping off point. As an artist, Monica's eye for color and composition rivaled Mom's, and the two of them whipped themselves into a design frenzy, feeding off each other's creative energy. Every excited cry of "what if we tried" or "wouldn't it be lovely," meant more toting, hanging, draping, or pinning for Cassie and me.

Not that Cassie minded. She was enchanted by everything about Monica.

First there was the artist herself, whose lifespan was impossible to determine. Monica's white hair was cut short, a mere downy glow on her brown scalp. Age had taken all structure from her facial bones, giving her back the amorphous softness of a newborn, but her skin was as creased and translucent as crumpled rice paper. On the other hand, her eyes were piercing and incisive, her body sleek and ramrod straight from a strict swimming regimen.

Monica's home provided intrigue as well - sparsely furnished with little to distract from her artwork that consisted of stark nudes, charcoal genitalia and sculpted I-don't-know-what's. Cassie was mesmerized.

"Lordy," she said of photos spread upon Monica's dining room table.

Peering over her shoulder, I saw a nude man casting quite a shadow on a plain white wall.

"You like?" Monica's laser eyes were upon me.

"Very nice." My Southern good manners came to my rescue.

"I can't decide." She cocked her head. "The composition's nice, and of course, he's fabulous. Still, I don't know. Should I have them framed, or just throw them away?"

"Framed." I felt my knees weaken.

"Or at least mounted," Cassie suggested.

Mom shot her a look.

Once the installation was underway, I knew I'd be cutting short all the pre-date prep I had planned.

Noon - no exfoliating, no sunless tanning.

Two o'clock - no softly curling updo, no experimentation with new eyeliner.

By four, it was no new pedicure and no stopping for conditioner. Retrieving the old bottle from the trashcan and swishing water in it would have to do.

By five-thirty, I had resigned myself to being late.

In the shower at six, I rubbed water from my eyes, so I could hear better.

Funny the way people get their senses all mixed up. My friend Jeanette Ernhardt does the same thing. Always afraid her car is burning oil, she'll turn down the radio, sniff and ask, "Do you smell that?"

Eyes dry now, I could clearly hear knocking on my front door.

Dana.

Early.

Damn.

I found a towel and dripped my way to the door. On the other side, I found not Dana, but Jacob.

Well, well.

CHAPTER 19

Jacob and I had been going out for almost two years. Casually at first then building steam over the last year. Our relationship had come to a head four weeks ago during what will hereafter be known, at least in my mind, as Incident at Crybaby Gorge (it's not on any map, don't even look).

Actually it was in Little River Canyon, a camping trip on which, hopped up on S'mores and insect repellant fumes, I had hinted to Jacob that I might be, *might be* thinking of marriage at some point. "To you, of course," I had clarified, seeing his blank expression.

This news had been received with the nervous high humor of an IRS audit, and things went downhill fast.

For years I had skipped over those magazine articles that told what to do when your man won't commit. Consequently, I knew a million ways to remove unwanted body hair (not that I have any), but was clueless as to how to deal with our present situation. So, I broke things off. Maybe not for good, but for good enough.

"If it's space you want, you got it," I had told him. "Not since the Louisiana Purchase has so much space been awarded so cheaply."

I had told him, "Remember your refusal to go out on our first Valentine's Day together, citing fear of 'all those lovers' the way one would say 'all those lepers?' Well, in one year eight months, we haven't come a long way, baby."

I had told him, "At first I thought maybe you did know best, you being the older more experienced one. But now I see that with experience comes baggage, and you, my dear, have an entire Louis Vuitton matched set from hatbox to steamer trunk." (The fact that I had used my mother's material was proof of my emotional distress.)

Finally I had told him, "Now I'm doing the thinking for both of us, and I'll disseminate this information to you on a need-to-know basis. Right now, all you need to know is that when the phone rings, it won't be me."

Ok, we all know I didn't say that to him.

To him I had said, "Fine! Let's see other people!"

To which he had replied (And this will echo in my mind forever), "Okey-dokey."

The good stuff I ranted to my steering wheel as I completed an eight-point, tire squealing turn out of his driveway after our last big blow up, one eye in the rearview mirror hoping he was following. The good stuff, I had told myself, I would say to him after we got back together for the sole purpose of picking the fight all over again, so that I could say the good stuff. Then I would step over his limp, recrimination-ridden body on my way out the door - for good!

But what was this?

Was fate smiling on me at last? Because here he was in my doorway, discovering me dripping daintily in nothing but a towel. Here at last I had the upper hand, and it was clutching that towel loosely, letting it edge eeeever so slightly downward.

Jacob's surprise showed on his face as he found it impossible to meet my eyes. "Just thought I'd drop by. Say hi. See what you were up to."

Really cute, this guy. Did I mention he plays soccer? I'm a sucker for soccer players.

He even sports a beard. I had never seen myself dating a guy with a beard and had even cancelled our first date when a friend of mine came into town, telling her breezily, "Oh, it wasn't a real date, he has a beard."

Now, I recognized that it added to his outdoorsy granola-boy persona. Plus, the beard had proven to be a great exfoliator. Truly. My skin has never looked better.

But…

One must be strong.

"I'm getting ready to go out." I cast my eyes downward. "I don't have a sec to talk. I'm running late as it is."

Jacob studied my face for a second, a pained expression filling his own. "Some other time then?"

"Sure." I held onto breezy and noncommittal. "I'll call you." Ha! Take that!

He turned, and I closed the door before I could call him back.

Life was good. I was good. Things were looking up.

Smiling, I returned to the bathroom, wiped condensation from the mirror and screamed. Mascara, left over from earlier that day, had run down my face in rivulets, forming black half moons under my eyes and caking in the corners.

Like a crazy woman my gaze shot from the shower (where I pictured myself using my fists on my face like squeegees) to the door (where I'd been so casual, so self-assured) to the phone (which was now ringing).

It was Jacob on his cell phone. "May I speak to Alice?"

Bastard. Already calling another woman.

"Alice doesn't live here," I said through clenched teeth.

"Are you sure? I was just up there, and I could've sworn I saw Alice Cooper in a towel."

"We are soooo over," I said with finality.

"Are you sure that's such a good idea? Not everybody's going to warm up to your new Goth look like I did. I think we should have dinner next week to discuss it."

For a moment, my hostility hummed along the connection between us. "Fine," I shot back. What choice did I have? I wasn't willing to going down – not this way.

"Fine." I heard the smile in his voice. "I'll call you."

CHAPTER 20

Two hours and two Coronas later, I felt like my old self again, mascara firmly in place, hair looking great (if a little under-conditioned) sitting across the booth from Mr. Six-Feet-of-Sex-Appeal, Jack Lassiter. Life can turn on a dime, can't it?

Dana had chosen the restaurant - a new Thai place where the drinks were strong and the lighting flattering. She had one eye on Jack (who looked particularly fetching in black pants and a light gray V-neck sweater) and one eye on the door, where her fiancé was supposed to appear at any moment.

Dana had revealed to me on the way over that she had a crush on Lassiter, though she would never act on it. Unless she got the chance. It was just talk, though, because Dana was way too excited about becoming Mrs. Daniel Carlson to stray off course now.

We chatted about inconsequential stuff until Dan arrived - late as usual, no excuses. We then ate dinner, chatted more (mostly about Dana and Dan's upcoming wedding, still no word on the dress), drank more and then headed to UltraViolet in Five Points. Good.

I had my own car, and Jack had his. Dana would ride over with Dan, and if she stuck to her usual MO, she and Dan would turn the five-minute trip into a thirty-minute ride either by fighting or making out. Just enough time for Lassiter and me to talk.

As usual the front room of the bar was crowded and smoky with a small band and dancing. Jack and I headed for the back where it was more quiet.

I didn't spot my mother immediately. She had her back turned. But the fact that she wiped her chair seat off with a linen handkerchief before perching on the edge of it made her identity unmistakable.

Hiding my irritation, I smiled and told Jack that if he bought the first round, I'd get the second. He headed off to the bar. I made a beeline for Mom.

"If it isn't Mata Hari in sensible shoes," I hissed, taking the seat next to her.

"Chloe! Hello, darling. I didn't expect to see you here."

"Spare me. You didn't think I could handle this alone?"

"Darling, I don't know what you're talking about. I'm here with Bunny Beaumont, going over some fundraiser stuff. She's at the bar." My mother craned her neck to look for Bunny. "My, it's crowded in here." Innocent green eyes turned back to me.

I had to laugh. Mom must've been desperate to endure an evening in a smoky bar with Bunny Beaumont.

"Nice trench coat," she said. "I see you and Banana Republic have patched up your differences."

"I'm working within the system." I smoothed my new short trench over a skirt that was roughly the same length, a fact that wasn't lost on my mother.

I was about to reassure Mom when a man tapped her on the shoulder. At a glance, tall, mid-forties, amazing facial tan, faded jeans and a Stetson.

"Baby, I don't want long walks on the beach, I don't want a deep soul-searching talks…" he began.

"I don't want to dance," Mom interrupted.

"Fair enough. Probably shouldn't be dancing anyway." To our surprise, he sank into a chair, leaned forward and lowered his voice. "Just had my appendix out, and the doctor said I should take it easy for a few days. Guess that includes dancing. Name's Rory."

"Rory, I don't mean to be rude, but we're talking - in private." Mom used a tone and gave him a look that I remembered well from my childhood.

"Don't mind me." He completely misread her. "I'm just enjoying the view. Anyone ever tell you you're the prettiest girl this side of the table." He laughed, willing to hit on us both equally. What a guy.

"I'm going to have to ask you to leave us alone." Mom smiled sweetly. "We're talking."

"Whatever you say, Sassy." Rory turned his attentions toward me. "I like me a sassy woman. Course I like all kinds of women, but I prefer a little spirit, something to challenge me. Can't stand a clingy woman, always needing a man around."

"Believe me," I assured him, "we don't need a man around."

Rory beamed. "Another sassy one. Must be my lucky night."

"Rory…" Amanda managed to look down her nose at him.

He slid his chair back a foot from the table and made a big show of turning his back on us. "There," he threw over his shoulder, eyes twinkling. "I'll leave you girls alone, but I'll be right here when you need me."

Mom and I exchanged looks.

Jack had finally reached the front of the line at the bar, so I got to the point. "I don't need a chaperone."

"You said Dana was going to be with you."

"She and Dan are probably parking their car."

"It's just that you're a little vulnerable right now," Mom whispered, glancing toward Rory. "You've got a job to do, so don't get distracted."

"Hence the crowded place, the separate cars and Dana," I pointed out.

"I'm just here as back up."

"I'm fine. Anyway, I don't sleep with guys on the first date."

"This isn't a date."

"Then, I guess that rule doesn't apply."

"Not funny, Chloe Elizabeth."

"Just kidding. Look, keep a low profile, and I'll fill you in tomorrow. Trust me."

She nodded, and I got up as Jack paid for our drinks. Bunny Beaumont, decked out in hot pink capris and a strapless white top, was talking to someone at the bar and would be for a while.

"She's all yours." I told Rory, gesturing to Mom.

His chair slid back to the table, and he spun around, giving my mother his full attention. "So, Sassy, what is it you look for in a man?"

"An appendix," Mom answered.

CHAPTER 21

Once Jack and I were seated, knees almost touching on overstuffed couches in the back of the bar, he preempted my carefully crafted information-extraction techniques, (plying him with more beer, delicately worded questions and maybe a little look-see at what a well-placed bra could do for a girl) by saying, "Word on the street is that you and your mom are investigating Saul and Oscar's deaths."

"Investigating?"

"Yeah. So imagine my surprise when I heard you wanted to talk to me. Did your mom send you to interrogate me?" His green eyes were mocking.

"My mom?"

"Is there an echo in here?"

"She's not my boss." I smiled, and he smiled back. Delish. "But since you're on to me." I forced myself not to picture that little scenario. "Mind if I complete my assignment?"

Jack leaned in, his blond hair slipping over his forehead. "Fire away."

I cleared my throat, all business. "Are the police convinced that Saul's death was connected to Oscar's?"

"That's a safe assumption."

"Any sign of Saul's computer discs?"

"None."

"Any indication that Oscar had them?"

"None."

"Because the way I hear it, Saul gathered information on people and then hold it over them, and you're one of those people." That threw him off guard.

"Your knees have crew cuts." He pointed to where I'd been razor careless.

I fixed him with a business-like stare as I wondered how unlucky I could be with guys and grooming.

He shot me a mocking smile. "I didn't know Saul that well. He was cultivating me as a source, an 'in' at the DA's office with Oscar now in private practice, but I don't chase publicity the way Oscar did."

"That might change if you grow political aspirations."

He shrugged as a group of twenty-somethings crowded into the back room with us. I noticed the appreciative double-takes a couple of the girls shot Jack, followed by speculative glances my way. "How did she...how serious are they...what if I...?"

Jack didn't seem to notice, and I remembered Dana saying none of the girls at work could attract his attention. A guy focused on his career.

"How about Robin? What's her story?" I restarted our conversation.

"What's yours?" he countered. "Why the Nancy Drew routine?"

I hid a smile, pleased at the comparison.

"No story. Just nosy I guess." I took a sip of my beer. "You were saying about Robin."

"Don't know her well, either. I know Oscar wasn't a fan. He thought she had gotten away with killing her husbands and Saul was a fool to mess with her."

"What do you think?"

"Innocent till proven guilty." His eyes restlessly scanned the bar, settling on no one.

I noticed Jack wasn't the only one getting approving glances from the opposite sex. A guy in the corner obviously liked what he saw when he turned his dark eyes in my direction, and I...

Nope. Scratch that. He was looking at Jack, too, although Jack was oblivious.

"What about Trianos?" I asked. "Also innocent?"

"Even I'm not that naïve. We'll get him. It's just a matter of time."

"So what's your theory on the murders?"

"What makes you think I've got one?"

"Everybody's got one." I was loving this cat and mouse game we were playing, willing to stare into those eyes all night if need be.

"I think it's cut and dried. Saul toyed with the wrong person. Oscar found out whom and had to be eliminated."

I sat back, trying to picture the scenes. "But how could Saul be killed in front of all those witness, the computer discs stolen and no one's the wiser? And why was Oscar killed so brutally when Saul's death was so devious?"

"Oscar's death looks more like a rage killing. In his own way, Oscar was just as creepy as Saul about passing judgment on people. Those 'Christmas presents.'" His derisive tone surprised me.

"What Christmas presents?" But even before the words were out, I knew - the Santa bag. I couldn't believe we had forgotten about them.

Jack looked sorry that he had brought up the subject.

"So spill it." I leaned closer. "Who got what?"

He rolled his eyes. "I can't remember everyone. There were thirty gifts in there."

"Hit the highlights. Start with Nancy."

Crinkling his eyes in the most adorable way, he tried to recall. "Not positive. Something innocuous. A gift certificate, maybe? Yeah, for Pilates."

Innocuous? Hardly. Oscar must've known about Nancy's affair. Had he learned about it from the missing discs?

"What about Robin?"

"Nothing for her. Nancy said they weren't expecting her to show up, but we found a wrapped gift in the study that we think he planned to give her - first edition Agatha Christie - *Murder is Easy*."

"Ouch."

"See what I mean? Creepy."

"Who else?" I asked. "Angela Jannings?"

"Mmm. A pair of handcuffs, I think."

I raised an eyebrow.

"Your guess is as good as mine."

"How about you? What were you getting?"

Jack shrugged. "There wasn't anything for me."

"Right. You just don't want to say."

"I'm serious. I was going to walk away empty handed."

"Interesting. Was I getting anything?"

"Your whole family was getting a week's use of the Browley's house on St. George Island. Nice, huh?"

"Very. I don't guess that constitutes a binding contract."

"Take it up with the widow."

Dana flopped down on the couch next to me. "Sorry we're late." She touched her lipstick self-consciously, hiding a smile. "Dan stopped at the bathroom, then he's getting us drinks."

A few minutes later, Dan brought over a round of beers. Jack favored the same dark, chocolatey beers Jacob did, their appeal lost on me.

"You should check out the condom machine they have," Dan suggested once he was settled. "Flavored. Colored. Glow in the dark." He shook his head. "Novelty stuff. Condoms aren't something you joke around about."

"I don't know," Dana said, already well into her beer. "A little good-natured ribbing can be nice." She laughed, hiccupped and flicked her eyes toward Jack.

From Dan's sour look, I suspected their ride home from the bar would not be as pleasant as the ride over.

CHAPTER 22

Dana and Dan didn't even make it through their first beers before their bickering reached DEFCON four.

Jack was looking at his watch. I was looking across the room to where Jacob was now sitting with some of his work buddies.

Not that the term 'buddy' adequately described the cute new interior designer they had recently hired. Bosom buddy was a more apt description. Spaghetti straps? Try angel hair pasta. And this the cold and flu season.

Still, Jacob wasn't the only one out with an attractive member of the opposite sex. I figured it wouldn't hurt for him to see me with a guy like Jack Lassiter. See other people? Don't mind if I do.

"Oh, like you never flirt, Mr. I Always Make Time for My Fans, especially the pretty ones."

Jack leaned over to me. "I'm heading out."

I looked at him in alarm. "Now? No! I mean, walk me to my car. Just let me say 'hi' to a couple of friends, and I'll be ready."

Jack nodded, obviously not happy about the delay. Dan called Dana a jealous harpy. I promised I'd make it quick.

Jacob's work friends greeted me with loud enthusiasm. This hadn't been their first stop. Where had I been hiding myself, they wanted to know.

I explained about the Christmas houses. They were more interested in the murders and the severed hand, but I waved them off. Occupational hazard.

"I love your coat," the new interior designer said after introductions.

"I really don't need you to be all cute and endearing," I said in my head.

Jacob pulled me aside. "I see you decided to lose the scary black makeup and return to your old sexy self."

"If it ain't broke."

"You double dating?"

"For now. Dana and Dan might not make it much longer."

I let him follow my gaze to where the unhappy couple sat with the absolutely adorable, if a little irritated, Jack Lassiter.

"They at it again? God, what's the point?"

"Apparently, they think they have something worth fighting for." Lame. I wasn't going to convince Jacob of anything using those two as Exhibit A.

"I know that guy. Jim? Jack?"

"Jack Lassiter," I said, loving the sound of it.

"Yeah. He's on the design review committee of his neighborhood. He approved the Farrington remodel I did. Nice guy."

"Nice? He's gorgeous. Can't keep his hands off me." It just kind of slipped out.

Jacob smiled down at me. "I doubt you'll get into much trouble with your mom sitting in the other room, pounding apple martinis."

Grrrr.

"As a matter of fact we're on our way out," I said, a little stiffly. "It was good seeing you."

"You too, Chloe. We're still on for dinner?"

Nodding, I signaled for Jack and headed off, sneaking one last look at the new interior designer as I went.

I had planned to breeze past Mom with Jack Lassiter, sending her maternal instincts into overdrive. After all, what better way to soothe my wounded pride than by driving my mother crazy? But the scene in the main bar stopped me cold.

Mom and Bunny were sitting at a two top crowded with empty martini glasses. Not good. Amanda Carstairs is strictly a chardonnay kind of gal - the butterier the better, throwing in an occasional cabernet just to mix it up. But sour apple martinis? Uh-uh.

If you've never had the pleasure, this bright green sour concoction is a curious blend of the sweet and the sour, tasting a lot like a crisp, ripe Granny Smith apple. It's so hard-candy harmless, it's easy to sip yourself sloppy.

Seeing Mom's over-bright eyes and over-wide smile, I said good-bye to Jack on the sidewalk, not even caring that he didn't seem a bit disappointed about no goodnight kiss.

Back in the bar, I maneuvered myself as close as I could without being seen by Bunny and sought Mom's attention. It took a second, but finally she looked my way. With eyes that had trouble focusing, she signaled for me to stay away.

Great.

I just prayed she was faking tipsy, thinking Bunny would dish the dirt easier to a drinking buddy than to a casual acquaintance from the same social circle.

From where I stood, I could see Rory across the bar, plying his charms on more receptive prey - a woman whose low-cut dress and grateful expression said the ink was still wet on her divorce papers. More importantly, I could hear Mom's conversation.

"I'm worried about Nancy. You checked on her lately?" Mom sipped her drink.

I made a slicing signal across my throat. Cut it out.

"I called her today," Bunny said. "Three sheets to the wind, but her sister's flying in this weekend so she'll be fine. When the insurance pays and the will gets settled, our little Nancy'll be rolling in it."

"But they were well off with Oscar alive," Mom pointed out.

"Yeah, but Oscar controlled all the money. He was generous, don't get me wrong, but she wanted it all. Now she's got it."

"Wonder what she'll do with it?"

"Poor Amanda. So naïve." Bunny signaled a passing waitress and, before I could protest, ordered two more drinks.

I glared at Mom.

Bunny continued, "I know for a fact Nancy ran off the man who cleaned their gutters last fall. The poor man felt violated by her behavior, even threatened to tell Oscar or report her to OSHA or some such nonsense, and him a happily married father of three."

"What did she do?" Mom traded her empty glass for the full one the waitress offered.

"A lot of walking past windows in the nude. A saucy bump-and-grind routine, when she 'had no idea he was working today.'" She mocked Nancy's innocent tone. "Stuff like that."

"And Oscar had no idea?"

"Please. He wouldn't have put up with that for a minute, not that he wasn't getting his own gutters cleaned, if you catch my drift."

"Anyone I know?"

Bunny waved Mom off. "Some paralegal with a pair of D-cups - old news."

"I hear Saul was kind of, you know, holding it over Nancy."

"Wouldn't surprise me."

"Why not?" Mom asked.

"He did the same thing to my first husband. The bastard."

I wasn't sure for whom the expletive was meant, but I found it interesting that Bunny and Saul had a history.

"You mean Saul knew about…"

"Uh-huh. But did he bother to let me in on the joke? No, ma'am. Every time I saw him talking to Gavin, I cringed, wondering if, once again, he knew something about my husband that was going to bite me in the butt."

"I can't believe you guys were still friends."

"It's too small a community to hold grudges. Best just to watch your back and keep dancing."

Loud laughter from the bar made it sound like plenty of people shared her philosophy.

"What will Robin do now?" Mom asked.

"Who knows? Who cares?"

"You don't like her?"

I wondered if Bunny resented Robin's youth and beauty.

"I just don't have much use for her. She's a snaky one. Didn't you see the way she was playing up to Tony Trianos? And to Jack Lassiter? A girl would be wise to watch her man around that one."

Ah… Competition. Bunny wasn't one to share the spotlight.

"You sure finished that one in a hurry," Bunny laughed. "I'm ready for a refill myself."

I looked down at Mom's empty glass in astonishment. How the hell had that happened?

"No way, Bunny. Uh-uh. I couldn't."

"Too late. I already signaled our server. Last call, I promise."

"You think there was something going on between Robin and Tony Treenos?" Mom tried again. "Tree-ah-nos."

I was going to have to drag her out of here.

Bunny laughed. "I think Robin wanted there to be, but with the dress I had on? She was out of luck."

"Don't you mean the dress you almost had on?" Mom teased.

"It was a knock out, wasn't it?"

"A knock off?"

Uh-oh.

"You feeling ok, honey?" Bunny asked.

Mom nodded. "Course, why you ask?" She licked her lips. "Why. Do. You. Ask."

The waitress put new drinks down. Mom carefully slid hers away, sloshing a little on the table.

"It's too full," Bunny chided. "Drink it down a little so it doesn't spill."

Mom did as she was told, despite my signaling like a third base coach, then pushed her glass away again. "You drink it."

"Sure. Just leave it there."

Mom looked around. "I can see why Chloe chose this place. It's funky."

When she turned back to the table her drink was back in front of her. That bitch was trying to get my mother drunk and succeeding beautifully.

"Chose this place for what?" Bunny asked.

"What?"

"You said Chloe chose this place. For what?"

I put my hands to my head, willing my mother to keep her wits about her. But apparently they had been drowned in a sea of sour apple.

"Questioning Jack Lassiter." Mom's words were graced with a slight 'sh' sound to them, particularly those that didn't contain the letters 'sh.'

"Questioning him. 'Bout what?"

"You know, this and that. Various and a sundry."

Cagey little thing, wasn't she?

"Give me a for instance."

"For instance, 'where were you on the night of December fourteenth?'"

"And why would she be doing that?"

"I'll ask the questions here!" Mom snapped.

Good cop, bad cop. Subtle, Mom.

Mom seemed to have forgotten I was hiding out. "Look, she's going home with him." She turned right toward me, pointing to where Rory was leaving with the woman in the low-cut dress.

Bunny turned.

Busted.

"Well, well. Guess it's my turn now to be questioned."

"What? No! Silly thing," Mom replied. "We know where you were the night of December fourteenth."

I pulled over a chair and sat next to Mom.

"Because I thought it was strange that you wanted to go out tonight." Bunny was talking to Mom, but her eyes were studying me with more shrewdness than I liked.

I wondered if she wore contacts. Her eyes really were a most improbable shade of green.

"Amanda?"

"Bunny?"

"Was that why you wanted to go out tonight?"

"C'mon. We never go out. I thought it'd be fun."

"It is fun. Another martini?"

"No!" I pulled Mom's half-half full glass over to me.

"So, did Gavin know Oscar and Saul before he married you?" Mom asked, back down to business.

Bunny looked amused. "Why, Amanda Carstairs, I do believe you girls are playing detective."

"Just simple, everyday curiosity," I took a sip of Mom's drink. Lethal.

Bunny laughed.

"So you got an answer or what?" Mom said sharply.

"Ok, I'll play. Yeah, he knew them both. He had been a consultant on a case Oscar prosecuted, and when Saul wrote a book about the case, he was a source. *Baby Brokers*, I think it was called.

"So they all got along?" I asked.

"One big happy family."

Raised voices and more laughter at the bar attracted our attention. By the looks of all the pretty young things in low-slung jeans, sheer tops and high heels, a bachelorette party was well underway. One of girls wore a cheap bridal veil, and the others were making her complete tasks on a crumpled list pinned to her shirt. The girls' drink of choice? The apple martini. I was getting too old for this.

I turned back to Bunny, ready to complete my questioning and head home. "And how about you? Saul ever try his little emotional blackmail schemes on you?"

Bunny laughed again. "I'm surprised at you two. You know I don't have any secrets. What fun would that be? Now, let's talk about you, Amanda. Monica Dupree isn't scared to have you decorating for her? Seems to me, your last couple of clients haven't fared so well."

"So you mentioned to anyone who would listen." Mom's eyes narrowed. "But no, Monica's just fine with me working on her house. It's going gangbusters."

"Brave soul. I don't think I'd risk it." Bunny leaned in, her tube top slipping precariously so that the deep line of her cleavage looked like an undiapered baby's bottom. "I mean, if you're really looking into this, you might consider that someone has it in for you."

"There would be easier ways to get at her," I scoffed. "In that scenario, Oscar and Saul would be innocent bystanders. Hardly the case."

"Maybe so," Bunny mused, leaning back. "Still, I bet the police are taking a long hard look at her. As a suspect, I mean. Close ties to both victims. Full run of both murder scenes. Who knows what she was up to."

"You're losing your mind, dear," Mom said. "As well as your shirt." She pushed my chair back "I think it's time we called it a night. I'm just going to slip back and say good-bye to Chloe."

"I'm right here, Mom."

"So you are, dear. I'm afraid I could use a ride home."

CHAPTER 23

"Did you puke? You might feel better if you puked."

"Chloe, if you say that word one more time, I swear I'll disown you."

The next morning brought Mom a pounding headache, a queasy stomach and a visit from her younger daughter. I found her on the couch nursing what I gleefully identified as a hangover.

"I'm just saying…"

"I know what you're saying, and I would appreciate it if you wouldn't say it in that annoyingly shrill voice of yours. Whisper."

"Did Dad see you this morning? Bet he got a kick out of it." Really, Christmas had come early this year.

"He did seem slightly amused." Mom cringed at the thought. "God. I only had three and a half drinks. Four if you count the wine I had before going out just to make being around Bunny more tolerable. True, I didn't have much dinner, but this is ridiculous."

"Hey, guys! How's our little patient?"

Mom winced at the sight of Bridget in the doorway and then fixed me with a withering glance. Her revenge would be swift and sure.

"She's hanging low," I said. "Very low."

"What are her symptoms?" Bridget asked, sitting next to me on the edge of the couch.

"Headache and nausea," I supplied.

Bridget put her hand on Mom's. "Any chance you could be…pregnant?"

Mom yanked her hand away and used one foot to kick Bridget off the couch. I could tell the movement sent an aftershock of pain through my mother's head.

"You girls need to leave now. My dying wish is to be left alone."

"Did she puke? You might feel better if you puke," Bridget said in all seriousness.

Mom spoke clearly. "I obviously failed to instill any sense of class or manners into you girls. You are both without the slightest bit of decorum."

Bridget smiled indulgently and dug into her purse, pulling out three bottles of Pedialyte. "Best thing for a hangover. I've got cherry and apple."

Mom moaned. "Don't say apple."

"What were you doing out with Bunny Beaumont in the first place?" Bridget poured juice into the water glass Mom had just drained. "Since when are y'all such big buddies?"

I jumped right on that one. "That's the best part. See, Mom was being her usual nosy self, making sure I was on my best behavior with Jack Lassiter. When really, in a deliciously ironic twist, she was the one who needed a chaperone, because she was the one slamming drinks like a sorority girl at a keg stand."

Mom grabbed my wrist and squeezed a little harder than necessary. "Didn't I tell you to keep your voice down? Now, get going, the both of you. You..." She pointed to Bridget. "Hand me that juice. And you..." This to me. "Be back here in three hours with chicken salad sandwiches and a large unsweetened iced tea, ready to work. I've put up with all I'm going to."

By the time I got back at noon, Mom looked more like herself. The iced tea helped, and the chicken salad soaked up the last of the alcohol. It would be a long time before she would have another cocktail.

I could tell she was in no mood to hear any more teasing, so as we ate we got right down to exchanging notes on the previous night.

Mom thought my news about the gifts in Oscar's Santa sack was quite interesting, while I was still intrigued that both Bunny and Gavin Beaumont had a history with Saul.

"Handcuffs, huh?" Mom referred to the gift Oscar had intended for Angela.

"Could be innocuous. Crime was her life. Or it could mean that she was somehow bound to Saul."

"Or something else entirely, maybe something with the severed hand? We need to think on that one some more. As for Nancy's gift, I would've liked to have seen her face when she opened that one."

Like the handcuffs, the gift certificate for Pilates lessons could have been given with either innocent or malicious intent.

"Did you find out about the Beaumonts?" she asked.

"I almost forgot about them," I confessed, "but as soon as I remembered, I asked. Jack said Bunny also got a Pilates gift certificate, which I thought was weird. If Oscar knew about Nancy's affair, was he also implying that Bunny was fooling around with Lance? Or was he simply handing out gift certificates?"

Mom didn't have a guess on that one either. Bunny and Lance? I'm not saying it was impossible, but Bunny hadn't even hinted at such a thing.

"What about Gavin?"

My mouth was full, so I signaled Mom to wait a sec while I chewed and swallowed. "Antique speculum," I said with a shudder.

"A what?"

"You heard me. Apparently Gavin collects them. It was wood, from like the 1860's and came with a matching obturator."

"And that is?"

"Some other kind of gynecological device, also wood, used to put medicine on the mouth of a cervix. Or, get this, direct leeches to the cervix."

Mom pushed away the rest of her sandwich and reached for her tea. "My goodness."

"I know. Apparently the cops had to get Dr. Beaumont to identify the gadgets because nobody else knew what the heck they were. Their best guess was some kind of shoe stretcher."

"Ah."

"Yeah. And Dr. Beaumont was all disappointed when he saw them because they would've been a nice addition to his collection."

"Moving right along. I say we head out to Saul's so we can catch up with Angela, ask her about the discs, the handcuffs and anything else we can think of. Then we'll put in a couple of hours at Monica's if you're up for it."

I said I was if she and Monica didn't get as manic as they had yesterday. Mom assured me she was in no mood for mania today, so we tidied the kitchen and headed out.

Saul's house had a slightly deserted feel when we arrived, so it was a surprise when the front door swung open. Even more of a surprise to find Meagan Taylor, Saul's daughter, on the other side of it.

Not to be uncharitable, but Saul's daughter wasn't exactly the delicate flower type. In fact, she was ugly, there was just no getting around it. Not in an interesting way either. Merely coarse and not at all feminine, despite a decent figure and decent clothes.

I despaired every time I saw her hard eyes under their thick brows in a their perpetual scowl. Her sloped shoulders made her look petulant, and her hands and feet were too big for her body. Part of me wondered if I put a dollop of hair mousse in one hand, could I casually trip and slide it into that mass of cowlicks she had stampeding across her forehead?

While Mom greeted Meagan, I stood there dressing the poor girl with my eyes, trading the dumpy dress and cardigan for something more tailored, mentally correcting her posture, putting concealer on those under-eye circles and a smile on that down-turned mouth. The changes would work wonders, but this was neither the time nor the place for an extreme makeover.

"Meagan, dear," Mom said. "I didn't know you were still home. Did you get my message? I'm so sorry about your father."

"Yeah, I got it," Megan said in her husky baritone. "What are you doing here?"

Now, from anyone else that would be rude, but I had met Meagan before and knew not to take offense. Like Angela, she had no social skills and had never been one for small talk. She was brilliant, mind you, with a string of degrees in biochemical-something or other, but not one for inviting guests inside, by the looks of things.

"Actually, we were looking for Angela," Mom said, "but I'm glad we'll have a minute to visit with you. You remember my daughter Chloe?"

"You're not the only ones," Megan said without even glancing at me.

"The only ones what?" I asked.

"Looking for Angela."

"Who else is looking for her?" I demanded.

"The police. That Detective McGowan was here this morning."

She had our full attention now, so I asked if we could come in. She nodded, not necessarily pleased with the idea, and led us toward the living room. It was the first time I had been back since the party, and let's just say the whole thing was depressing.

The Bradford pear tree that Saul had pulled over when he fell was back in place, but the partridge was nowhere to be seen. The greenery on the mantle had dried out and looked faded and dusty. As we passed the study, I could see the pipers still keeping their silent watch, forlorn and tired in the harsh daylight.

When we had settled on the couch, the five golden rings still sparkling over the mantle, Mom quizzed Meagan as to why McGowan was looking for Angela.

Meagan lifted her sloping shoulders and let them fall. "More questions, I guess. Something about missing discs."

"And he couldn't find her?" I asked.

"She's been living in the guest house for three years, but after the lawyer told us about the will, she moved out without telling anyone." Meagan delivered her report as if she were reading from the phone book.

I tried to make sense of her announcement. "Saul's will?"

Meagan nodded. "Angela got nothing. Everything was split equally between Robin and me."

Mom's gasp told me she was as stunned as I was. Robin, the woman who once had no motive, now stood to inherit yet another fortune. Meagan gave no sign that she shared our dismay.

"And Angela was upset?" I asked.

"She called Robin a gold-digging bitch and said she would show everyone who was the real talent behind my father's books."

"That qualifies as upset." I glanced at my mother.

"And this was when?" Mom asked.

"Two days ago."

"When are you heading back to Berkeley?" I asked finally.

"First week in January. Maybe sooner, if things get settled here."

"When did you get here?" Mom asked, probably hating to think of Meagan traveling by herself, having just heard about her father's death.

For the first time, Meagan looked uncomfortable. "I'd flown into town the day it happened. I just didn't want to come to the party. Crowds make me nervous."

I thought back to that night and how Saul had gone to make his nightly call to her and received no answer. Did that make her a suspect? It made my head spin to think so. We hadn't cleared anybody yet, and now we were adding new possibilities.

Eerily, Megan seemed to read my thoughts. "I was having dinner with my grandparents - my mom's parents. The police checked it out."

"It's probably better that you weren't here." Seeing Meagan's blank look, I added, "Since the party ended so tragically."

Meagan nodded. "It looked fun, though, not the death part, but before."

Again, I was baffled. "What do you mean it looked fun?" I pictured her watching through binoculars, but her explanation was much more reasonable.

"I got an invoice from the videographer. He apologized when I called, said he had mailed the bill before. I paid it, of course, and got a copy. The police said it was ok, they had their own."

I got the same feeling I'd had when I heard about the gifts in the Santa sack. As Lily would say, "well, duh." I'd forgotten that Saul had a videographer recording the party, a perfect record of the night's events.

Meagan's expression was almost dreamy. "He offered to edit the end of it, but I said not to. Part of me had to see it. It made me feel closer to my father somehow, to be there when he passed from this life. The moment was really quite fascinating."

CHAPTER 24

We were tempted to skip Monica's house and head right home to watch the DVD Meagan had loaned us. But Mom wasn't about to get behind schedule, so we spent a couple of hours in Monica's two story great room decorating six antique white goose feather trees of various sizes.

I don't know about you, but feather trees don't really do it for me. From a distance, they look too much like those artificial toilet brush type trees you find in places where Christmas decorating is an after-thought, like convenience stores or the DMV. It's only on closer inspection that you see a feather tree, or a Nuremberg Christmas tree as they're also called, is made of downy-soft goose feathers and that its square wooden base has cracked and faded paint applied with an artist's hand.

Mom assured me that feather trees, first created in late 1800's Germany to save a dwindling fir population, are highly collectible. Two of the trees we were working on were circa the 1920s.

I still wasn't convinced, but then, what do I know. I once left a Christmas tree up so long that Mom claimed it had gone from Noble Fir to Chernobyl Fir and finally to straight-up fire hazard. I just hang ornaments where I'm told.

With Monica busy in her studio, Mom and I had plenty of time to discuss Meagan's revelations.

"You're building a rapport with him. We can use that to our advantage," she said, when I balked at the idea of calling McGowan to pump him for more information. I had nothing against the guy personally, but working together would be like trying to make low-slung jeans work with granny panties. Not happening.

Mom was adamant. "Something might have happened to Angela."

"It sounds like she just went off in a snit because Robin inherited and she didn't." I placed another delicate white glass ornament on an equally delicate branch. Thank goodness Monica didn't have a cat.

"Maybe so, but there's a murderer out there and Angela could be in trouble. Not to mention the fact that it looks suspicious for her to disappear like that."

I agreed to nothing, but knew compliance was inevitable. This is my mother we're talking about here. "Speaking of the will," I changed the focus. "I about died when Meagan said Robin was in it."

"Me, too. Saul was out of his mind. I don't know which was worse, putting Robin in his will or constantly telling her she wasn't." Mom opened another box of ornaments, clear etched glass with sculpted silver tops. Gorgeous.

"Surely the police consider her the number one suspect. The one thing she lacked was motive, and now she's got that in spades."

"They would have to prove Robin knew about the will, though, and she could provide dozens of witnesses, us included, that heard Saul tell her she wasn't."

"But she was," I argued. "There are ways she could've found out. She had the run of the house, and on the subject of money, I bet she made it her business to know."

"You're preaching to the converted, dear. I think she's a dandy suspect, and she has all but admitted to killing twice before. We don't have proof, though, and till we do we might as well keep digging."

I sighed and stepped back to see where the next ornament should go. Locating a gaping hole up high and to the left, I moved over to fill those branches. "You know, Jack brought up a good point. These were two very different types of murder. One a precisely planned poisoning. The other, what he called a rage killing. Are we off base thinking one person committed both?"

Mom shook her head, never taking her eyes off her work. The largest of the trees was six-foot tall and the smallest just thirty inches. The latter was the one she was working on, and it took an especially steady hand to hang such tiny ornaments.

"I can't make myself believe we have two killers in one neighborhood," she said. "This isn't some mystery novel where crazed killers crop up everywhere, no matter what Gavin Beaumont says."

"So the two different MO's mean what?"

"They mean something happened to force the killer's hand with Oscar. Either it was a spur-of-the-moment murder, or there was a plan in place that somehow went awry."

"I can't wait to look at that DVD. The whole party caught on tape."

Mom gingerly placed her last ornament and stepped back. "What do you think?"

"Amazing!" Margie from Flower Fantasy said, appearing in the doorway to drop off the last of the poinsettias, two gigantic pots. I took one from her and looked over the room.

Did I say I didn't like feather trees? I stand corrected. With an array of white, silver, and clear glass ornaments now dangling from each of the randomly spaced branches, the trees looked terrific, like the snow-tinged firs you might find in a German forest.

"Awesome," I breathed.

Margie winced. "Are you shouting? I told Cassie I don't need these things." She reached up and pulled out two small hearing aids.

Mom and I traded exasperated looks.

"I think that'll just about get it." Mom gave the room another once over. "A little cleanup, and we can go watch some TV."

A short time later, I was watching Bunny Beaumont make her big entrance at Saul's.

"We can start this party now!" Bunny crowed to the camera, throwing her fur to Gavin.

After finishing at Monica's, we had returned to my loft, and I'd gone downstairs to the health food store to get us fruit, cheese and crackers to snack on for the big screening. Jimmy James, the storeowner, was a friend of mine - a cute twenty-three-year old who had opened Sprouts N Stuff with the settlement he'd received from a skiing accident a couple of years before. The accident had cost him a kidney and, to hear him tell it, any hope of finishing college.

Young as he was, I'd briefly considered dating him (you know me and those granola boys). But, alas, I had matured past the age where you date those who live with three other guys and stock their bathroom with fast food napkins instead of toilet paper. Somewhere along the line, brokerage accounts had become sexy.

So far the DVD hadn't revealed much. I was keeping a list of everything Saul had eaten or drunk.

Mom was admiring her design work. "Those precious little calling birds. Just the right touch."

In the foreground, Saul and Robin were chatting with the Browleys, Nancy's eyes resting everywhere except on her host. Saul had a wine glass, and I made a note of it.

"Those darling Waterford maids," Mom cooed. "So elegant."

Using the remote, I skipped over parts that didn't have at least one of our suspects on the screen. We watched as Angela circled the party, not really talking to anyone, and noted how Oscar's angry scowl found Tony Trianos again and again.

"The geese really do look lovely, don't they? Silk was a good choice."

"Could you focus?" I chided. "This isn't about you. We need to… Oooh, there I am in my Nanette Lepore. Check out that rack."

Mom cleared her throat and pointed out that Saul was at the buffet. I noted the hors d'oeuvres he had heaped on his dish. Since he had served himself, though, there was little chance the food was tainted.

"Maybe Marco froze digitalis in the swan punch bowl, and it slowly dissolved during the party," I ventured.

Mom shook her head. "The police tested the food and drinks. Besides, the killer couldn't afford for everyone to ingest the digitalis. Someone else might have been killed."

Still, somehow an overdose of the drug was in Saul's system, and if it hadn't been in something he ate or drank, how had it gotten there?

On screen, Oscar brought Saul another drink, the second time he had made that gesture. It was an opportunity, but what was the motive?

"Interesting." I paused the disc. "I didn't see that, did you?"

"I don't think so, or it didn't seem remarkable if I did."

On screen, Robin spoke to Jack Lassiter, their heads bent together in a moment of shared intimacy. I hit play again, and we watched as Robin bent even closer, her lips almost grazing Jack's ear. He looked enchanted, his eyes searching hers for an answer.

Robin seemed to put him off, but lightly. His disappointment, while obvious, was manageable.

"Now, here's where I would've done it," Mom said as Saul went to make his phone call. "Go back a few frames."

I held down a button on the remote until we could see Robin and Tony Trianos, their backs to the camera, talking with head's close together. Over Robin's bare brown shoulder, Angela was unlocking the door of the study to fix Saul's nightly Scotch.

"Love a man in uniform," Mom said happily, as the camera caught sight of the ten pipers piping.

Angela stepped out of the frame for a brief moment to get a glass and the decanter from the sideboard, before taking both to the desk and pouring a generous serving. She left the glass and decanter within easy reach of the phone and in plain sight of the camera.

"At the beginning of the party, the study door was unlocked for just under an hour," Mom recalled. "Saul was in the foyer the whole time greeting guests as they arrived. When he joined the party, he locked up."

I nodded. "So the discs had to be in the study, or there would have been no reason to lock up." But even as I spoke, I realized something else. "At least, Saul thought they were in the study."

"Right. Now, see there. Angela poured his drink, and the study is unlocked for a few minutes between the time she leaves and the time Saul goes in to make his call." Mom narrated what we both could see, at least part of the door in every shot the videographer was getting.

"There." I said. "Saul goes in and makes his call. Meagan's obviously not there. He tosses back the Scotch and comes out, relocking the door."

"We know that's not when he was poisoned, because the glass and decanter where right where Saul had left them and there was no trace of digitalis in either. I was thinking that was a window of opportunity for someone to steal the discs." She picked up a cracker. "And yet, no one went into the study, and the outer doors and windows were locked."

"Looks bad for Angela. She had permission to go in there, and if she knew Saul wasn't going to survive the night, he would never have missed the discs."

"Angela's the one person without a motive to steal the discs," Mom argued. "They contained her research, and she could've copied them. Plus, she's the one who called attention to their absence in the first place."

"Which McGowan would say was done to throw us off track." Something else occurred to me. "Now, I know Meagan said the police had cleared her…"

"Not that we're taking her word," Mom interrupted.

"I know, but isn't it interesting that her father didn't know she was in town?"

"Good point. He wouldn't have called her if he had known she was having dinner right here in Birmingham."

"There." I paused the disc as Saul popped something in his mouth. "I'd forgotten that Saul snagged a lobster puff from Gavin Beaumont's plate. Maybe Gavin was the intended victim, and that puff was poisoned."

Mom shook her head. "I don't think Gavin's on digitalis."

"Then maybe Gavin poisoned one puff to give to Saul."

"Maybe, but did you see Gavin's face?" Mom added a bite of cheese to the cracker. "He looked crestfallen that Saul took his last puff, and he couldn't have known Saul would snatch it."

Not wanting to let go of my theory, I hit the remote, and we watched the rest of the party play out in silence. Saul gave Mom the CD of Christmas music and playfully patted her behind, Robin offered Saul his medicine, and he painfully died. The videographer hadn't even flinched in the face of Saul's collapse as the camera had rolled.

"I can't believe Meagan watched that," Mom murmured.

"And she didn't seem overly upset. Remember what she said? That it looked like a fun party."

Some fun.

CHAPTER 25

After we finished watching the DVD, I walked Mom to her car, assuring her the whole way that, yes, I would call McGowan. No, I wouldn't let it sound like we were worried about Angela, thereby making her disappearance look like a flight from justice. Yes, I would call Mom the minute I learned anything, and, no, I wouldn't antagonize the man. It was a lot to ask of one phone call, so I put it off as long as I could.

First, the mail. No checks. Then back to Sprouts N Stuff for dinner fixins. Roasted asparagus and blue cheese quesadillas, maybe. One look at Jimmy's new skate boarder haircut and my fantasies came to a halt. Ah, well.

"Somebody left this for you." Jimmy brushed his bangs from his eyes.

"Oooh." I recognized the distinctive gold box - Godiva chocolates. Someone loved me. "Who? Where?" Chocolate has this effect on me.

Jimmy shrugged. "They were in with our mail, but your name's on the card."

Loft mailboxes are in our secured lobby. Commercial tenant boxes are out front. Friends had left stuff with Jimmy when they couldn't get to my box before.

Showing remarkable restraint, I opened the card first.

Something special for someone special. J.

Ha. Not jealous, huh? Forgot that seeing other people could work both ways, didn't you, my little Jacob? Unless...

Unless he had done something he shouldn't have, and this was a half-pound of dark chocolate guilty conscience. No, no, mustn't jump to conclusions. This was a sweet gesture, and I should take it as such.

I mean, Jacob only has a handful of emotions in his repertoire, and guilt isn't one of them. But then, jealousy isn't either. So what did that leave? Hunger? Arousal? Fear of commitment? Affection? That one worked. Affection. Yes, that was it. Sweet.

"That was exhausting," Jimmy said.

"What was?" I was surprised to find him still there.

"Whatever was going on in your head. Sometimes chocolate is just chocolate." He was looking at me strangely, so I paid for my asparagus and blue cheese wedge and headed upstairs.

Before I called Jacob, I decided to call McGowan and get that chore out of the way. Suddenly, talking to McGowan didn't seem like such a pain. Nothing did.

Life was good. Jacob and I were good. Chocolate was good.

I decided to have a piece - just one. Then another one tomorrow. One a day. My kind of vitamin.

I picked out a gooey clustery looking thing. Don't be coconut, I thought, as I fished McGowan's card from my wallet.

Coconut.

I chewed the half I had bitten into, threw the other half away and tried again as I dialed.

Orange crème.

Disgust.

I would be dropping subtle hints about my love of truffles when Jacob and I were back on solid ground.

McGowan answered just as I found a caramelly nutty thing that smelled like almonds. I took a bite.

Jackpot.

"Are you at home?" McGowan asked after we exchanged greetings.

Savoring a decadent piece of ganache, I said I was.

"I'm in your neighborhood. Mind if I come up?"

I made a face. I had asparagus to roast. A phone call to Jacob to script. And I wasn't about to share my chocolate. But Mom was expecting information, so I agreed.

"How'd you know this was my neighborhood?" I asked when I opened the door.

"Hello, to you, too. Are you going to invite me in?"

"How do I know you're not a vampire?"

McGowan smiled. "Vampires can't enter without being invited, right? Here." He slipped past me without an invitation. Cheeky.

"I've always wanted to see inside these places." He wandered around my loft, also without an invitation.

He touched things, picked up things and generally made himself a nuisance. I felt the beginnings of a headache.

"You didn't answer my question." I flopped on the settee, not because the light from the tall windows was most flattering there, but because I felt a little worn out by the day.

"I saw your address on the police reports." He had known without prompting the question I meant. That was nice.

Come to think of it, the light flattered him, too, although blond hair on guys really doesn't do it for me. Even when it's paired with navy blue eyes, a nice tan and really cool Cole Haan slip-ons.

"So, you called me." He took a seat on the green couch.

"I wondered what you thought of Saul's will, and the fact that Robin was in it?"

"News travels fast." He shrugged. "It was interesting, but I don't think I found it nearly as interesting as Angela did. Sounds like she was furious."

My stomach was tying itself into knots. "You sure have a one track mind."

"Just going where the leads take me. I'd love to talk to Angela and clear up a few things."

"You should. I bet she'll be happy to sit down with someone who's already convinced she's a killer."

McGowan ignored the sarcasm. "Trouble is, Angela's disappeared."

I managed a shaky laugh. "Disappeared? Hardly. Just because she's not taking your calls, doesn't mean she's on the lam."

"Is she taking your calls?"

"I haven't called her."

"Has your mother?"

"You would have to ask her, but I doubt Mom's taking your calls either." All this back-and-forth was making my head spin.

McGowan looked me over. "You don't look so hot."

The nerve! "You're not hot either."

"No, really, you're sweating."

"I ate too much chocolate." I felt nauseated just thinking about candy. Nauseous and self-conscious. I sweat more than your average girl.

McGowan moved onto the settee and felt my forehead. "How much did you have?"

"One piece. Maybe two. Six. My boyfriend sent me Godivas."

"Where's the box?" He was in scary cop mode. Both of him.

"Kitchen." My stomach rolled when he got off the settee.

It seemed like an hour before McGowan returned.

"There were only nineteen pieces in the box. There's supposed to be thirty."

"No math," I moaned.

"You ate eleven pieces."

What a pig. A big sweaty, nauseous pig. "I threw some away. The fruit. Coconut."

"I called an ambulance."

I was shocked. And scared. And sooooo dizzy. "I'm just sick to my stomach." I tried to get up, but it wasn't happening.

"The card was typed."

"You read my card?"

"How did you get the chocolates?"

"Jacob left them in the mailbox of the store downstairs for me."

McGowan made phone calls, and I watched the room spin.

I dimly remembered eating a PBJ for breakfast and wondered if I'd developed a peanut allergy. Then I wondered if I would blow up like a life raft after eating eleven Godiva chocolates in one sitting?

I heard sirens downstairs.

McGowan remained seated beside me on the couch. "I don't think the box was from Jacob. I think you did what your mother always told you not to do. You accepted candy from strangers."

I did something else my mother had told me not to. I antagonized the man by throwing up on his nice shoes.

CHAPTER 26

When I opened my eyes, McGowan had been replaced by Jacob, and we had jump cut from my loft to a hospital room. I had dim recollections of an ambulance ride and people yelling questions in my face.

"What are you doing here?" I croaked. My throat burned, and I had a terrible taste in my mouth.

"Just keeping you company till your parents get back."

"My parents are here?"

"They've been here the whole time."

"And you've been here?"

"The whole time."

Tears welled up, but I blinked them away.

"How do you feel?" he asked.

"Death would have been easier."

"I didn't send you chocolate."

"You should have."

Jacob smiled at that. "I thought we decided against the Goth look for you."

I tried to rub under my eyes, but gave up. Everything hurt. "Did I miss Christmas?"

"What? No. It's Saturday. You were sick all last night, and now it's morning."

Crazy. It felt like weeks had passed.

"What happened to me?"

"They thought it was cyanide at first. Which would've been worse."

I didn't see how, but ok.

"But it turned out to be something called nitrobenzene that's used in different kinds of polishes, insecticide. There was some in the stuff you and your mom use to clean ornaments."

"And I had it on my hands?" Pigging out on chocolates and licking the fingers of my unwashed hands. Charming.

He shook his head. "Somebody tampered with the chocolate."

Again with the tears, only this time it was harder to hold them back.

The realization that evil had found its way to my doorstep, had disguised itself as affection and played so cleverly on my emotions both stunned and frightened me. I wasn't ready to face the idea that someone knew just how to get to me and had done so without hesitation.

Jacob took my hand and squeezed it hard, bringing me back from a dark place. I gladly turned my attention to him.

"Where are my parents?"

"They went downstairs for coffee."

"You didn't want coffee?"

"I'll go when they return."

I studied Jacob, looking for some hint that my near-death experience was making him re-evaluate his recent decisions. Nothing.

He stared back just as intently, like he had the same question about me. We didn't say anything.

Over his shoulder, I saw the door open, and my parents came in.

"She's awake." Jacob leaned over, gave me a brotherly kiss on the cheek and said the three words every girl longs to hear. "Feel better soon."

Then my mom was beside me. This time the tears fell.

Just as Mom had pronounced my face to be mascara free, the doctor arrived and said I could go home. As poisonings go, mine had been rather mild. The way my muscles ached as I clutched my hospital gown together in the back and hobbled to the bathroom contradicted that diagnosis.

"Shit, Mom!" I called out, catching sight of myself in the mirror.

Mom rushed to help. "What?"

"What the hell happened to my mouth?"

Mom was in no mood for cosmetic emergencies after a night of medical ones. "It's the charcoal they gave you for the poison. It made your lips a little black."

"A little? You couldn't have run a wet washcloth over them? Jacob was here." I grabbed a towel and started scrubbing.

"We all had more important things on our minds." Her tone was stern. And something else.

"Why do I keep crying?" I said into the towel.

"Let's go home."

Home was my parents' house where they took me to convalesce. I had made a couple of perfunctory protests, but had given in pretty easily. Their couch and I are old friends.

McGowan dropped in bearing gifts.

"Saltines. My favorite." I said, taking off the bow.

"When I saw them, I thought of you."

"Sorry about your shoes."

"Me, too. They were my favorites."

"I'll pay for them." Embarrassing.

"What happened to his shoes?" My mother came in with a glass of tea for McGowan and water for me. I still tasted charcoal.

"Collateral damage." McGowan's face sobered. "And no, you don't have to pay for them. That's how they would've wanted to go - in the line of duty."

My mother sat next to him on the love seat. "Detective McGowan. Max. I can't thank you enough for your quick thinking. We're so grateful to you."

"I'm just glad I was there, Mrs. Carstairs. It was luck more than anything."

My stomach was too delicate for such touching scenes. "Any leads?" I nibbled a saltine.

They looked at me blankly.

"You know. Fingerprints. Bank statements. Any of our suspects bought Godiva chocolates lately?"

They exchanged grave looks before McGowan spoke. "Look, Chloe. I know you and your mother wanted to help Angela, but now, it's too dangerous."

Amanda agreed.

"This was all your idea," I protested. "I didn't want to do it, but you insisted."

Mom's look was patient. "And now, I'm insisting we stop."

"But someone tried to kill me." I would've yelled, but my ab muscles were too sore.

"Exactly why you should leave police work to the police," McGowan stated, a new firmness in his tone. "It's too dangerous for amateurs."

A flicker of irritation passed across Mom's face, but she nodded. "It's too risky."

"Tell me something I don't know. I'm the one they came after. I thought this whole thing was a lark, but now it's self-defense."

"No. It's what's it's always been," McGowan said. "A police investigation. Speaking of which, I'd like to ask you two a favor."

I wasn't in the mood to play nice, but Mom assumed her how-may-I-help face.

"I'd like to keep the poisoning quiet. Let us continue our investigation and see if anyone tips their hand."

"You don't think they'll try again, do you, thinking she didn't eat the chocolates?" Mom asked.

"The mere fact that she's still alive could prompt them to try again, whether they know she ate the chocolates or not. That's why it's important for you both to be careful and stay out of this."

I was tired of being talked about like I wasn't in the room. "What about Angela?" I faced Mom. "A.K.A. suspect number one?"

"Honey, I think we can all agree that's no longer the case," Mom said. "More tea?"

McGowan frowned. "Angela's still a prime suspect."

Mom arched a brow. "Why would Angela hurt Chloe? We were trying to help her. Only someone who thought we were a threat to them would try to hurt us."

I thought she made a good point.

"That only works if Angela's innocent," McGowan pointed out. "If she's guilty, she might be scared that you would prove it."

Mom and I made identical derisive sounds.

McGowan ignored us. "You might already know something that's a threat to her and not realize it."

I rolled my eyes. Mom shook her head.

"Look. I know you two think I'm railroading your friend, but that's not the case. I think there's a possibility she's guilty. How is that more unreasonable than your knee-jerk, completely baseless belief that she's innocent?"

"It just is," I explained.

Mom took McGowan's not-quite-empty tea glass from his hand, put it on the tray and stood. "It just is."

He had no choice but to follow her to the door.

"You will both stop poking around?" McGowan did a little jog step to keep up with Amanda as she marched to the entryway.

"Neither of us has a death wish, Detective." Mom threw open the door. "We'll leave the police work to you."

"Glad to hear it. Call me if you need…"

But the door closed, and McGowan was on the other side of it.

Mom returned to the living room.

"So that's it?" I was ready to start the argument all over again.

"We'll leave police work to the police," Mom repeated as she picked up the tray. "But our work is far from done."

I smiled, shoved a whole saltine into my mouth and settled back onto the couch to think.

CHAPTER 27

It felt good to be upright again, so Monday afternoon I made Mom go with me to my bridesmaid's dress fitting. This was to by my first glimpse of the style Dana had chosen, and I figured I could use the moral support.

Mom was just as curious as I was, but warned she could only stay for a half hour before she had to pick up Lily from ballet.

"What was Dana thinking?" I said to my reflection, which was swathed in ten yards of pale green taffeta. "This looks like a sack."

It was obvious what Dana had been thinking when she chose the empire waist bridesmaid dress. It would be her day, and no one would upstage her.

"I think it's cute," Mom said helpfully.

The seamstress, Marva Lowenstein, pinned the bottom. A buxom woman of about fifty with yellow hair that still bore hot roller tread marks, she wore a yellow caftan and a matching wrist corsage of straight pins, blooming from a yellow cushion. I'm guessing the woman liked yellow.

"It's the Jane Austen look," Marva offered.

I held my curls in a messy updo.

"Stop squirming," Marva ordered.

Mom almost hid a smile and didn't meet my eyes until the dress was all pinned.

"You look lovely." Marva's tone told me she wouldn't indulge complaints. "This style flatters all figures."

"What did she mean by that?" I demanded when Mom and I were alone.

No exercise and a steady diet of beige-colored comfort food had put back any weight I had lost on the Godiva diet.

"Just what she said, I imagine. Be careful, you'll rip out the hem." The dress was filled with pins.

"How do I get out of the thing? There's no zipper."

"Well, see if you can... Good Lord, how are you supposed to get out of it?"

"Here, you pull, and I'll back out of it." I bent over, and we carefully bunched fabric toward my head.

"Ouch! Pins. Very sharp pins," I complained.

Mom fought a major case of the giggles, watching me wiggle around with my arms in the air, my head lost in the folds.

"Behold the dance of the honeydews," she said, unable to stifle her laughter.

"That's not funny. I'm claustrophobic in here."

"My God, Chloe, what happened to your legs?"

I paused in backing out of the dress, my pink-pantied butt and legs leading the way. Had cellulite completely taken over my thighs, and my own mother was horrified?

It wasn't until I was free, gulping for air, that I realized what she must have been talking about. One of my legs was bronze, the other lily white.

"I ran out of sunless tanner after doing one leg," I defended myself as I smoothed down my curls.

"And you left them like that?"

"Give me a break. I got distracted."

"By what?"

"My toast popped up or something."

"For Heaven's sake! Don't get into an accident on the way home. What would the paramedics think?"

"I'm more embarrassed that they saw my two pasty white legs Friday." I reached for my jeans, sending up a silent prayer that McGowan hadn't seen those legs or worse my underwear. These things should be carefully choreographed.

"Heard anything from Jacob?"

"He left a message saying to call him if I needed anything, and that we're still on for dinner this Friday, if I feel up to it."

Mom frowned. "If it's any consolation, he was upset at the hospital."

"He didn't act like it."

"Well, he was, and it was no act."

I pulled my shirt over my head. "Did you tell him about our investigation?"

"A bit. He seemed to think that you've lost your mind."

"What'd he say?"

"He said, 'that girl has lost her mind.'"

For some reason, this cheered me up. "So why isn't he rushing to protect me?"

Mom cleaned my glasses and handed them back to me. "He and your father might be under the impression that we're no longer looking into this."

"Where would they get that idea?" We hadn't discussed the case while I was still at my parents. I had thought she and my father were trying not to stress me out. Apparently not.

"Not from me. They seemed to have taken it for granted."

I had to laugh. "Never a good idea."

"Any word from McGowan?"

"Another message asking if I was feeling better." My cell phone was getting more action than I was these days.

"Angela is still MIA, I'm afraid."

When we reached Mom's MG, I tried looking on the bright side. "We're getting closer, don't you think? We've asked the hard questions. We've rattled some cages. We're a threat to someone. Surely something's about to pop loose."

Mom shrugged. "We haven't proven anything, and it's time to get serious."

"Serious how?"

"I wonder what Tony Trianos could tell us."

"Are you kidding? He'll tell us to sleep with the fishes."

"Think about it, Chloe. He's connected."

"Yeah. To the mob."

"I meant to this case." She started the car. "He was at Saul's party. He had a grudge against Oscar."

"He's a criminal, and he's out of our league." The thought of questioning Trianos made my heart race. That and Mom's driving. Always just a tiny bit too fast.

"You said it yourself. No stone unturned."

"I was kidding. You know me. Always with the jokes." I slid onto the tiny seat, prepared to take my chances with the driving.

"We need to know why Saul was so interested in him and if Trianos saw anything. He's a suspect, and we have to question them all."

"We haven't questioned Gavin Beaumont," I pointed out.

"I forgot about him. Ok, first Gavin. If our clever interrogation techniques don't coax a confession out of him, we question Trianos."

"And this is something we have to do in person? We couldn't just make an anonymous call?"

Mom smiled over at me. "Every suspect, no stone unturned. He could be our guy."

"Oh, great. So we accuse a mobster of murder. Brilliant, Mom."

CHAPTER 28

That evening, Mom seemed to understand my leeriness about eating in. I didn't say anything, and she didn't ask. We just pulled things out of her refrigerator and started dinner.

Still nervous about questioning Tony Trianos, I tried another tack. "Are you going to tell Dad about your little plan for tomorrow?"

Her little plan for tomorrow was to join Trianos for lunch at his downtown restaurant.

"I don't see why not," she said, surprising me, "if it comes up."

Ah. She was taking the ignorance-is-bliss approach. One of my favorites. "So you admit, it's not something he would approve."

"I'm a grown woman who doesn't need his approval."

Which was true, but we both jumped when we heard Dad ask, "What's for dinner."

He kissed Mom on the side of the neck. "Did I startle you?"

"No, I thought you were watching the news." She ignored my smirk.

"It's all bad. You staying for dinner again?" He gave me a rough one-armed hug.

"Veggie pizza. Like I'm going to pass that up." I grabbed a fat, red pepper, sliced it into slivers, and added them to a skillet in which onion, garlic and mushrooms were already sautéing.

For a few minutes, the three of us worked together not saying much. I kept shooting Mom looks, daring her to say something about Trianos, still trying to make her realize what a harebrained scheme it was.

"Have you heard anything downtown about Angela's disappearance?" she asked Dad, ignoring me.

"Ran into Detective McGowan just this morning, as a matter of fact." He stretched dough for the crust, his flour-coated hands deftly smoothing it onto a pizza stone sprinkled with cornmeal. "He said he's not treating Angela's disappearance as a missing person case yet, but he's as interested in talking to her as we are."

"Did he give you any insight as to where the rest of the investigation stands?" I slid the crust into the oven to blind bake for a few minutes.

"Still no connection between the guy who got his hand chopped off and Saul or Oscar. They're treating the deaths as related homicides, no surprise there. No sign of the missing discs, and no real idea of how or when they were stolen. And last, but not least, no clues on who tried to poison Chloe. Other than that, he was very cagey, our friend McGowan."

"No, wonder. He doesn't know half the things we know." I filled Dad in on all we had learned. Nancy's affairs, Robin's quasi-confession, Jack Lassiter's possible connection to Robin if their whispering at Saul's party was any indication.

"And Robin inherits half of Saul's estate," Mom dropped the bombshell before I got the chance.

"You're kidding?"

"Nope. Meagan told us last week," I offered what little I still had.

My mother signaled me to turn off the heat under the veggies, now just shy of crisp tender. Homemade sauce thawing since that morning simmered in a pan.

"I just wish we had come up with something tangible, just one bit of concrete evidence." Mom scanned the cheeses in the deli bin.

A gooey mozzarella? Something unexpected, like crumbled gorgonzola? Who was I kidding? Fresh goat cheese wins it every time.

"The cops aren't having any more luck." Dad held the oven door open for Mom to peek in. "That's the way these things work, sometimes. You think you're getting nowhere then everything falls into place."

The crust was slightly brown around the edges. "Looks good to me." Mom handed him the oven mitts.

"I don't see why McGowan is so focused on Angela." I ladled sauce onto the middle of the crust. "Even if Angela took the discs, Robin and Tony Trianos make much better suspects."

Mom shot me a look, knowing exactly why I had brought up that name.

"I don't think he sees two different people committing the murder and the theft," Dad said, "but it's a possibility. Angela might have taken the discs as a way to protect her work and launch her own career."

"What about Nancy's theory that Oscar might have stolen them?" Mom asked.

"Interesting but unlikely." Dad crumbled the goat cheese as my mother spread the veggies onto the pizza.

"Why unlikely?" Mom asked. "That's the one theory that's working. The discs were stolen after the murder, either by Oscar or Robin. Angela, maybe, but it's a stretch. The police were swarming all over that place."

"Why would Oscar risk it? That's tantamount to tampering with evidence." Dad poured wine into a glass, then held up the bottle, offering to pour us some.

I accepted. Mom didn't.

"Evidence that might've been damaging to his wife," I argued. "Or better still, might've helped him nail Tony Trianos." On went the cheese, and into the oven went the pizza.

We sat down to dinner in the dining room, one of my favorites. Dominated by a beautiful 17th century Spanish refectory table with walnut lyre legs, vintage Lalique sconces cast a soft ambient light over the room and its Italian triptych landscapes on one wall and elaborate Venetian mirror on another.

Mom waited till Dad had taken his first bite of pizza, the crust crunching nicely, the goat cheese puddling around fragrant veggies. Then, casually, she called my bluff. "So tomorrow Chloe's going to talk to Gavin Beaumont in the morning. Then in the afternoon, we're questioning Tony Trianos at his restaurant downtown."

I almost fell out of my chair.

Dad sprinkled more crushed red pepper flakes on his pizza. "No."

"No?" Mom acted as if she wasn't sure she had heard him right.

"Not a good idea," Dad clarified, like that explained everything.

I gazed into the art glass bowl in the table's center and wondered how this would play out. Dad had bought her that bowl in London. Perhaps, I should move it to a safe harbor.

"Did you just say, 'no?' Like I was one of the girls asking for the keys to your car?"

Hey, a good offense.

"If you were one of the girls asking for the keys to my car, I would've said, 'Hell no.'" Dad said pleasantly.

"I've always loved the wallpaper in this room," I decided a change of subject might be in order.

"Your father and I put it up together along with the wainscoting - a team effort. How could I have known that underneath his enlightened exterior beat the heart of a no-wielding caveman? I had no idea we had the kind of relationship where he…"

"Amanda," Dad interrupted. "We both know you're making an issue about the 'no' to distract me from the real issue - your hanging out with gangsters or our town's version of a gangster, which is way out of your league." He caught her look. "Mine too, for that matter."

"Don't lawyer me, Alex. You know I hate to be lawyered. I have a solid argument about why we need to see Tony Trianos tomorrow, and if you will return from whatever 1950's time warp you've slipped into, I'll be glad to share it with you."

He put down his pizza and gave her his full attention. "Fine. Let's hear it."

Mom laid out the argument about Tony being a suspect and our needing to question everyone involved with the case. She mentioned that we needed to know what Saul was working on when he died and how it involved Trianos. She argued that Tony might tell us things he would never share with the cops.

She got nowhere.

"You have forgotten that someone tried to kill Chloe," Dad pointed out.

My smile could only be described as beatific.

"I certainly haven't forgotten, which is why this is more important than ever. Someone struck out at our family, and Angela is in danger as well. These things make me more determined, not less."

Hate to admit it, but Mom made a convincing case. The snap in her green eyes, the set of her mouth, the cocky little way she tilted her chin. I was ready to follow her into the breach.

"Then let's consider the dangers associated with Tony Trianos. People sometimes disappear when they talk to him."

"Questions, Alex, that's all I'm proposing. In broad daylight. I'll be careful."

"Can you at least wait until I can go with you?" Dad met her halfway.

"Theoretically I could, but Trianos will clam up around a lawyer. Two chicks from the suburbs aren't as threatening."

"Clam up. Chicks. Since when do you refer to yourself as a chick?"

"I'm getting into character."

Dad looked at me. I kept my face neutral, resigned to my fate.

"Ok, fine, but I can't say that I like it, any more than you would if I were putting myself or our daughter in danger."

Mom rolled her eyes. "Jeez, Alex, it's not like we don't have another daughter. You know I always keep a spare on hand."

"Hello. Sitting right here, you two," I interjected.

Against his will, Dad smiled. "Yeah, well, just don't get any bullet holes in my cars or my family - in that order."

Mom kissed him and wiped pizza sauce off his chin. In that order.

I just sat there. What does one wear to question the mob?

CHAPTER 29

Good daughter that I am, I volunteered to question Gavin Beaumont on my own Tuesday morning, so that Mom would be spared another encounter with Bunny. Since there was no way I wanted to see the good doctor in his professional capacity, I opted for a house call. Bunny already knew what we were up to, so there was no need to be coy about it.

The Beaumonts' old ranch-style house in the heart of Mountain Brook had been popped on top to create an enormous Georgian mansion that dwarfed its modest lot. I didn't think they had kids living at home, although I recalled a daughter from Bunny's first marriage who had graduated college and was off traveling. Honey, I thought her name was.

I rang twice, breathing in the pungent fragrance of the door's huge eucalyptus and bay laurel wreath, before a slim black woman answered, her irritation evident. A little older than I, tall and graceful with the carriage of someone who studied ballet, her makeup was spare and skillfully applied, emphasizing large dark eyes whose direct gaze was hostile. She wore a chef's jacket, baggy pants and black clogs. Her dark hair was pulled straight back and clipped at her neck.

"Hi, I'm Chloe Carstairs. Are the Beaumonts here?" My tone was apologetic in the face of her annoyance.

"I thought they were, but I also thought they would get the door. Shows how much I know."

"Lucy? Was that the bell? I was out back and couldn't get to it in time." Bunny rushed into the foyer, pulling off gardening gloves in her haste, having adopted the same apologetic tone I had. Lucy, it seemed, knew how to get respect.

"I'm not the maid, Ms. Beaumont," Lucy said firmly and, I assumed, not for the first time.

"Of course not, dear. I was just…"

"I'm a professional personal chef. I don't do doors."

"Yes, I know. It's just that I was…"

"Mmm-hmm." Lucy was already moving toward the kitchen.

"It won't happen again, I promise."

"Mmm-hmm."

I expected Bunny to be a bit miffed that I had witnessed this little household drama.

She waved it off. "The attitude is horrendous, but so worth it come dinnertime," she said, then addressed my presence. "So, dear, what can I do for you before 10:00 a.m. Selling Girl Scout cookies?"

I smiled and let my eyes drift over her outfit. Speaking of things we were a little old for.

Tight dark denim jeans, cuffed at the bottom, and a red gingham shirt, tied at the waist so that a tiny swath of belly was visible when she moved. Her makeup was vivid, and her hair was in, I kid you not, pigtails. The effect was cute, but a little cartoony, like the stereotype of a slutty farm girl you might see in a men's magazine. Gardening? Squatting in those jeans would have staunched blood flow as effectively as a tourniquet, but then the look Bunny was going for was more va-va-voom than verisimilitude.

A man wouldn't have questioned the look. A woman seeing a man pitching hay wearing nothing but cowboy boots and a neckerchief would've had only one thought - chiggers.

If Bunny noticed my amusement, she didn't let on. I hoped I hadn't interrupted her and Dr. Beaumont in the middle of some weird role playing game. If he came out dressed like a pirate, I was out of there.

I told her I wanted to speak to her husband for a minute.

"Whatever for?" She smiled maliciously. "Oh, let me guess. This and that. Various and a sundry, right? Honestly, you girls and your snooping. Did it ever occur to you that folks might find all of this just a tad bit offensive?"

"Not even once. So is Dr. Beaumont busy?"

She feigned nonchalance. "He's around back, washing the car. Right this way."

"What kind of gardening were you doing?" I asked as we moved through the foyer and into their soaring great room with its two-story windows flanking a marble faced fireplace. I barely had time to take in her tree, a fifteen-foot white number covered in jewel tone glass ornaments.

"Just piddling. Where's Amanda this morning?" She opened the door to the sun porch and motioned me through with an after-you wave of one hand.

"She ran out to Miss Dupree's to take care of a few last minute things. Monica's having a private showing tonight."

"Really. Y'all going?"

"I'm not. I don't know about my parents. They were invited, but Dad's helping out with some big case so I think they begged off."

"Two murders in two weeks in that neck of the woods, I wouldn't risk it either."

I started to point out that it was a good thing then that she wasn't on the guest list, but decided to take in their nice set up out back instead.

An outdoor kitchen took up most of the back patio, spilling into the pool area. The yard was tiered, a quaint little seating vignette on the top, a more expansive dining area closer to the house. Plantings were structured, but a lush water feature kept things from getting too fussy. To the right, a stamped concrete drive snaked around the corner of the house and ended in a private parking pad where Gavin was giving his Lexus LS a serious rubdown.

"Just follow the drive down when you're finished, okay, sweetie?" Bunny suggested as she held the door open for me, but this time her gesture said, "Hit the road, kid." Such hostility.

As I approached Gavin Beaumont, who was looking like Santa's most eager, but least able elf, I had to wonder. What was he doing sudsing up his car, when his wife was inside dolled up like the farmer's daughter? Very strange.

"Chloe Carstairs, what brings you out this morning?" Gavin caught sight of me as he began going after his hub caps with a fat sponge soaked in soapy water.

"Nothing much." I was surprised to find myself smiling. Sure, Gavin Beaumont was socially awkward and maybe even a little creepy at times, but he was kind of endearing, too. In a weird sort of way. "I just wanted to ask you a few questions about Saul and Oscar."

He nodded, attacking a wheel well with a vengeance. "Bunny said you and your mom were looking into things, and I must say that I'm glad. I don't think the police have a chance with this one, do you?"

"I don't know. There's an active investigation."

"Yes, but we took Nancy some flowers and such the other day, and she said they're after Trianos." He looked over at me as if we could both agree that this was absurd.

"I guess they think he's the most likely suspect, given his reputation."

Gavin snorted. "Yes, but what about access? He couldn't have set something like that up in Saul's house, and Oscar never would've let him get close enough to stab him."

"It doesn't take much access to stab someone in the back. I doubt that Oscar even saw it coming."

"Does that sound like Tony Trianos to you? Stabbing one man in the back, and poisoning the other? He seems more direct to me - more mano a mano."

"I didn't realize you knew him."

"Sure. I delivered his sister's kids - seven healthy boys. Tony was very grateful. Sent me a case of first growth claret with each one."

"So what's your theory?"

"Who says I have one?" Gavin stepped away from the car and picked up a hose, gesturing for me to watch myself. He rinsed the wheel thoroughly, the spray casting a watery rainbow around his hands, the water's metallic tang reminding me of summer.

"I just thought you might. You seem more observant than other people. More intuitive."

"Less apt to be snowed by a pretty girl?"

See? Endearing. In a weird sort of way.

I didn't think he was going to tell me his theory, if he had one, but he surprised me.

"You're not going to like it. It might hit a little too close to home."

I rolled my eyes. "My mother? Please. Just because she decorated the houses? Give me a break."

We moved along, so he could do the left rear wheel.

"Actually, I was thinking more along the lines of your father."

"My father? You can't be serious." Had the man lost his mind?

"It makes a certain amount of sense, you must admit."

"What are you talking about? How do you figure?"

"I told you that you wouldn't like this."

"I don't like it," I said hotly, "but keep going. I can't wait to hear your logic."

"It's just that we had dinner with Saul a few months ago, and he said your dad was as good as they come - a real straight arrow."

"Exactly my point. Not a murderer."

"But he also speculated that if he dug for a few months he could turn up something on anybody, even a Boy Scout like your dad. You could tell the idea really appealed to him as a way to take his books to the next level - an exposé. Instead of just recounting a story, he would create one."

"And you think that's what he was doing when he died? Digging into my father's life?"

Gavin tossed his sponge into the bucket and picked up the hose. "Why not?"

Water again roared into the wheel well, and I waited till he shut off the spray. "There's nothing to find."

"How can you be so sure? Everyone cuts corners now and then, bends the rules."

"Even you?" I wanted him to see how it felt to be accused.

"Even me."

"What would Saul have found about you, if he 'dug around for a few months?'"

Gavin laughed. "I could think of a few things."

"So maybe Saul found out something about you, and you wanted to shut him up."

"Maybe, but he wasn't looking into my past. He was looking into your father's."

"We have only your word for that," I pointed out.

"You could ask Angela."

"No one's seen Angela for days. Nobody knows where she is."

Gavin took the news in stride, not a bit concerned. "Look. Do I think your dad is a murderer? Not really. I'm just saying it's not as far outside the realm of possibility as you might want it to be. Saul was burnt out writing about criminals. He wanted to expose the bad side of basically good people, and he was a man who didn't care who he hurt."

CHAPTER 30

Tony Trianos owned a small hole-in-the-wall restaurant downtown that served some of the best Mediterranean food in the South. Called simply Tony's, the place had the corporate crowd lined up out the doorway on weekdays to order thick slabs of Moussaka, rich, hearty Stifado or steaming bowls of lemony Avgolemono. On Friday and Saturday nights, the entire complexion of the restaurant changed. The lights lowered, the tables were pushed aside and a small stage gave dancing girls room to do their stuff.

Thankfully, today was Tuesday.

Mom and I went after the lunch rush, going on the rumor that Trianos always ate at his own place, ordering the same thing day after day - a steaming wedge of spanakopita and a Greek salad. His real money was made, at least on the surface, in the laundry business. He had a chain of dry cleaners and commercial laundry services throughout the Southeast.

"How do they know on the wiretaps if he's talking about laundering money or laundering sheets," Mom had asked when I picked her up. "That was smart thinking on his part."

On the way to the restaurant, I filled Mom in on Gavin's obnoxious theory. She wasn't nearly as upset as I had been.

"Ridiculous, dear. Saul could've dug all he wanted to, it wouldn't have meant a thing."

"Yeah, but..."

"But nothing. If anything, Gavin distracted you from questioning him by getting you riled up about Alex. I can't believe that you fell for it. Now tell me again what Bunny was wearing."

We exhausted that subject, catty comments flying, then got back to the case. Mom was interested in Gavin's assertion that

Saul wanted to do more of an exposé than his usual true crime narration.

"I thought he was doing a story on Tony Trianos," she said thoughtfully.

"Yeah, but if that were the case, why would Tony be cooperating?"

"We can ask him."

Parked in front of the restaurant, we sat for a moment and collected ourselves. For this venture, I had chosen a pink paisley knee-length skirt, white tank and brown cropped jacket - a look that was smart, casual and easily spotted should my body be dumped in a landfill.

Mom had on her favorite A-line silk dress, nipped in at the middle to show off her tiny waist. When I turned fourteen, we knew my wearing her wedding dress down the aisle was no longer a possibility. I wondered if Ms. Hospital-Corners chose to wear red today, so that her outfit wouldn't show bloodstains.

"You're not putting on lipstick?" she asked.

"We're not on a double date. This is business. No use getting all dolled up just to die."

"Stop being so dramatic." Mom checked her own perfectly glossed lips in her compact mirror. "Nobody's going to die. At most we could be sold into some sex slavery ring. No biggie." She snapped the compact at me.

"It's not too late to back out."

"You're more than welcome to wait in the car."

Right.

We got out. Amanda smoothed her dress, fluffed her hair and waved at a van parked along the street.

"Who's that?" I asked.

She shrugged. "Could be FBI. If it is, I want my face on video. That way if I go in, someone will at least wonder if I don't come out."

"You watch too much TV."

"You're probably right, dear."

And I probably was, which meant that my mother was wrong. However, our track records in that area didn't stack the odds in my favor. I waved at the van.

Inside, the restaurant was almost deserted, just one older couple at a table sharing the moussaka. I wondered if the woman had a Tommy gun in her oversized handbag.

In a booth, sipping tea and dipping pita into what looked like Taramosalata dip, was Tony Trianos. I'd seen him on the news, file footage accompanying stories of how he beat yet another racketeering charge and, of course, at Saul's party. At this proximity, I was struck by his quiet intensity. And again by the fact that his face, though his skin looked like it had never known sunscreen or moisturizer, was downright handsome.

Mom, never one to be shy, marched right up to him. "Mr. Trianos? I'm Amanda Carstairs, and this is my daughter Chloe."

"She a dancer?" He asked Mom, flicking topaz colored eyes in my direction.

"A what?" I asked.

"Girls come in all the time looking for jobs." Trianos chuckled. "First time anyone's brought their mother."

Mom hid a smile, clearly enjoying this.

"Ok. Let's see what you got here." He looked me up and down. "Cute. Good general muscle tone."

"She works out," my mother said helpfully.

"A little on the skinny side."

Bless his heart.

"I could see her working some kind of school girl angle," Tony said.

"Eight years of Catholic school," Mom said. "Probably still has the uniform."

"Excuse me." I said.

"Course, we would have to make a few cosmetic adjustments." He nodded to where my chest would be if I had one.

Mom tilted her head, conceding the point.

"Excuse me!" I said, more forcefully this time. "I am no dancer."

"It's true." Mom grimaced. "Not very graceful, I'm afraid." She slid into the booth across from him. "Actually, we're here to talk to you about Saul Taylor."

"Ballsy little thing, aren't you?" Tony now checked out my mother. "I like that."

Oh, brother.

Mom smiled prettily and gestured for me to join them. Even sitting down I could tell Tony was powerfully built, just a little soft around the edges. Nice hair - thick, dark and shiny. An attractive man. As mobsters go.

"We don't want to interrupt your lunch," Mom began.

"Nonsense. I haven't even ordered yet. You girls eat with me. Nothing whets a man's appetite like dining with beautiful women."

Was I mistaken, or had my mother actually tittered?

We spent a moment looking at the menu.

"I'm having the spanakopita," Tony said helpfully.

"Eggplant parmesan sounds good," I said. Calories be damned, this could be my last meal.

"I hear y'all do a wonderful Greek salad," Mom said.

"The dressing's a family recipe," Trianos replied, pleased.

"Then I definitely should try it."

Yesterday, I would've sworn there was nothing worse than watching your fifty-something mother flirt. Now I knew better. It's far worse to watch your fifty-something mother flirt and see that it's working. Who knew how many years of therapy it would take to undo the damage of this little get-together.

Tony called over his waiter, a young guy who would've been right at home on page twenty-three of any men's sportswear catalog, and ordered for us.

"This is Chloe," he told the waiter, who nodded in my direction. "And my new friend Amanda."

Clearly, I had slipped into an alternate universe. Surreptitiously, I dug into my purse, turned my head and put on lipstick.

"So, what can I do for you ladies?" Trianos asked after the waiter had left us. "I take it this isn't a social call."

"We were at Saul's party."

Tony was already nodding in Amanda's direction. "I remember you. Red dress. It's a good color for you."

Gag.

"And we were at Oscar's party," Mom continued.

"Trouble seems to be following you ladies around."

"Occupational hazard, I guess."

"Oh, right, you're interior designers or something. I liked what you did with Saul's house - kind of over the top. I'm a little over the top myself."

Mom laughed. "I'll keep that in mind. You created quite a stir showing up at Saul's party like that."

"I had an invitation, same as everybody else."

"Which is interesting in itself. What was your connection to Saul?"

Tony shrugged. "Man liked to hang around interesting people. I guess I qualified."

"We heard he was working on a book about you," I said.

Tony looked surprised to find me still there. "I'm not really the tell-all type." His tone flattened - deadly serious.

"So he just hung around to, what? Try the Taramosalata?" I pressed.

"That's reason enough, but no. We just shot the sh…breeze for a while. He was interested in my dealings with Oscar Browley. Told him that wasn't one of my favorite subjects."

"Why not?" Mom asked

"Guy was a putz, using my reputation - apocryphal as it is - to build his own. Things like that can get a man in serious trouble."

"It didn't seem to hurt you much," Mom pointed out, with a hint of coyness. "None of the charges ever stuck."

"Like I don't have better uses for my money than paying lawyers." He leaned across the table towards Mom. "Tell me something. Being in the decorating business, you know a thing or two about ornaments, am I right?"

"You are."

"My sister Marie in there," he gestured to the kitchen, "collects them. What should I get her this year? Something special, now. I'm not talking a plastic snow globe or nothing."

"What kind of collections does she have? Blown glass? Polonaise?"

"This and that, but she's obsessed with it. A real, what would you call it? Aficionado."

"If you're talking really special, you might consider the '02 Waterford Hope for Healing ornament that commemorated the World Trade Center tragedy."

"That's a good one?"

"A very good one, and it's highly collectible as well as being a sentimental favorite."

"You got one?"

Mom shook her head. "I wish. They show up on eBay from time to time, but bidding forces them into the six-hundred dollar plus range."

A bone of contention, here. Mom has the disc - the flat, easier-to-find ornament - but eBay squatters had twice beaten her out of the crystal ball. With her connections, she could've scored one, but she preferred the thrill of the hunt.

Tony nodded. "Thanks for the tip."

The waiter brought out our food, and for a moment we busied ourselves digging in. My parmesan was amazing - thick slices of breaded eggplant slathered in a richly pungent, delicately seasoned red sauce.

"Incredible." I sopped up some of the sauce with a piece of soft country bread.

"To die for," Mom said and got a quick kick under the table from me. No need to give this guy any ideas.

"The way we hear it," she resumed, "is that Saul was using you to..."

"Saul wasn't using me for anything."

"My apologies. What I meant is that Saul wanted you to play a role in his next book. I was wondering if he gave you any indication of what that role would be. Source? Character? What?"

"Taste this. You have to taste the spanakopita," Trianos said to Mom, then shouted at the kitchen, "You've outdone yourself today, Marie!" He cut off a piece of the thick spinach pie with its flaky lattice crust and offered it to Mom on his fork. She ate the piece daintily, closed her eyes and savored.

"Excellent," she said, blushing. "Thank you."

Tony laughed appreciatively.

Jeez, why didn't they start kissing right there. I sent another kick Mom's way, aiming upward because, of course, her feet didn't touch the floor. But she moved her ankles.

"Tell you the truth, I was as surprised to see Oscar at the party as he was to see me. The way Saul talked about him, I didn't expect to see them so cozy, you know what I mean."

"They were good friends," I said.

He shrugged. "Well, nobody told Saul. He wanted to nail the guy. Had this whole angle about Oscar fixing evidence so trials came out in his favor. Wanted to know if that had been my experience."

Mom tensed beside me. This fell right in line with what I had learned from Gavin that morning, only Dad wasn't the topic of Saul's exposé. Oscar was. Curiouser and curiouser.

"And had it been your experience?" Mom asked.

"No, my lawyers would've torn him apart. Much as he wanted to bring me down, Browley knew he better play by the book."

"So the rumors might have been false," I said.

"Not necessarily. I told Saul about other people that had felt railroaded – associates I heard were unhappy."

"That could just be guilty people talking," I protested. "Thinking it's everybody's fault but their own."

"Yeah, these people were guilty alright, but that don't make it any more legit, what Browley was doing."

Mom nodded her agreement, doe-eyed.

"See, that was Oscar's thing. Like a waddyacallit? Vigilante. He fixed cases on people he knew were guilty. Made things up, like a wiretap that wasn't entirely kosher. He'd fudge the paperwork to get it through, or he might lean on his experts to be more aggressive with their testimony than they felt like being. End justifies the means and all that."

"You just gave Oscar a great motive for killing Saul, but who killed Oscar?" Mom took the last bite of her salad and eyed my eggplant. I pulled the dish closer.

Tony shrugged. "That Jannings gal has her sights set on Robin."

Now I leaned forward. "How do you know Angela?"

"Saul brought her around sometimes - smart girl. She got me reading Joseph Wambaugh. I got her eating something besides chicken fingers and pizza. She came here after Oscar died. Said she was picking up where he left off, but she needed to lay low for a while. She wanted me to know her book was no threat to me, and she wouldn't tarnish my good name." He laughed as if the idea was ludicrous.

"She didn't say where she was going, did she?" I asked.

"I let her use an apartment in this little building I got downtown. Nothing fancy, but quiet enough for her to write."

"Why would you do that?" I was intrigued.

"She seems like a good kid, kinda pathetic but nice enough. I don't mind helping out."

"Was she on the same trail as Saul?"

"Hard to say. I think she was doing something about Saul and Oscar's murders. Like I said, she figured Robin for at least one of them."

"What's your connection to Robin?" I asked. "At the party, I got the impression you two knew each other."

"We don't. Maybe she was tired of Saul and got the idea to trade up. Not my type, though." His eyes rested on my mother.

"Could you give us some of the names you gave Saul?" Mom pretended not to notice his interest. "The associates who felt Oscar railroaded them?"

"You don't need to hang out with people like that," Tony hesitated.

"I think we can take care of ourselves." Tony still didn't look convinced, so Mom added. "Just pick an easy one, and we'll start there."

"Sid Weinstein. He's doing work release now outta that halfway house on the west side. Small potatoes, but he's got a good story to tell. You go see him, and we'll go from there."

When we got outside, I turned on Mom.

"What the hell was that?"

"Chloe, please. Don't make a scene."

"What? Am I offending your delicate sensibilities, Little Miss Spanakopita?"

"Chloe, I don't think it's a good idea to be arguing in front of what could very well be an FBI van."

"It's not an FBI van. Would you stop saying that?"

"But it could be."

"So what if it is?"

"I'm just saying the camera adds ten pounds, dear. Those grainy surveillance cameras probably more. Paisley is an ambitious look at the best of times."

We got in the car.

"I hope you know he's going to have Dad rubbed out now, just so he can have you."

"Stop being so dramatic, darling. You get all screechy. We learned some valuable things from Tony, and I don't think my techniques were any more brazen than your questioning of Jack Lassiter."

"I'm not married," I said virtuously.

"I know, baby, but give it time. You're a late-bloomer, that's all."

I gripped the steering wheel and tried some yoga breathing in an effort to keep from flipping out. In with the good air. Out with the bad.

Having decided she had pushed all my buttons, Mom chose to ignore my meltdown.

"Well, I for one think that went well," she said cheerfully. "We're really plumbing the depths. This visit to Sid will help us unravel everything. You wait and see."

CHAPTER 31

The halfway house to which Tony Trianos had directed us was a Southern gothic two story that had seen better days. I shuddered at the havoc that had been wreaked on the old beauty.

The front porch was sagging and crowded with an odd assortment of salvage yard finds, and lawn care didn't seem to be part of the men's rehabilitation. The house's interior had been retrofitted with all the trappings of an institution - shabby furniture, a ping-pong table and an old console television in what had once been the front parlor. A battered fake fir and a haphazard draping of twinkle lights enhanced, rather than dispelled, the overall feeling of weariness and gloom.

The little man working the desk in the foyer squinted. "Weinstein? Oh, you mean Sid the Shiv. What'd he do to rate so many visitors this month?"

"Who else has been to see him?" I asked.

"I ain't his social secretary."

"I'm sure it was Saul Taylor, the true crime writer," Mom said to me. "He was working on a book, and Mr. Weinstein was going to be in it."

"Really? I hadn't heard that." I played along.

"Yeah, that was the one," the man confirmed. "Real character, that guy. His book sounds like a snooze. Sid ain't had what you'd call an illustrious career."

"What's he in for?" I asked.

"I ain't his PO."

"I heard he was strictly small-time," Mom confided. "I can't imagine what Saul wanted with him."

"Whatever it was, they were real sneaky about it." Our informant rubbed his hand across a scratchy expanse of stubble. "Whispering and looking around to see who was listening. Like the rest of us give a shit."

"Could we speak to him if he's available?" Mom asked.

"Try the rec room." He pointed to a large open room to our right.

"What's he look like?" I caught the guy's suspicious glance. "We met in an internet chat room."

"Bald guy. Can't miss him."

Mom had one more question. "Has a another woman been here to see Sid yet? Red-hair. About so tall?" There wasn't a lot more to say when describing Angela Jannings.

I beat the man to the retort he was obviously going to make. "Mom, he ain't no dating service. Come on."

Everyone in the room was experiencing some degree of hair loss, your basic white-collar criminals in need of visits to their stylists, their gyms and their tailors.

We stood uncomfortably in the doorway, ignoring the stares we were attracting from the roomful of men, who apparently had not been enjoying conjugal visits as part of their work release freedom. Picture two fluffy pink bunnies dropped into a cage of hungry Rottweilers.

Ok, that's an exaggeration.

Far from looking threatening or dangerous, these were the nerds of the criminal world - your basic tax evaders, insurance frauds and company embezzlers. The currency in this place was probably stock tips rather than the cigarettes and sexual favors traded in real jails. Trianos would've had a good laugh at their expense.

"Sid Weinstein?" I asked the man closest to me - a tall, trim gentleman who looked harmless enough, unless the red and green snowman sweater he wore was evidence of mental illness rather than alarmingly bad taste.

"He'll be down in a minute. Are you ladies friends of his?" Like the rest, he wore faded jeans, the collar and cuffs of a chambray work shirt peeking from under his sweater, but he held himself in a manner so stiff and correct, you would've thought he had on a silk smoking jacket and ascot.

"Friends of a friend," Mom enlightened him. "The writer, Saul Taylor."

She got a nibble on the first cast.

"Ah, Saul. Tragic, that. Though I daresay the old chap had a way of making enemies. I'm Jeremy Longtham, by the way." His tone was courtly and British, but I detected an unmistakable trace of a Southern accent. Country Southern.

"Wait a minute," I said, light dawning, "Jeremy Longtham? Mr. Lonely Hearts?"

Jeremy blushed modestly. "My reputation precedes me."

"A reputation for swindling rich elderly women," I said.

"A tragic series of misunderstandings, I assure you."

"You said Saul had a way of making enemies," Mom prompted, seeing an opportunity.

"Well, he wasn't very savvy, was he? Seeking out a bore like Sid, when there are much more colorful stories to be told."

"Like yours?" I asked, pointedly.

"I daresay my life would make an interesting read, but I'd want complete creative control. Mr. Taylor and I never saw eye to eye on that."

"Did other people come to see Sid in reference to Saul's book?" Mom steered us back to our quest.

"Now that you mention it, there was someone else."

"Red head, about so tall?" Mom asked.

"No. Blond guy, very pulled together."

Mom's eyes met mine. It could only be Jack Lassiter, but we had no idea what their meeting meant.

Longtham couldn't tell us much other than the fact that their conversation had been heated. Once we assured him we weren't in the market for a suitor or interested in helping with his rehabilitation, he started to move away.

"Wait a minute," I called him back.

Longtham turned hopefully.

"Why does everyone call him Sid the Shiv?"

"A joke, my dear, only as a joke. Harmless little man, really. Worked at an accounting firm and was convinced no one appreciated his genius. One day he pulled a silver-plated letter opener on his boss when she told him he wasn't getting a raise. Unfortunately for Sid, she takes kickboxing classes at her gym and disarmed him handily. Still pretty bitter about it." He nodded significantly toward a chubby guy who had just entered the room, newspaper in hand.

The man took a chair by the window and scanned the front page as we approached.

"Sid?" Mom asked. "Mr...Shiv?"

"Who wants to know?" The bald man looked us up and down. Did I say Rottweiler? This guy was pure basset hound.

Mom made introductions and explained the purpose of our visit. We pulled two wicker chairs toward his seat.

"Nice sweater," I said, eyeing its reindeer appliqué complete with googly eyes and a little red light bulb nose.

"My kids sent it. Heard about what happened to Taylor. I'm not real broken up about it."

"You didn't like him?" I asked.

"Mr. Got-Rocks thought he was better'n the people here. Like he was too good to set foot in this joint."

Sid was obviously affecting the persona of a street hustler, an image completely at odds with his fat fingers, weak chin and droopy eyes.

"He was pretentious, wasn't he?" Mom commiserated.

Weinstein shrugged. "If he had helped me get even with that S.O.B. Browley, I coulda put up with a little condescension, know what I mean?"

"And how was he doing that?" I asked.

"He was going to expose some irregularities with my case, namely the fact that I was innocent." The reindeer sweater fixed us with a lazy-eyed stare and dared us to disagree.

"I bet everyone in here would say that they're innocent," I pointed out.

"Not Nathan." Sid nodded toward a bearded man working a Sudoku puzzle. He got even with his company by hacking onto their server and sending porn to their customers instead of the weekly newsletter. He says he'd do it again, the way they treated him."

I smiled. "With the exception of Nathan and one or two victims of the system, I'm sure a lot of guys here would cry foul."

"Yeah, maybe."

"So what's the story?" I didn't show my impatience. "People saw you pull the letter opener. Heard you make threats. Yet your conscience is clear?" I was ad-libbing, and he was quick to contradict me.

"No one saw anything but her manhandling me. It was my word against hers. I shoulda filed assault charges on the bitch."

"What about the letter opener?" Mom asked. "What about fingerprints?"

"Weren't any," Sid said, smugly. "I'd wiped 'em off with my tie, while she was calling security. 'Cept the joke was on me 'cause the police report said otherwise."

"Maybe you weren't as careful as you thought," I suggested.

"Maybe. But nobody said nothing about prints until they found out I did a little freelance bookkeeping for Tony Trianos. Suddenly, Oscar Browley hot shit DA is taking a personal interest in my case. Suddenly, there are prints where there weren't prints, and this guy's telling me he can make my case go away if I tell him what he wants to hear."

"About Trianos." Mom remarked.

"About Trianos. That kind of trouble, I don't need." He glanced around the room at the guys playing cards, working puzzles and listening to their iPods. "This is a good use of my time if it keeps me off Trianos' radar."

We sat in silence, wondering how it all fit. Was this the reason Saul had been killed?

It gave Oscar the strongest motive yet, but it still left too many nagging questions. Like how was Saul killed? And why was Oscar killed and by whom? And who left that damn hand on the doorstep?

"What did Jack Lassiter want?" Mom asked.

Another good question. And how did Jack even know about Sid? From Angela? Or more likely, Robin, if they were as cozy as they appeared to be on that DVD Megan Taylor had given us.

"Him? He wanted to know what Saul wanted. Like I'd tell him, the dumb bastard. I wasn't looking to the DA's office for justice this time around. Saul and me was going to get it real public like, making for a good book and an even better lawsuit."

I didn't point out that, in a twisted way, justice had already been served. After all, he had committed the crime. I didn't care for Oscar's methods, but I didn't have much sympathy for Sid Weinstein either.

"Was Jack here before Saul's death or after?" Mom asked.

"Day or two before."

"And did Saul know any other stories similar to yours?" I asked.

"He had a few. He didn't share the details with me, but then, I wasn't interested in any case but my own."

It was all too incredible. Saul and Oscar were pals, had been for years. I remembered them at the party, backslapping and joking around. Yet all the while, Saul was gathering evidence that would ruin his friend and send him to prison. Not to mention emotionally blackmailing Oscar's wife. I couldn't believe my family had socialized, even casually, with such whack jobs.

I was worn out by the time we got back to my parents' house. Mom invited me in for an iced tea, feeling as drained as I was.

She tossed the mail on the center island and went to fix our glasses.

"You think Saul would've published a book about Oscar?" I wondered. "It would've completely discredited all his other books, at least the ones that used Oscar as a source."

Ice tinkled into the glasses as Mom answered, "I don't think he could resist such a huge story. We're talking national. Saul would've loved the publicity and drama of it all."

"You think Angela will call?" Tony Trianos had been reluctant to tell us exactly where Angela was, but had agreed to pass along our urgent plea to get in touch.

"Not likely." But as Mom passed the phone, she hit the playback button on the answering machine.

Bunny Beaumont's voice filled the kitchen.

"Amanda, honey, word on the street has it that you were seen leaving a halfway house for convicts. One minute you're going to bars, the next you're hanging out with men behind them. Do tell. It's a little late for a midlife crisis but don't worry, doll, your secret's safe with me." She gasped. "Unless Alex picks up this message first. Oops, hope I didn't let the cat out of the bag. Alex, if you're listening, hey you sweet thing. What are we going to do with that naughty wife of yours? Anyway, whoever gets this message, call me. Inquiring minds want to know!"

Mom hit the delete button, pushing it far harder than necessary. "That woman's as subtle as a goiter."

I poured tea and offered her a slice of lemon. "Dad will flip when he hears about Oscar. I can't wait to see what he has to say."

"You're going to have to. He's in Montgomery taking a deposition and won't be in till late." She pulled a small manila envelope out of the stack of letters she had brought in. "A present already?"

"From whom?"

"No return address. No postmark either. Someone must've put it in the box."

"Letter bomb." I backed up. "Candy from strangers."

"Don't be silly." But she opened the envelope gingerly and away from her face.

No sparks, no suspicious powders. Just six discs neatly labeled in Saul's familiar script.

CHAPTER 32

Mom was putting a batch of homemade orange sablé cookie dough in the freezer when I called from the gym.

"Are you going to tell Dad?" I asked.

"Eventually."

Dad would insist we turn the discs over to McGowan. Immediately. But we hadn't even looked at them yet because they were password protected.

The plan was to find Angela tomorrow no matter what it took. With the discs as bait, she was sure to come out of the woodwork. Failing that, we would be spending quality time with a computer trying to crack the pass code. But none of that would happen if Mom suddenly got a conscience.

I needn't have worried. "We'll turn them over as soon as we look at them," she said.

"Good. 'Cuz we need to study them before we hand them to McGowan. No offense to Dad, but this is no time to be all law-abiding. Somebody sent us Saul's discs for a reason, and I want to know why. So, what's your theory? Why us? Why now?"

We hadn't talked much after discovering the discs because I had to train a client at the gym. The six discs had been labeled Research I, Research II, Notes, Outline, People and Letters.

"Maybe the person who stole them was finished with them," Mom theorized.

"Do you think they changed them in some way? Deleted stuff that was damaging to themselves?"

"We won't know that till we look at them."

"Why not just destroy them?"

"Maybe the killer realized they couldn't incriminate him or her, so why not give someone else a motive."

"I still think..." My attention veered toward a familiar figure strolling to the sauna. "Damn. Guess who I just saw?"

"Who?"

"Robin."

"Did she hear you? We can't let anyone know we have the discs. It could be dangerous."

"She didn't hear me, but that reminds me. Nancy could be lurking around somewhere, too. Maybe even Bunny Beaumont."

"I thought you had a client. Where are you?"

"She's doing twenty minutes on the treadmill first. I'm in the locker room."

"Well, be careful. We're not exactly on the side of the angels here, keeping evidence from the police."

"Fine. Sheesh."

Mom was silent for several seconds before speaking. "You and your father don't keep secrets from me do you?"

"What? No, of course not."

"Uh-huh."

"I'll call you when I get home. You can help me pick out something to wear for my date with Jacob later this week."

When we hung up, I did some light weight work with Gloria McClanahan, my sixty-something client who was taking a New Year's cruise with her husband. She planned to wear a red bikini, just like she had on their honeymoon forty years ago. I thought she'd look damn good in it.

When I got back to my loft, Dana was waiting outside my building. I was so not in the mood. I could barely deal with my own love life much less Dana's train wreck romance.

"You want to get some frozen yogurt?" she asked.

What I really wanted was to crawl into bed and hide out till the world started making sense again, but a girl's got to eat and preferably not by herself, so if she's poisoned someone will be there to call 911. I would just have to steer the conversation away from Dan.

In the car, though, it was Dana who was doing the steering. We had both finished our white chocolate mousse waffle cones, and Dana had wanted to ride around looking at houses. It didn't dawn on me until she slowed the car and cut her lights that she had driven over to Dan's townhouse.

Dana shouted, "Drive-by!"

Instinctively, I slipped down in my seat.

"Don't stop," I warned.

She stopped.

"Who's car is that?" she asked slowly.

My heart sank.

"Look at the bumper sticker - a tanning salon," she said as if she had never been to one of those dens of inequity.

"What are you doing?" I demanded. "And can't you take me home before you do it?"

"I think Dan's cheating on me."

"Again?" I couldn't help asking.

Dana wasn't pleased with my reference to ancient history. "It's been two years."

"Is little Courtney two already? So cute."

Sorry, but we had been over this before.

"I can't do this alone," Dana pleaded her case. "It's stalking if you're alone."

Ah, such a fine line.

She cut the engine.

"Oh, no," I said. "There's no way we're going to sit here all night. That car could be anybody's. I don't have time for this."

"That's why we should take a quick peek in the side window."

"Absolutely not! You get this car moving." I used my sternest voice.

She opened her door.

"The light," I hissed. "Close the door."

She did, but she was on the other side of it. She came over and crouched beside my door. I cracked it open, cursing the light.

"Come with me. I need to know if he's seeing someone."

"Why?" I asked. "If he is, seeing them together is just going to hurt. If he's not, you're going to look like a fool. Ask him. Talk to him. Or better yet, trust your instincts."

"I need to know. Wouldn't you love to know where you stand with Jacob - the real reason why your relationship isn't moving forward? I have that chance."

"This isn't going to tell you anything." I whispered. "And I'm telling everyone we know. Don't think I won't."

"You won't if you come with me. Then you're an accomplice."

"I'm not coming with you."

"Yes, you are." She stood up and backed away from the car. "Because you worry about me, don't you? I ain't right." She ran, hunched over, toward the house.

"I'm telling." I stage whispered, but she was gone.

I sat there imagining a hundred scenarios - none of them good. I got out and crept after her.

We made our way to the patio and squatted in front of the sliding glass doors. The gauzy white curtains, draped just so, didn't do much to block our view, and I wondered if Dana had been in charge of the decorating and had chosen them for that reason.

In the kitchen, Dan was slicing something on the cutting board - alone.

"You see?" I said. "Let's go."

She saw, alright. A blond came into the kitchen and took the knife out of Dan's hand, laughingly fussing like he was doing something wrong.

Dana started pounding on the glass doors.

I tried to jump up and get back to the car before Dan caught us. Unfortunately, my legs don't recover from a squat as quickly as they once did, so I toppled onto my butt. That's where I was when Dan flung open the door (as much as you can fling open a sliding door).

"What the hell," was all he managed before Dana pushed past him into the room.

The blond came forward, still holding the paring knife, and Dana momentarily lost her focus.

"That's my knife!" She yelled, pointing her finger accusingly.

The blond held out the knife handle first, the idiot, but I intercepted. Great, now my fingerprints were at the scene.

Even my surprise that a hip little thing like Dana had opted for a country Christmas, with primitive ornaments and folk art Santas, couldn't distract me from the scene unfolding before me.

"I live here, you know," Dana told the blond who nodded as if that explained things.

"Not yet you don't. Goddamn it, Dana this is the craziest thing you've ever done." That was Dan, and I had to disagree. Had he forgotten the time she had called his mother and pleaded with the woman to make Dan propose?

"You bastard," Dana yelled. "Is there a turnstile in our bedroom?"

"She's just a friend, you psycho," Dan said.

Lovely.

"We're getting married in two weeks, and you're making gazpacho with some other woman."

"It's fajitas," the blond interjected.

"Who puts cucumber in fajitas?" Dana demanded.

"I think you two better leave," Dan suggested.

"I think she had better leave," Dana disagreed.

"I'm not leaving. Should I leave, Danny?" the blond girl asked.

"No, Dana's leaving. You!" Dan pointed to me, "Get her out of here."

The nerve!

"It's my townhouse, too." Dana yelled. "I gave you rent money this month!"

"My name's on the lease." Dan was calm.

"I'm canceling the check I gave you."

"I already cashed it."

Dana's hands flew to her hair, and I actually thought she might tear out handfuls of her shiny black locks. In the end, though, vanity won out, and she settled for raking her hands through its length.

"It's over!" Dana shouted. "The wedding's off! You'll never see me again."

Dan took the news well, even holding the door open for Dana to walk through. I handed the knife back to Dan, blade first.

"She didn't start out like this," I told the blond.

"They never do." She got her purse and followed me out.

Dan didn't even call after her, just slammed the door. As much as you can slam a sliding door.

Back at the car I took the wheel. Beside me, Dana whiplashed through the stages of grief.

Denial: I can't jump to conclusions about this. She could just be an old friend.

Anger: Old friend my bleep cheating mother bleeper, I've known the bleep for ten years. Where the bleep would he get a friend he could bleep in my bleeping bed the minute I turn my bleeping back?

Sorrow: I loved him so much. We were perfect together.

And finally, acceptance: It's over. It's really over this time. Who could've seen this one coming?

At her apartment, I sat with her as she totally wigged out, now moving without pause through the seven deadly sins. The anger was back, and so was her potty mouth. Then for a while she lazed on her couch - makeup tear-streaked, shoveling cold pita and hummus into her mouth with alarming speed and bad manners. Gluttony did double duty if you also count glutton for punishment, which manifested itself in a phone call to Dan despite my protests and a brief wrestling match. (Dana's slim, but she's scrappy.)

I told her God wouldn't begrudge her a little pride, but it was the one sin she didn't seem interested in.

She asked Dan to come over and finish this once and for all. By the time he came roaring up on his motorcycle, Dana was hell-bent on letting him know exactly how he had ruined her life and how much better off she would be without him.

I took a beer out on the fire escape to await the inevitable. I was grappling with several emotions - sad that my friend was in pain, relieved this had happened before she got married and not after, happy that I wouldn't have to wear a honeydew bridesmaid dress, and frustrated that I'd already paid for the damn thing. I didn't even bother listening to the scene unfolding inside. The inevitable took less than twenty minutes.

The front door clicked, a death rattle came from the apartment ("He dumped me!") and, finally, the receding whine of a motorcycle. I could almost hear the tuneless song Dan hummed as he roared away.

I went inside to help Dana reclaim a sense of self, rising like a phoenix from the ashes of despair, or break out the Hagen Daz and put on an angry-women-of-rock CD. She wanted none of it.

I called my mother to come pick me up.

Since it was after ten and Dad still wasn't home, I had let Mom talk me into spending the night, instead of going all the way back downtown. I was seriously bluesing after the drama filled day. First lunch with Tony Trianos, then the visit to the halfway house, followed by the mystery of the discs and finally Dana's histrionics. The only thing keeping me going was my curiosity about Saul's discs and the knowledge that eight-hundred threadcount sheets in Mom's guest bedroom were only moments away.

At the house, I dropped my purse on the kitchen's island and went straight for the wine glasses. Mom looked as tired as I did. Neither of us spoke.

I was about to offer her a glass when she stopped mid-step and stared at the floor. I followed her gaze and noticed a footprint. Had I tracked something in on her freshly mopped floor? Wouldn't have been the first time.

But aggravation was Mom's usual reaction. This was different.

I looked closer. It was only an outline of a shoe not a full print, bigger than my foot. Had Dad been home?

But even as the thought formed, I knew my father hadn't made the prints. The size was wrong, and the hint of tread belonged to one of those rugged wet-dry sandals. Dad didn't own sandals like that.

Almost unwillingly, I raised my eyes a few inches. Sure enough, there was another print not far from the first. And another. I counted seven in all, as I followed their progress across the kitchen and received another jolt when I realized the last one disappeared into the pantry.

One wall of Mom's kitchen is filled with lovely old built-in drawers and cabinets, as well as a pantry that's wide but not deep. You would only be in the pantry with the door closed for one reason - to hide.

Then I noticed the knob on the pantry door turning.

CHAPTER 33

I stood, transfixed, watching the knob slowly turn, my brain unable to process what my eyes were telling it. Someone was in the house. Someone who had been hiding, but who now thought it safe to come out.

It was the telephone that jolted us into action, the jangle of the ringer especially loud against the suspense-charged silence.

Amanda and I both jumped, and I think the person in the pantry did as well. The knob paused a moment, and I heard a tiny gasp of surprise behind the door. Mom headed toward the front door, and I headed toward the back. Instead of going anywhere, we bumped into each other—a mistake that cost us the split second of opportunity we had to escape.

Mom pulled me down behind the island, and we crouched, listening to the unmistakable whisper of pantry hinges swinging open. We were poised for action, although neither of us knew what that action should be. The center island stood between us and the phone. To get to the front door, we had to pass the pantry.

"Back door," I mouthed.

"Deadbolt," Mom mouthed back.

Ah. Good point. No time to fumble with a key. Think! I ordered myself.

Right then we had an advantage. We knew the intruder's location but he, from the size of the footprints, didn't know ours. I wracked my brain for any self-defense moves I knew. Stop, drop and roll? Probably not a good idea.

The person on the other side of the island seemed to be listening as intently as we were. We heard the answering machine click on, and Dad's voice asked the caller to leave a message. As quietly as I could I eased open one of the island's cabinet doors and surveyed the contents. Angela's voice now filled the room.

"Mrs. C. It's me!" She waited then sang, "Hell-oooo? Tony said I had to call, so that's what I'm doing. I know you're trying to help, but I'm fine. Stop worrying."

I felt around in the cabinet, willing Angela to keep talking. My hands encountered casserole dishes, Tupperware bowls, cookie sheets. Nothing that would do any real damage. In the middle cabinet there was olive oil, various cans and jars. Useless.

Angela said something about working on her book.

Don't hang up, I begged silently.

She hung up.

Mom nudged my shoulder. In the cabinet closest to her, she had found the five-inch cast iron skillet she used to make corn bread. If she could get enough force behind it, this would make a pretty handy weapon. Trouble was, she couldn't quickly pull out the skillet without a cacophony of crashing glass, stainless steel and ceramic.

I prayed that whoever was in the house would think Mom had gone upstairs to the bedroom or bathroom. But there had been no footsteps overhead. No rush of running water. In fact, there had been no sounds anywhere, and I could feel the intruder's brain working it out in his head, growing suspicious of the strained silence that filled the house.

His shadow stretched across the kitchen floor as he moved toward us. Mom's hand closed around her weapon, and after a moment's hesitation, I grabbed mine, ignoring her look of disdain.

Again, a sound startled both of us. This time it was Josie coming in through her doggie door, the innocuous jingle of her tags absurd in such profound quiet. Luckily she was distracted by our visitor.

Miniature Schnauzers aren't as visually imposing as, say, a Doberman, but I knew she would protect Mom if her life were threatened. The only problem was, Josie didn't know Mom was in danger. So she did what I'd always suspected she would do if our house was broken into. She greeted our guest with happy whimpers, danced eagerly on the kitchen floor, and rolled over to invite anyone who was interested to scratch her tummy. She was killing him alright - with kindness.

And how was the intruder taking all this? Impassively according to his shadow. Then I heard him growl, "I'll get you, Mrs. Carstairs, and your little dog, too."

I watched in dismay as two shadow arms reached toward Josie, who cried in pleasure thinking she was in for some serious belly rubbing.

Mom and I went into action. Without a second thought, I jumped from my hiding place and fired my weapon - a stinging blast of butter-flavored non-stick spray right into the intruder's eyes.

Direct hit!

At the same time, Mom tore the skillet free of the other dishes, the crash loud and violent, and with a wood chopping motion, brought down with all her might five pounds of cast iron onto the intruder's head.

Jack Lassiter went sprawling.

Josie yelped and hightailed it back out her doggie door. So much for her status as watchdog.

Blood pooled under Jack's head at an alarming rate. Had we killed him? Should I feel his pulse? Elevate his head? Perform CPR?

Like hell I would! The man had bought me drinks under false pretenses.

I grabbed my purse and took off with a speed and dexterity that surprised me. Mom was faster, even more surprising. I'm ashamed to admit a strangled scream tore from my throat. As Mom fumbled with the front door latch, I expected any second to feel Jack's bloody hand snaking around my neck, his hot breath against my cheek or a bullet rip into my spine.

It wasn't until we were safely in the Cadillac, doors locked and barreling down the driveway that I started to feel safe. I fumbled for my cell phone and called 911 as Mom parked across the street. With the engine running, the car in drive, we watched the house.

I told the operator what had happened as I fought to control my voice, but I was seriously freaked and Mom was, too, her hands trembling on the steering wheel. I checked the back seat, irrationally terrified that Jack's bloody form would rise behind us.

The 911 operator, her name was Paula, kept us company until two police cars roared up. She tried to get us to go to a neighbor's house, but Mom wanted to make sure Jack didn't get away.

What Paula thought of our claim that one of our city's assistant district attorneys had tried to kill us, she wouldn't say. We hung up with her promise to call Dad and our sincere thanks for her calm, gentle manner. I envisioned one of Mom's homemade pineapple upside down cakes in her future.

We gave one set of officers, Brubaker and Conner, our statements as the other team, Dawson and Jemison, entered my parents' house. An ambulance arrived. Neighbors trickled out of their homes. Gina from next door brought me a sweater and Mom a fleece hoodie. Before I knew it, I felt Dad's arms around me.

It was almost one a.m. before our house emptied of everyone who wasn't a Carstairs by birth or by nature - me, my parents, Bridget and Lily, completely wired, in her pjs.

Very protective of my mother, Dad tucked an antique quilt around her feet and rubbed them gently as she reclined on the living room sofa.

Mom suppressed a shudder. "Is the kitchen clean?" I knew she meant the floor.

Bridget nodded. "I did it myself. One of the cops said Lassiter's got a hell of a knot on his head. You really let him have it."

There was no mistaking the admiration in Bridget's voice, and I could tell Mom was pleased.

"I didn't exactly escape unscathed." She gestured toward an ice pack on her shoulder.

It wasn't until the excitement had worn off and the adrenaline had stopped surging that she had realized her shoulder was throbbing dully. Thankfully, it wasn't dislocated.

"I can't believe y'all pulled it off." Bridget's voice again filled with amazement. "You smoked out a killer. "Had y'all suspected Jack?"

"He was on our list," I lied.

"Along with about six other people," Mom admitted.

"Yeah, but we must've done something right. We forced his hand and got him to make a mistake. And we were there to nab him." I yawned. "Now that we know the killer it's just a matter of filling in blanks - a piece of cake."

Mom didn't share my confidence. "Jack Lassiter? Why?"

"It has to have something to do with Robin. It just has to," I said.

"I wouldn't jump to conclusions," Dad interjected. "What we have is a suspect in an alleged breaking and entering. That's a long way from proving he's a murderer."

"Alleged? He broke. He entered. There was nothing alleged about that," I said.

"There is till we have all the facts," Dad stated.

Talk about a buzz kill. But before any of us could reply, a knock on the front door made us jump.

"Who in the world could that be?" Mom asked as Dad went to the foyer.

Max McGowan led their way back. "Sorry, but I thought you guys would be up, and I figured you would want to be informed. Lassiter's conscious, but he's not saying much."

"Lawyered up, didn't he?" I crowed.

"Not quite." McGowan wasn't impressed. "Jack doesn't think he needs a lawyer. Says he was looking for evidence related to two murders, acting on an anonymous tip." It suddenly occurred to me that McGowan was controlling his temper. "Evidence you two were keeping from the police."

I could feel Dad's eyes on me, but I didn't return his gaze. "Once you see what's on those discs, you'll learn the real reason Jack was after them."

McGowan's eyes narrowed. "What discs? I told Lassiter if you two had those discs you would have called me immediately."

"Where are they, Amanda?" Dad asked.

Mom told him in her office on her desk.

We waited in uncomfortable silence while he got the discs from upstairs and gave them to McGowan.

"Lassiter said he entered the house only after seeing signs of a break-in, a broken lock on the back porch. He was just making sure everyone was ok. When he heard you two coming in, he thought you might be the intruder, so he hid in the pantry."

"He threatened Mom! He said he would get her and her little dog, too!"

"Not according to him. He said he only wanted the discs and to tell you two that Saul and Oscar's deaths were police matters and you should stay out of it."

A fact that seemed all too clear now. What impact would our mistake have on the case? We had been too cocky, too careless.

"I'd just about ruled you two out as suspects," Detective McGowan said. "But now, I'm not so sure. You're either completely brainless or in this up to your eyeballs."

"Max…" Dad interrupted.

"No, Alex, they compromised my investigation."

There was nothing Dad could say to that, and I was sick knowing I'd put him in such a bad position. I couldn't blame McGowan for being angry, either. Terms like "chain of evidence" and "due process of law" were just catchphrases to Mom and me, plot points in our favorite TV shows. Dad and McGowan dealt with the realities of these ideas every day.

"I think we had better get together tomorrow to talk about everything you guys have learned." Dad's voice was tight. "Lunch here, maybe."

"You're lucky I'm not hauling you both downtown," McGowan made his position clear.

"They know that. Lunch tomorrow." Dad rose, and the two men decided on a time as they walked to the front door.

"Not good," I said.

"Not good at all," Mom agreed.

"I knew we should have turned over the discs."

"Please."

"I mean, in my heart, I knew." Not even a night of throwing up nitrobenzene-laced candy had felt this bad.

CHAPTER 34

The next morning, the mood at my parents' house could only be described as grim.

Dad had slipped out of bed without waking Mom. His cereal bowl and coffee cup were in the sink, and we could tell from the distant whine of his circular saw that he was in his shop. Mom said his mood didn't bode well for the guestroom window seat he was building for her, and she suspected the storage compartment wouldn't be getting the removable bins she had requested.

"Fine, two can play this game." She checked to see if she had the makings for tofu stir-fry, knowing Dad considered tofu to be the same as eating Styrofoam packing peanuts.

Nancy called just as I finished blending a fruit smoothie. Mom put her on speakerphone, so I could listen in.

"Amanda, I just heard. Are you ok?"

Mom assured her that she was.

"A break-in. I can't imagine. You should get an alarm or a dog or both."

Mom took a sip of coffee. I took a sip of smoothie. We let Nancy ramble on. It was easier that way.

"The wife of one of Oscar's lawyer friends filled me in on everything. Dreadful woman, such a gossip and very thick ankles for a woman her size. She said Jack was some kind of sexual deviant, a peeping Tom or worse, and she's never liked the way he looked at her." A derisive snort punctuated this.

Mom raised an eyebrow, but Nancy was off again.

"She also said the police had Saul's discs, which I just Can Not Believe."

Mom was testing her skillet-wielding shoulder, which seemed to be in fine working order this morning, and missed her cue to respond.

"Amanda! The discs? Jack? Are you there?"

"I'm here. The police have the discs."

"But how did you get them, and why didn't you tell me? I thought we were in this together, Amanda."

News to us. In what?

"I mean, true, I don't have as much to lose as you, your husband still being very much alive and all. Still, I would've hoped you would have let me in on the fact that you had the discs and were planning to destroy them."

Nancy still thought Saul had been playing his emotional blackmail games with Mom, and Mom should have destroyed the discs to protect her marriage and/or reputation? Really!

Another possibility occurred to me. Nancy might just be feigning outrage to cover up the fact she had sent the discs herself.

"I had the discs less than twenty-four hours," Mom explained, taking Nancy's ranting in stride. "Never even opened them. I can't imagine who sent them to me, but I'll tell you one thing, I've never been unfaithful to my husband."

"Is he there?" Nancy whispered.

"What? No."

"Do you think he heard us?"

"Nancy, he's not here."

"Call me back when you can talk." She clicked off.

Mom sighed and finished her coffee.

"What are you doing this morning?" she asked.

"Working out, and finishing up a concept board. I'll be back here for the inquisition. You need me to pick up anything?"

She didn't. I think she just wanted to be alone for a while. Being on the outs with my Dad makes her edgy.

She handed me a to-go cup for the rest of my smoothie and gave me a ride home.

When I called a little while later, I could hear the dejection in Mom's voice over the speakerphone. "Is he still mad?" I asked.

"He's not happy, that's for sure."

I could picture her in her office, die-hard multi-tasker that she is, sorting through bills, printing out invoices. She would be dressed to entertain guests, of course, maybe a little twin set and skirt combo, lipstick on, every hair in place.

I was at my loft, about ten minutes away, doing intervals on my elliptical trainer. By the time we hung up, my labored breathing sounded like something you would expect to pay $9.99 a minute to hear. If you were into that sort of thing, which we, of course, were not.

"Did he say anything?"

"Not a word."

"Ouch," I said.

"See you at lunch."

"I guess."

Knowing I couldn't put it off any longer, I rode my bike over to my parents, both to get in some additional exercise and to prove to my family that the bike wasn't just another fitness fad I had gotten into and would soon drop, although it kind of was.

Birmingham is so hilly, even a short ride is a major workout. Too major for the pleasant little jaunts I had envisioned. Plus, I had allowed the salesman talk me into getting a top-of-the-line road bike (necessary to accommodate my petite frame, was the line I fell for) with clipless pedals. If you've never tried riding with clipless pedals, take it from me, it ain't easy.

You need special shoes that lock into the pedals, shoes that can't be unlocked with the normal, instinctive pulling-up motion you've handled well all your life. I could now manage a short ride every now and then. Besides, riding the bike also provided me with a way to put off seeing my father as long as I could.

Luckily this route took me by some of the most spectacularly decorated houses in Birmingham, including some Mom and I had done ourselves. At the Powell's, we had flocked their seventeen-foot Fraser Fir with a mixture of water and no-dyes, no-perfumes washing powder. That thing looked like something growing wild in the snowy foothills of the Smokey Mountains, absolutely beautiful. And for the Changs, we had done a festive combination of Christmas (their version of Santa is called Dun Che Lao Ren or Christmas Old Man) and the Chinese New Year.

I concentrated on taking deep cleansing breaths of the mild December air (hard to believe Christmas was less than a week away) and cleared my mind of everything except the soft breeze stirring the red-ribboned wreaths that hung from each of the Farr's upstairs windows. Slowly, my dark mood lifted.

By the time I got to my parents', I was almost optimistic about the upcoming meeting. I rode up just as Bridget came along the walk from the house, and I yelled for her to catch me and my clipped on shoes, just in case. She grabbed where she could, and together we managed a clumsy stop that left us both in relatively upright positions.

"Get regular pedals!" she demanded as I got off. "It isn't giving up. It's accepting the reality that you suck on this thing."

"I know." I pulled clogs from my backpack. "But all the cool kids have clipless."

"Jacob has clipless?"

"Isn't he coolest?" I said with mostly pretend adoration.

She rolled her eyes.

"Did you see Dad?" I asked.

"Yeah, who left his cake out in the rain?"

"Still mad, huh? It's your mother's fault."

"Oh she's my mother now? Wait till you see them. They're both acting completely bizarre. Very polite with each other. 'Alex would you like some iced tea?' 'Not right now, thank you.'" She shivered.

"Did they say anything about me?"

Bridget smiled. "They didn't have to. You're so dead."

Sibling rivalry was still alive and kicking in our relationship. In addition, our squabbling drove our parents nuts - always a plus.

"Thanks for your concern." I headed for the door.

"Come on, I'm sorry. Anything I can do?"

"Take my side for once."

"Anything but that. I've got to get to work."

"You're not staying? What if I get The Look?"

My father has a look that can reduce a witness under cross-examination to tears. And we're talking male witnesses, here. Hardened criminals. The Look even humbled Mom.

"I'd say it's pretty much a given," Bridget smirked.

"Great. Just great." I hadn't gotten The Look since April of '92, when it was revealed that I had financed my spring break trip to New Orleans by not renewing my car insurance. I still have night sweats.

"Your detective friend will protect you." Bridget pointed to the curb.

McGowan, carrying a black leather briefcase, was getting out of a '68 Mustang. "What Dad's going to do to you, I can't believe he would want any witnesses."

"Aren't you supposed to be at work?"

"I'm going. I'm going."

Before heading up the walk I paused to admire the twenty-foot wreath that hung from the chimney, illuminated at night by a spotlight tucked among the gardenia bushes. The eaves were draped with the white lights mandated for historical houses, plush red velvet bows punctuated the pine garland draping the porch wall and paper luminaries lined the sidewalk. This was what Christmas should look like.

I sat on the front steps and changed my shoes, watching as Bridget chatted for a sec with the detective. I couldn't hear what they were saying, but I noticed the way Bridget tossed her hair when she laughed. And I noticed McGowan noticing it, too. Interesting in a sort of unsettling way. Bridget had been divorced for barely two years. She didn't need to rush into anything.

They said their goodbyes, and McGowan approached, looking a little calmer and quite attractive in charcoal pants and a crisp white shirt. Attractive for a Yankee, I mean.

"Nice car." I stood up.

"Thanks, it's a Mustang."

"I know. A three-ninety GT."

"You girls know your cars," he said.

"Our Daddy brought us up right."

"It's your mother I'm concerned about. The two of you have been up to no good."

"I don't know what you're talking about."

"Your wide-eyed innocent look works better than any polygraph. 'Cause I know there's nothing innocent about you."

I gasped. "How can you say that? I'm as innocent as a lamb. As pure as driven snow. As good as…"

"Chloe."

"Yes?"

"You're talking in clichés. You stalling just so you don't have to go in?"

"Yes."

"We're going in."

"Cover me."

Dad actually seemed pretty cheerful, at least while he was greeting McGowan.

"Is that you, Max?" Mom came in from the back porch. "Thank you for joining us."

In gracious hostess mode, she reminded me of a mint julep - all sweet and Southern, but with a kick you don't see coming. Apparently McGowan didn't drink on duty.

"Hello, Mrs. Carstairs. What've you been up to lately?" he asked.

Mom looked at Dad. Dad looked at me. I looked at my clogs.

"Why don't we talk over lunch?" Mom suggested.

We moved into my parents' sunny eat-in kitchen, where the table was already set and a mound of chicken - not tofu - and crisp-cooked veggies waited for us in the wok.

In the light of day, with all surfaces gleaming and the air fragrant with enticing aromas of teriyaki sauce and jasmine rice, it was hard to believe an intruder had almost attacked us the night before. An intruder I had casually flirted with over drinks just a few nights before. I really had to hone my screening skills, if I was going to hit the dating scene again.

When we had filled our plates with stir-fry, Mom and I spilled the whole story, sparing them nothing. Nancy's alleged affair with her Pilates trainer, among others. Robin's quasi-confession to killing her first two husbands. Jack Lassiter's relationship with Robin. Angela's career aspirations and her dismay over Robin's inheritance. Meagan Taylor's presence in Birmingham without her father's knowledge. Tony Trianos's claim that Oscar Browley was fixing cases. And Saul's proclivity for digging up dirt on people and then holding it against them, possibly even his buddy Oscar.

McGowan listened carefully, interrupting only twice to compliment the stir-fry.

When we had finished, McGowan shook his head. "Oscar fixing cases? I'm going to need a lot more than Tony Trianos's assertion and Saul's theories to believe that." He accepted another glass of iced tea from Mom. His plate was so clean, running it through the dishwasher would be a formality.

"Speaking of Trianos." He reached down and retrieved the briefcase he had at his feet. "Thought y'all might be interested in these."

He handed a folder to Mom. Inside were grainy black-and-white photos of her outside Trianos's restaurant standing next to a paisley sofa.

I gasped and looked closer. That was me in my paisley skirt! Or should I say Bridget's new paisley skirt?

"The FBI has a surveillance van on Tony Trianos," McGowan informed us.

Mom cut her eyes at me.

"Remember what I told you about Moriarty and the illegal gambling operation?" McGowan asked.

"Moriarty?" Mom looked blank.

"One-hand man," I clarified.

"Yeah. Gambling might be the tie-in between Trianos, the severed hand and, by extension, Saul."

I couldn't hide my exasperation. "That's what we've been saying from the beginning - Trianos."

"Yeah, but you two haven't been the only ones getting cozy with Trianos lately. Feds have plenty of shots of Angela hanging around him, too. Funny how it always comes back to her."

"Hilarious." I closed the folder on the incriminating (read: unflattering) photos.

Dad set down his tea glass. "What about the discs? Have you opened them yet?"

McGowan nodded. "Lot of the same stuff you guys just told me. Interviews with Sid the Shiv. Oscar fixing cases. Saul was doing his homework."

"That's it?" I couldn't believe it. Considering all the trouble we were in for not turning over the discs, they should've at least told us something we didn't know.

McGowan didn't appreciate the irony either. "Nothing about anyone else connected to the case. Just interviews for a new book about Oscar."

"Which means Oscar's the only person who had a reason to steal the discs," I said.

"But no one knew what those discs contained, so someone's imagination could've gotten the best of them," McGowan pointed out. "Oscar was the only one with a legitimate reason."

Dad wasn't buying the whole Oscar-fixing-cases story. "Then why didn't Saul ask me about Oscar? Interview me for his book? I defended clients Oscar prosecuted and never saw any evidence of wrongdoing."

"But would Saul know about those particular cases?" Mom asked, not talking directly to my father, but rather addressing remarks somewhere over his shoulder. Tensions were high, folks. Repeat: tensions were high.

"In Saul's first book, *We, the Jury*, I defended one of the bank robbers he wrote about in that one. We dealt the case down, so my client didn't go to trial. Because of his testimony, his partner got the death penalty, and you can bet the eyes of the world were upon Oscar when he prosecuted a capital case. There was absolutely nothing irregular about it."

Dad got up and helped himself to another serving of stir-fry, offering to serve Max as well. Of course, he accepted.

"Not a lot of people knew this." My father returned to his seat. "In fact, maybe not even Saul, but Shearer, the guy who actually killed the security guard, confessed right before he was executed. He even sent a note to the guy's widow asking for her forgiveness. His confession didn't make the book because it was such a sad footnote to such a hard case, and it was Oscar's idea to keep the confession private out of respect for the widow."

"What about the other cases Saul wrote about? The black widow cases for instance," I asked, crunching on a snow pea. "According to *Lady Killers*, Oscar prosecuted one of the three women in that book, but he couldn't make a case against Robin."

"Under Saul's theory, Oscar could've just conjured up a case if he had wanted to," McGowan said. "Why let a little thing like lack of evidence stand in the way?"

Mom shook her head. "Trianos made it sound like Oscar only twisted little things. Cut corners here or there."

"Again, not the most credible of sources, Tony Trianos," Dad stated.

Mom bristled at his tone, "He's never been convicted of a crime, dear, and he had nothing to gain by telling us what he did."

"If he killed Oscar and Saul, he has everything to gain by throwing the investigation off track." Dad didn't back down.

"You don't think he killed them, and you know it." Mom refused to give up. "It isn't his style."

"Shouldn't we be starting from the end here?" I suggested. "We know Robin and Jack are the killers, why can't we just work backwards to prove it?"

"I've warned you about jumping to conclusions. We don't know anything for sure," McGowan spoke up. "Jack's sticking to his story that he was acting on an anonymous tip and entered the house only when he saw signs of a break-in. Also, there's nothing to tie Robin to anything. That girl's slick. Believe it."

"Please. She and Jack had the most to lose, or they wouldn't have tried to break in here," I argued. "Why make things harder than they have to be?"

"Who sent you the discs in the first place?" McGowan asked.

"My money is on Trianos," I announced.

Three sets of eyes turned to me in disbelief.

"He did seem interested in helping us, but of course, Mom was shamelessly flirting with him at the time. That's another story, though." I moved my ankles before they could be kicked under the table. "And he has a way of getting his hands on things. Maybe Angela or Tony had the discs all along. Whatever. But we know Jack and Robin were the most afraid of being incriminated by them."

"So much for that," Dad said. "Saul didn't have anything on the discs to incriminate Robin or Jack. Something we all could've learned sooner if you two hadn't hidden evidence."

"Alex, we know, okay?" Mom said. "We know."

"I'm not sure you do. You were careless, and things became dangerous - again."

"The thing you have to learn about men, dear." Mom spoke as if there weren't any in the room. "Is that when they do something dangerous, they're being brave. When we do the same thing, it's foolish."

"Dead is dead, that's my thinking." Dad glared at me as if I was the one who had spoken.

"No one is dead." Mom's tone reflected her exasperation. "Stop blowing this out of proportion. You just don't like my using my feminine wiles on anyone but you."

"Feminine wiles?" My father actually sputtered. "Is that what you were doing? Oh, forgive me, I thought you were chatting up gangsters with our daughter in tow. Hiding evidence. Obstructing justice."

Dad really is a good lawyer. If I had been on the jury, I'd have voted to convict. Daughter in tow, indeed. What had my mother been thinking?

"And you." He turned on me. "Are you out of your mind? Do you not have the sense God gave a peanut?"

My mouth opened and closed several times, but no sound issued forth.

"People, what's done is done," interrupted McGowan, which was lucky for Dad because I'm sure my comeback would have been blistering. "We need to focus on what we do know and hope it helps us fill in the blanks. Now, who wants to start?"

Of course, Mom did. "So we're thinking Robin was afraid Saul had evidence against her, and Jack was stealing the discs to protect her. But could Jack have a motive of his own? Jack told Chloe there was nothing in Oscar's Santa sack for him. Is that true?"

"No…" McGowan was obviously trying to recall. "He got something insignificant, but weird. An apple. A big ripe Red Delicious apple."

"What the hell is that supposed to mean?" I demanded, and for a moment, my parents were united in their disapproval. Whatever.

McGowan shrugged. "There were other food gifts. Chocolates. Mixed nuts. Maybe it was nothing."

"One big shiny apple, though, has to mean something." Mom looked my way.

"An apple a day keeps the doctor away?" I suggested. "Maybe some connection to Gavin Beaumont?"

"Who's a gynecologist," Dad pointed out. "What connection could he have to Jack?"

"Maybe it's the apple in the Garden. Adam and Eve." Mom said. "Jack should resist the temptation that Robin represents."

"I like that." I got up to clear the plates.

McGowan rolled his eyes. "Hokey."

"Well, you come up with something." Mom held his gaze.

"I did. It's an apple. Big deal. Tasty treat, nothing more. Alex?"

"I don't attach much significance to it either."

Mom and I looked at each other. Clueless, these guys.

"We haven't even talked about the hand." I shifted our focus. "Jack Lassiter is in law enforcement. He could get a hand if he wanted to."

"Bullshit," McGowan declared. "You can't just sign one out of the evidence room. That hand's got everyone stumped, so to speak."

"It's gotta mean something."

McGowan's look said he didn't appreciate my stating the obvious, as he pushed away from the table. "So that's all you ladies got? 'Cause we don't want any more surprises. No more discs? No more secrets?"

We shook our heads, both wishing he hadn't mentioned the discs again.

McGowan recognized our crushed expressions and took pity. "You've done some good work." He tossed us a bone. "You got a lot closer to Trianos than we ever could."

"Feminine wiles," Dad reminded him.

"Pretty powerful stuff," McGowan replied.

"Tell me about it." Dad's voice was just a tiny bit softer.

I knew he wouldn't be able to stay mad at Mom for long, and I suspected he, too, was secretly impressed by our resourcefulness. Maybe not by our methods, but by our results. Jack Lassiter had broken into our house, and even if we didn't know how or why he had killed Oscar and Saul, we had helped catch him.

After a few more minutes of fruitless speculation and another warning from McGowan to mind our own business from now on, Dad said he had to get to the office, and the two men stood to go.

When my father touched my arm, I yelped, "Help! Police!"

McGowan kept walking.

"We're not through talking about this," Dad said.

"I know."

My mother remained quiet.

McGowan thanked Mom for lunch.

"We'll let you know if we learn anything else," I couldn't resist saying. "While we're minding our own business, I mean."

McGowan gave me an oddly speculative look, shook Dad's hand and started down the front steps. Weird.

Dad turned to me. "Where's your car?"

When I boasted that I had ridden my bike over, my parents exchanged amused glances before they remembered they were still annoyed with one another.

McGowan turned, not in on the joke. "Be careful on that thing. One of our detectives is laid up for the next three months with a broken back. Out riding with her bike club a couple of days ago and bam! Hit and run."

"How awful," Mom said, the born worrier.

I knew from her look that my street riding days were numbered. Thank God.

"Anyone I know?" Dad asked.

"Margulies. Margaret-Anne. Little blond thing with braces."

"Young girl?"

"Forties, I'd say. The office is sending flowers. Any suggestions, Amanda?"

Mom suggested that Margie at Flower Fantasy would do up a nice arrangement and send it over. McGowan thanked her again and headed to his car.

Dad hung back. "Love you," he said. Grudgingly. "Both of you."

Mom and I smiled at him gratefully. And guiltily.

But when he left, we indulged in a slightly exuberant high-five.

"Your dad's right," Mom said a few minutes later, as we finished cleaning up the kitchen. "It's not enough that we think Jack is guilty. We have to prove it, and we start by finding out who sent us those discs."

"We should ask Angela. If Jack didn't take them when he killed Saul, then she must've. You've got to make Trianos tell you where she is."

"How am I supposed to do that?"

"He's probably still at the restaurant. Call him. You're the one he has a crush on."

Mom shot me a withering look, which might've stung had she not been blushing like a schoolgirl.

"Marie?" she asked, when the phone was answered at Tony's restaurant. "This is Amanda Carstairs. I had lunch with Mr. Trianos on Saturday…the Greek salad. It was wonderful…Yes, he mentioned it was a family recipe…Anyway, I need to talk to Angela Jannings. Mr. Trianos said she was staying in one of his buildings, and I wondered if you could ask him real quick which building…Yes, I'll hold…Oh, Mr. Trianos, I didn't mean to bother you during your lunch…Ok, Tony, then." She turned away from me, so I couldn't see how pink her cheeks had turned.

Gag.

"Yes, it was delicious…Next time, I promise, but right now it's imperative that I get in touch with Angela Jannings…No, I wasn't hurt at all, just a little frightened…No, no. No need for that. We'll just let the justice system deal with him…I'll keep that in mind. Now about Angela?"

Mom listened for a few moments more, making a note on the scratch pad near the phone. With a couple more giggles, some more blushing and a sharp poke in the arm from me, she said her good-byes and hung up. "Piece of cake."

CHAPTER 35

We loaded my bike into Mom's Caddy and headed off to find
Angela, making only two detours on the way. The first was a
stop at the coffee shop because I was having a Chai latte craving
and refused to do any investigating until I got my fix. Mom
knew it was useless to argue and a mocha cappuccino went a
long way toward soothing her irritation.

Our second stop was at Robin's high-rise apartment. Mom
wanted to hear her take on Jack's "alleged" break-in before the
couple could get their stories straight. We rang her condo from
the lobby. After a moment's hesitation, she buzzed us up.

Years ago Mom had done the remodel of a unit in this
building and knew them to be spectacular. The view was
stunning, the floor plans spacious and airy. Robin had exquisite
taste (or, at least, her decorator had), having furnished her unit to
look like a Bauhaus dream - all cantilevered this and tubular
steel that, lots of leather and a couple of Mies Pavilion chairs I
coveted. Mom thought this look was cold and sterile, but I loved
it.

Reading my mind, my mother whispered, "Alas, darling, for
this decorating scheme, slobs need not apply."

"I should have known you two would show up sooner or
later." Robin led us into a living room done in blinding white.
Robin herself was as simply and elegantly dressed as her
apartment - white shift, black slides, casual chic costing a
fortune. Her ponytail was high and sleek - a silky, swinging cat
o' nine tails.

Mom perched on the edge of an Eames lounge chair while I
slid into a Ludwig Mies van der Rohe. Slid and kept sliding.
Those things really aren't practical.

Our hostess stood by the terrace windows, admiring the view
she had paid seven figures for. Looking around, I saw no signs of
Christmas.

"Since you were expecting us, we won't have to mince words," Mom said. "Why did you send Jack over to my house to secure the discs?"

"What makes you think I did?"

"Come off it," I said. "You overheard me at the gym, talking on the phone, and you sent Jack to get them."

"And you can prove this, how?"

Smooth. Very smooth, this one.

"You think Jack's going to go down for this alone?" Mom asked. "Pretty soon he'll start talking, and when he does, the police will have all the proof they need."

"Proof of what, exactly?"

"Proof that you conspired to commit two murders and attempted two more." I said.

I don't know what I expected. A little fear might've been nice. A confession wouldn't have hurt. I'd have even settled for a wicked 'catch me if you can' cackle.

What I got was a stare so blank, so unfathomable, that I thought for a moment Robin had come unplugged. Then, seeming to reboot, she moved restlessly toward the kitchen, visible beyond a waist-high bar lined with sleek stools. The kitchen was stainless steel everything, as welcoming as an OR.

Leaning against the bar, she traced an abstract design on the metal surface, quiet for a moment before meeting my eyes. "Wrong."

"Which part?" I asked.

"The murder parts, for sure. The attempted murders, I couldn't say. I don't believe Jack meant you any harm."

"He was going to kill us!" Mom insisted. "And my dog."

"Please. Jack loves animals. You're overreacting."

"You can't be serious." Mom was incredulous.

"One thing at a time," I said. "You sent Jack over to get the discs. True or false?"

"I'm not up for games today, ladies. I didn't kill Saul or Oscar. I told you that. I've been quite candid with you, and frankly, it's insulting that you would doubt my honesty."

"Did you send Jack over for the discs or not?" I demanded.

"You make it sound like Jack is a puppet that can't think for himself."

I wouldn't let it go. "Did you or didn't you? Impress us again with your honesty."

"Let me tell you this..."

"No. Tell me what I asked."

"You'll find this more interesting, trust me. I could've gotten the discs from Saul any time. He loved me. He didn't publish what he knew about me. What I had told him quite freely. We were like that with each other - no secrets, no deceptions. Because I knew he loved me, I didn't worry, but I couldn't stop him from writing it all down. It's what he did, who he was. When he died, and the discs were missing, that's when I started worrying. Jack didn't want me to worry, that's all."

Now we were getting somewhere.

"How long have you and Jack been involved?" Mom asked.

"We met at one of Oscar's Christmas parties last year, and we hit it off."

"And Saul didn't know?"

"He didn't care. To Saul, everyone was a potential source."

"So you sent Jack over to get the discs?" I said again.

"Jack didn't want me to worry," was all she would say.

"The police think Jack is the murderer," Mom offered, after a moment of uncomfortable silence. "They only question how you were involved."

"I'm not concerned. Jack wouldn't want me to worry."

I couldn't believe her. "But aren't you worried about Jack? He's in a lot of trouble."

"Jack can take care of himself. He's very resourceful when he has to be."

We pushed, but she wouldn't elaborate. "Oscar was going to give Jack an apple at the Christmas party. From his Santa's sack. What was that about?"

"I was never interested in Oscar's little games. He thought he could pin my husband's deaths on me. He was wrong."

"The way we heard it, if Oscar really wanted to pin a murder on you, he would. Evidence or not." I held her gaze.

"That was my experience."

Talk about candid. The woman was nothing if not forthright. The cops who hadn't caught her for her husbands' murders hadn't been asking the right questions.

"So you're saying Oscar tried to frame you?" Mom doesn't rely on nuance.

"He tried."

"But he couldn't. Why not?"

She wasn't saying, but for the first time I saw how a woman like her might benefit from having a friend in the DA's office. Was this a motive Jack had all on his own? Had he destroyed some evidence, real or created, against Robin?

We didn't get any more out of her.

"I meant what I said about the movies," she said to me as she showed us out. "Call me sometime."

"Um…okay," I agreed.

"Over my dead body," Mom said when we were on the elevator.

In the car, we tried to make sense of what we had learned.

"It's plausible." Mom waited for a green Audi to pass before she pulled out of the parking spot. "She only worried about the discs when they fell into the wrong hands. Maybe Jack did, too, or maybe he was afraid of them all along."

"If it's true that she didn't take them in the first place. To help him, if not herself."

"Does she ever help anyone besides herself?"

Neither one of us had an answer for that one, but were eager to find out what Angela had to say on the subject of the discs.

"What are the chances Robin will come forward to help Jack?" I asked as we made our way downtown.

"Slim to none."

As we headed further downtown, my cell phone rang. I looked at the screen and winced. Beaumont. I couldn't imagine why Bunny would be calling me, but I did wonder what she would say.

Gavin was on the line, though.

"Chloe, glad I caught you."

"Mr. Beaumont. Hi. This is a surprise," I said for Mom's benefit.

Her look registered a mixture of bewilderment and distaste.

"I wanted to see how you and your mother were. We heard about the break-in. I hope you weren't hurt."

"No, no. We're a little shaken up, but basically ok."

There was a pause as I waited for him to get to the real point of his call. Concern for my welfare just didn't ring true.

"I also heard, that is Bunny and I heard, that you had Saul's discs. Is that what Lassiter was after?"

Now this was interesting. "The discs? Yes, Jack apparently broke in to retrieve them."

"So the police have them now?"

"What's all this about, Mr. Beaumont?" I hedged. "What's your interest?"

"No interest. Just curious."

"I am, too. Why don't you level with me? The discs contained some interesting stuff."

"So you opened the files?" He sounded tired, resigned.

"I did."

"Then, you understand my interest."

"Why don't you explain it to me."

"A thing like this…It wouldn't do for it to get out…reputations could be compromised."

"Mmm-hmm." Enough with the euphemisms. I needed nouns. Verbs. Details.

"But the police have the discs now."

"They do."

He clicked off without another word.

What in the world?

CHAPTER 36

Adaptive reuse are the big buzz words in downtown Birmingham right now. Angela's hideout was ex-retail space that was now being turned into lofts, a few blocks from Tony's restaurant in one direction and from my loft in another.

We found a parking place up front, which was lucky. This area of town isn't one you spend a lot of time walking around in. Not that my block is much better, but I have underground parking - an "it's a nice place to live, but I wouldn't want to visit" set-up that are common to this area of town.

Judging from Angela's lack of surprise or enthusiasm, Tony had told her we were coming.

"This needs to be quick, I'm on a deadline," she said.

The loft was in early construction phase, which is to say stripped to the studs in some places, crowded with sawhorses, tools and painting equipment in others. In a space the size of a three-car garage, Angela was occupying a powder-room sized section - enough room for a card table with a laptop, another table covered with papers, a printer on the floor, an air mattress and a hot plate. More papers were tacked to a bulletin board leaning against one wall. A construction-sized garbage bag overflowed with crumpled rejects and take-out boxes. There was only one chair, and she didn't offer it.

Charming.

"Mind if I smoke?" Angela lit up without waiting for a reply, cranked open a window and blew the smoke from the first lusty drag out over the street. Appearing to be an oft-repeated ritual, her movements provided a chance to study her.

Not holding up well, our little Angela. Her red hair was wild and frizzy, as if nervous hands had been raking through it. Her shirt was on inside out, her bare feet looked dirty. A Tic-Tac would have improved her situation.

"Heard y'all had a little excitement at your place the other night." She exhaled another lungful of smoke.

I smiled. "Nothing we couldn't handle."

"And the discs?"

"With the police," Mom said.

Angela stared out the window and shook her head. "Not good."

"What was on those discs," Mom prodded.

Angela shrugged. "I wasn't sure."

"Why not?" I asked. "You made it sound like ninety percent of what Saul wrote was based on your work. Your research."

"Probably closer to seventy percent, but yeah, a lot of it was mine. The good stuff anyway. How'd you get them in the first place?"

"They were sent to us. Not by you?" My eyes wandered over the bulletin board, where I noted clippings of the murders and pictures of the suspects tacked in haphazard groupings.

I was surprised to see my mother's face staring back at me, an old magazine shot that had accompanied a story about the Christmas houses. The word 'Access' was scrawled across her face.

Behind Robin's picture, there were articles about her husbands' deaths. A picture of Jack hung much too close, held in place by a cheap plastic pushpin shaped like a red apple.

What were we missing?

Horns had been drawn on Bunny's picture with savage slashes, while Nancy's head had been stuck on the body of a scantily clad woman. Gavin looked off the board, and Meagan, Oscar's daughter, stared into the camera as if daring onlookers to challenge her presence there. There was also a crude sketch of a human hand with a dead rat in it.

Angela caught our interest. "You like? It helps me to free associate. Though I must admit, I didn't see the Jack thing coming. Who knew he had it in him?"

"Angela," Mom said, her voice gentle. "We need to know what's going on. Given your research skills and journalistic instincts, I'm sure you know more than anyone about these murders."

"You've got that right. I'm sure Robin did it - once a killer, always a killer. I think Jack's in up to his ass, but how did they pull it off?" She took a hard drag on her cigarette and whooshed more smoke out the window. "At the party, I watched Robin practically the whole time. I thought she was up to something with Jack and couldn't believe Saul was so blind. He considered himself shrewd, smarter than the rest of us, but his girlfriend was screwing around under his nose and he didn't have a clue."

I didn't correct her. Drag, exhale.

"And what was up with her and Trianos?" Angela asked. "Snaky, that girl, but she didn't spike any drinks or tamper with any food. That much I know."

"Maybe Jack did." I suggested.

Angela sucked her cigarette down to the filter and used its last blinking ember to light another one. My lungs ached just watching her.

"I don't know. On my suspect list, he wasn't even in the top three. Y'all?"

"Not even in the top five," I admitted. "We were thinking maybe Robin, maybe Nancy. Maybe even you."

Angela's laughter turned into a coughing fit. "It's not like I didn't think about it, but bottom line? I needed my job, and the perks that came with it."

"Such as?" Mom asked.

"Access. Credibility..."

"Proximity?" I said. "To Saul, I mean."

Angela attempted another laugh, but we saw the tears before she blinked them back. "Okay, I admit it. He was a mentor to me, and I read more into it than there was. Now who's not as shrewd as they thought they were?"

We didn't push, and as it turned out, we didn't have to.

"When I heard Saul left Robin half his estate..." She shook her head and drew on her cigarette. "What a joke. What a lousy joke."

"Tell us what you know, Angela," I prompted. "There's got to be more to it."

"I know Meagan isn't heartbroken about her dad. Saul chased away her last boyfriend. He was bisexual, but seemed to truly care about Meagan. Saul threatened to tell his parents. After that, Meagan only came home holidays."

"What about Jack and the apple?" Mom pointed to the apple pushpin on the bulletin board.

"I think Oscar knew about or at least suspected, Jack's affair with Robin. The apple was a warning - an Adam and Eve thing."

Mom shot me a look, which I ignored as I kept the ball rolling. "And what about Nancy?"

"Saul knew about Nancy's affairs, and he told Oscar. Not in so many words, but with broad enough hints that Oscar would've been a fool not to have picked up on them."

Now that was news.

"How did Oscar take it?" I asked.

Angela shrugged and tossed another cigarette butt out the window. "Best I could tell, he got off on it."

"What!" Mom was shocked.

"Nice, huh. He let Saul have his fun, blackmailing Nancy with the affair, while meanwhile Oscar was kind of encouraging her. Did he really need that work done on his pool house, and how many times a year do gutters need to be cleaned? Nasty."

"What about Bunny and Gavin?"

She shook her head. "Something's up there. Saul could smell it a mile away, but if he ever found out what, he didn't tell me."

"Did he have any suspicions?" Mom asked.

"Not really. Maybe they're swingers. Maybe she's really a man, or he's really a woman. I don't know what it is, but I can't stand either one of them."

"What else?" I pressed.

"I've told y'all plenty. You want the rest? Buy the book."

"Come on," I pleaded. "Just one really juicy thing."

Angela considered my request, and I could tell she was tempted. "What the hell. But you're going to die when you hear this."

That got our attention for sure.

She smiled. "The hand - I know something about it."

We were practically salivating now for the scoop.

"Saul was in on it."

"No freaking way!"

"You're joking," Mom said.

"No ma'am. Some of those crooks Trianos set Saul up to interview? Seems some guy cheated them in some gambling thing, pocketed some money he wasn't supposed to and got himself killed."

We nodded. That much we knew.

"Anyway, the guys invited Saul to watch them interrogate the guy. Basically, they were calling his bluff, seeing if he could hang with the big boys."

"But he didn't have the stomach for it," Mom guessed.

"Not even close. Things started to get out of hand – no pun intended – and Saul split. When he found the hand on his back doorstep, he thought Trianos's friends had sent it as a warning to keep his mouth shut, but he couldn't resist using it to his advantage."

"And you were in on his scheme?"

"Hell, no. I never would of gone along with something like that. That was what I was trying to tell you about integrity. I have it. Saul didn't."

"But you figured it out?" Mom asked.

"Almost from the beginning. The pinkie ring? The rat? Saul added those. It's the same kind of melodramatic crap I always had to ghostwrite out of his books. He always overplayed scenes."

"So it was all a publicity stunt?" I still couldn't get my head around the situation.

"Basically. Saul figured Stumpy couldn't tell the truth about what happened, even if the police did find him, so he cooked up his little PR scheme." She cranked the window closed. "But the joke was on him, wasn't it? Because Trianos told me his boys didn't leave the hand for Saul. Someone else did."

None of it made any sense.

"I gotta get back to writing," she said. "Truly, I don't have everything figured out, but it's only a matter of time. The police aren't much competition, and persistent as y'all are, you two don't stand a chance - no offense."

CHAPTER 37

No offense, indeed. I was still fuming over that little parting shot three days later. Mostly because, at that point, Angela's words seemed truer than ever.

We had called McGowan right after talking to her to tell him what we'd learned about the hand.

His first reaction had been underwhelming. "Sounds an awful lot like y'all are still investigating."

Even after I had assured him we weren't, that we had happened upon the information in a casual conversation with Angela, he hadn't been impressed. "We still don't know how the hand wound up on Saul's doorstep, and Trianos's claim of innocence doesn't carry much weight."

The part of our story that did interest McGowan? The fact that Angela had known something all along about the hand and had kept the information from him. I ended our phone call somewhat abruptly.

The case stalled completely on Thursday, and there was the little matter of Christmas to attend to. We Carstairs celebrate our Christmas on the twenty-fourth because Lily spends the twenty-fifth with her father. You wouldn't think being shorted a single shopping day would make that much difference, but it does. It really does.

I spent Thursday fighting crowds at Brookwood Mall, looking for those inevitable last minute gifts. No matter how carefully I plan, no matter how early I shop, I always find myself at the mall the week before Christmas. True, I didn't have the panicked, frazzled, lost look I usually have this time of year, but that was little consolation as I drove from parking deck to parking deck in search of a space.

After several hours I returned home with three books, some scented soaps, a blouse, a pair of slippers and the solemn conviction that I wouldn't set foot in another mall until February. That, of course, was before Bridget called and asked if my parents and I wanted to go with her and Lily to see Santa. At Brookwood Mall. What auntie in her right mind would pass that up? So it was more parking deck roulette, more crowds, more last-minute gifts - all completely worthwhile.

On Friday, Lily, Mom and I baked up a storm - Latte Crisps, Snickerdoodles, Gingerbread men and Red Velvet mini cupcakes. These joined the Espresso Truffles and Orange Sablé Cookies Mom had already made in little cookie boxes Lily gold stamped before we delivered them to neighbors, Lily's teachers and other friends.

All the while, like a low-level hum in my head, I worried obsessively about the case and my upcoming date with Jacob.

Talk about stress. Try getting ready for a date with your boyfriend of two years, when negotiations are at their most delicate stage and two unsolved murders hang over your head. I had to give Jacob some clue as to what he was missing without looking like I was trying too hard. My outfit had to project a sense of confidence with a hint of vulnerability.

Since technically we were broken up, my clothes should say "Look, but don't touch." My makeup must appear fresh and dewy, a testament to my youth and ability to bear many children. A sexy tumble of curls for my hairdo was required, hinting at how I'd look waking up next to him, without in any way recalling the fright wig my mop usually resembled in the morning.

Oh, and my mascara had to stay in place. Firmly.

With an uncharacteristic lack of procrastination, I had completed the prep work for our date twenty-four hours early. The outfit had been chosen (swingy skirt, clingy halter, black boots, leather jacket), and there was a back-up outfit selected (pink-and-brown wool sheath, brown boots, pink car coat) in case outfit number one fell through. I had stopped all salt, soda and simple carbs the day before, so I retained no water. My sunless tan was streak-free, and a quick visit to Angelo, my hairdresser, had left my curls bouncy and manageable.

Jacob didn't stand a chance.

Consequently, I was ready for my seven p.m. date by four-thirty. Not good.

Running early is as bad as running late because you second-guess yourself. Do these boots make my calves look chunky? Chunky calves, the kind rarely glimpsed outside a roller derby, are my secret shame. What if I tried to fix that one errant curl? Is that a zit trying to form? You know the kind of thing.

I also second-guessed my gift to Jacob, now neatly wrapped (ok, gift bagged) and ready by the door. I'd settled on a half-zip sweater and a pair of cashmere-lined leather gloves, striking the right balance between affectionate (on the off chance that he gave me a piece of small, but tasteful jewelry) and impersonal (in case I came home with a stuffed animal and a Christmas ornament).

These are the things that can be fraught with drama and disappointment.

For instance, last Christmas, my friend Heather bought her boyfriend some achingly expensive Bose speakers. He got her a velour tracksuit - size-small top, size-large bottoms - with the store's security sensor tag still attached. They're currently seeing other people.

So. Mustn't dwell.

I could have balanced my checkbook. I had probably trained more clients at the gym in the last two days than I had in all of October. Everybody's desire to look fabulous at holiday parties meant I was rolling in cash. But who are we kidding? I never balance my checkbook.

I could have wrapped presents. I still had three to go, Mom and Bridget's broaches and a computer game for Lily. But, I decided not to risk a paper cut.

Before I could do anything, though, someone called me. McGowan.

"Thought you might want to know, Jack's talking a lot more and I don't much like what he's saying."

"Why not?"

"Because it doesn't bring me any nearer to closing the case."

"You had to know he'd deny everything," I was only half-listening, too busy looking at myself in any reflective surface I could find.

"But I didn't know his denials would make so much sense. Jack's sticking to his story that when he got to your house, the back door latch was already broken. He wasn't there to rob or hurt you, but was looking into an anonymous tip."

"Sure. Uh-huh. Very plausible."

"And in an instant of rare candor, he said he wouldn't have killed Saul or Oscar - period. But if he had, he would've made damn sure he had those discs beforehand. And if he had the discs, he never would have sent them to you."

I didn't know what to make of that.

"And it gets worse. Jack's making noises about charging you and Amanda."

"For what? If he's trying to say we assaulted him, he's right. He was threatening to kill us."

"Actually the charge is Hindering Prosecution, for not turning over evidence. It's a class C felony."

I smiled, picturing my tiny mother in an oversized bright orange prison jumpsuit. But when the picture changed to me in a similar outfit, the image wasn't nearly as amusing.

"It's obvious what Jack's thinking. Best defense is a good offense, right?" I checked my teeth for lipstick. Funny that I was so calm as our case fell apart.

"If so, he's got a point. I gotta tell you, Chloe, I'm going with my gut on this one. I'm not ruling anything out, but I don't think Jack's our guy."

I didn't argue the point further and got off the phone to think about the case some more. The case that I had once thought might be fun to investigate. The case that had resulted in my being poisoned, my parent's house being broken into and now the real possibility that, instead of clearing Angela, Mom and I could face criminal charges.

What was my gut telling me?

On our list of suspects, Jack hadn't even been in the top five. I tried to imagine him calmly slipping poison into Saul's drink or cruelly plunging an icicle into Oscar's back. He was more the pistols-at-dawn kind of guy. I could see him defending a woman's honor out of some misguided sense of nobility. But devious or violent? Not so much.

Frankly, I had to blame Mom for jumping the gun on this one. I had just gone along because she'd seemed so sure.

Now I was more at loose ends, with still a good hour left before my date. I picked up the TV remote and aimlessly started flipping through channels.

An infomercial for a Pilates video got me thinking about Nancy having a torrid affair with her personal trainer. What was her deal? Why men in the service sector? Pool boys, trainers, gardeners. Did she have control issues, or just like men who were good with their hands? And why was Oscar not only tolerant of her behavior, but secretly encouraging it? Pilates gift certificate, indeed.

I landed on a special about spiders. Which, of course, got me thinking about black widows, and in turn led me to Robin. On the one hand, a total bitch. Practically admitting to two murders and ruining the career of another man she supposedly loved. On the other hand, there was something likeable and unpretentious about her. As murderers go, a charming woman. But was she audacious enough to kill her boyfriend in front of a room full of people? Could she drop her ice princess act long enough to stab someone in the back?

I flipped some more and came to a claymation Christmas special that reminded me of Oscar-Santa passing out presents to the naughty and the nice. The explanation we came up with for Jack's juicy red apple made sense, but what about Angela's handcuffs? Or Bunny's Pilates gift certificate? Was there any special significance to Gavin Beaumont's antique gynecological equipment beyond just the surface cringe factor?

And speaking of odd, what about Bunny's outfit that day I had gone to her house? What a flake. But was she up to something that Saul had found out about? And besides being a crime of fashion, was that a secret she would kill to protect?

None of which even addressed the whole issue of Oscar fixing cases and Saul writing a tell-all book about his friends' dirty deeds. The whole thing was maddening, and stressing over it was taking the bounce from my curls.

I threw the remote on the sofa and looked through my DVD collection for a movie, something I could watch for fifteen minutes to take my mind off both the murders and my love life. Something festive and familiar.

It's a Wonderful Life fit the bill. I could start anywhere, get immediately absorbed and then turn the familiar plot off at any point without regret.

Apparently that's what'd I'd done last year, because when I hit play, the movie started in the middle, with the folks of Bedford Falls demanding their money. The scene reminded me of Cassie saying her dad was the president of an S&L, but in a good way, no scandals.

The movie was as relaxing as I had hoped, and I watched for a few more minutes before something trickled into my subconscious.

What was it? Bank runs? Bedford Falls?

Yeah, the name felt familiar. Hadn't Cassie said she was from New Bedford or something like that? I'd have to tell her that her dad's life was a lot like the movie.

But then the trickle became a gush as I remembered other things Cassie had told us about her dad. That everyone in town loved him. That he had wanted to be an architect. That he was deaf in one ear. A litany of facts from the Christmas classic.

What the hell?

On our list of suspects Cassie wasn't even in the top one hundred. But if you've got someone with access to two crime scenes, who has completely fabricated her background, that's got to mean something, right?

Damn right!

But what?

I picked up the phone and dialed Margie Ryan's cell. If anyone knew Cassie, it would be her.

"Margorie Ryan speaking."

"Margie, it's Chloe Carstairs."

"Hey sweetie, whatcha need? I'm at the shop, so if your Mom's wanting more poinsettias, now's the time to ask."

I laughed. "No, we're good. If I don't see another poinsettia for twelve months I'll be ecstatic. I was actually calling…"

"Speak up dear, my cell phone's not the greatest."

No, you're not wearing your hearing aids, I thought. But out loud, emphasis on the word loud, I said, "I was calling to ask you something about Cassie."

"Cassie's on a delivery. Two days before Christmas and still hard at work. Such a blessing to have an employee like that, especially this time of year."

"I didn't want to speak to her." I was relieved the coast was clear. "I wanted to ask you something about her father."

"I don't know anything about her people, dear."

That old Southern expression. Who are your people, Cassie, I wondered.

"How did she come to work for you?" I asked.

"Just filled out an application one day. Was great with flowers."

"The application. Do you still have it?"

"Of course. Chloe, what's going on?"

"I need some information about her contacts. Next of kin, that kind of thing."

"Dear, I don't think we have a good connection, maybe tomorrow…"

"No!" I shouted. "I'll speak up. I need you to tell me about Cassie's contacts, her references."

"I don't feel comfortable giving out that kind of information," Margie shouted back.

I was clutching the phone in frustration. "Margie, you don't need to shout. I can hear you, but I need those numbers. Please. I wouldn't ask if it weren't important. Life or death."

She coughed up the info. I almost wept with relief.

The third number I tried was one of Cassie's references, a Ashley Brewer, working the evening shift at a veterinarian's office in Metairie, Louisiana.

"Her father? Why would you bring all that back up? The holidays are hard enough for her without you talking about him," Ashley chided.

"It's just that I'm worried about Cassie. I think she may be having a nervous breakdown, and I don't know how to help her without getting the whole story."

"How long have you worked with her?"

"Long enough to really care about what happens to her." I wasn't lying about that part. "Just tell me what about her Dad."

"He was convicted of armed robbery over there in your neck of the woods. Felony murder, too. He got the death penalty. Sandy's never recovered. How could she from a thing like that?"

"Sandy?"

"Short for Cassandra. Her dad's nickname for her. I knew the family, of course. Her mother died when she was a baby, and after that thing with her Dad, she lived here with relatives. Not much of a life for a girl, being raised by a couple that never had much use for her, I'm afraid."

"Why did she come back to Birmingham?"

"I'm not sure. Just up and turned in her notice one day. Said it was time to go home. I tried to talk her out of it, but when Sandy sets her mind on something, that's it."

I sat in bewildered silence.

After a moment, Ashley added thoughtfully, "She told me once her last happy memory was of Christmases spent with her dad. They never had much money. He lived a hard life and ran with a bad crowd, always in one scrape or another, God love him. Still, he was devoted to his daughter and made Christmas special for her - just the two of them, decorating the tree, watching old movies…"

Like *It's a Wonderful Life.*

"That's what she was looking for," Ashley said, her tone sad. "That happiness again, even if it meant going back where she had also been the saddest."

I thought Cassie had a more specific and far less innocent agenda, but I didn't mention it. Instead, I thanked my informant and clicked off, still holding the cordless in one hand.

A father who got the death penalty. A daughter with access to the homes of the attorney who prosecuted him and the jury foreman who recounted the story in his first true crime book, *We, the Jury.*

Cassie.

It had to be.

CHAPTER 38

I clicked on the phone then clicked it off. The time was just a little before six. I knew I'd be cutting it close, but my parents' house was on the way to the restaurant where Jacob and I were having dinner. Why not go over there and see what Mom thought of what I had learned.

I grabbed my purse and jacket.

In the car, I called Jacob and told him not to pick me up. Instead we arranged to meet at seven-thirty at our favorite cozy café within walking distance of my parent's house. Overstuffed cushions, wine in jelly jars, lighting that made everyone look like they were about fifteen. Love that place.

He agreed and sounded as excited about the evening as I was.

I screeched into my parent's driveway, burst into the house and demanded Mom come up to her office. Dramatic as hell, but I couldn't keep the information to myself a second longer. The stunned expression on Mom's face told me I had been right to feel so anxious.

"Our Cassie?" Mom responded, when I told her what I had learned from Ashley in Metairie.

I nodded, feeling heartsick. She was our Cassie, wasn't she? We didn't hang out or double date, but I liked her, felt genuine affection for her.

Mom gaped at me. "So everything Cassie told us about her father was a lie?"

"Exactly. Her real father was the subject of Saul's first book *We, the Jury*."

"But she wasn't even at Saul's party."

We were stumped on that one. Knowing who the killer was hadn't filled any blanks. There was still the problem of all those locked doors, all that poison-free food and drink.

"Let's look at the DVD Megan Taylor gave us again," Mom suggested. "Maybe we didn't see Cassie at the party because we weren't looking for her."

She tried to pop the DVD into her laptop, but there was already a CD in the slot.

"The *Twelve Days of Christmas* CD Saul gave me." She tossed the disc on the desk and slid in the DVD. "I had expected the traditional rendition I prefer. Instead, it was Robin's obscure ten ladies dancing, nine pipers piping, eight maids-a-milkin'."

"What did Saul mean he liked this version better? Better than what?"

She shrugged. Tapping a few keys on the laptop, she got the DVD going. "Maybe the band played the traditional version, although I had specifically asked them to stick to the way Robin liked it."

She began zipping backward through the DVD, which was still cued up on the death scene. Midway through the party, she let the scene run, turning up her computer speakers.

Over the crowd noise, I could make out the band playing in the basement. Saul, returning from his phone call, asked Robin to dance. Straining to block out conversations in the foreground, I listened to the background music. Unable to make out all the words, I heard snippets of the crowd singing along - twelve drummers drumming, eleven lords-a-leaping, ten ladies dancing, just as Robin had requested.

"Better than what?" I asked again.

Mom backed up the DVD to where Angela prepared Saul's drink. "Again, if I had tampered with Saul's food or drink, this is when I would've done it. No one did, though, because the police checked the Scotch glass, the decanter and the cigar. Nothing."

We stared at the scene, looking for a glimpse of Cassie's blond hair or her petite frame.

The videographer swung to the left to include some party guests, but at least part of the doorway was still visible. No one but Angela went in or out. He swung back to the right, and I got another full-frame shot of the study. Angela replaced the decanter while ten pipers looked on.

What in the world?

Mom saw it, too, freezing the shot of Angela replacing the decanter. But she wasn't alone. The pipers were with her.

I counted again, half out of my chair. Instead of a back row of five and a front row of four, there were now two rows of five. Ten pipers, where before there had been only nine.

"You see it?"

"I see it!"

Adrenaline surging, I hit keys on the computer, going back to the beginning of the DVD - Saul, welcoming guests with the study doors wide open. Nine pipers. Back to the middle, Angela pouring a drink. Ten pipers.

Had someone brought a piper in from the garage where the two extras had been stored? When? How? It occurred to me that the pipers where life-sized - smock, tights, boots, black caps. Someone could easily have borrowed the outfit and slipped into the study.

Everything fell into place with an almost audible click. I closed my eyes and pictured Cassie putting her head on the piper's shoulder that day we were in the study - exactly the same height. Same blond hair, the length of Cassie's easily tucking into a black cap. Plenty of time to slip into the garage for a smock, which she would return after she had slipped in the poison.

I saw the scene clearly. Margie checking her work before the party, and Cassie nervously putting an extra pin here, a strip of floral tape there. Had she unlocked the study's exterior French doors, put floral tape on the tongue of the lock, and pulled the door shut so that we were none the wiser? I suspected she had.

Then during the party, when she was sure the study's interior French doors were locked, she had slipped in dressed like a piper and waited until the drink had been poured. She had only to lean forward, pour some digitalis into the Saul's glass and return to the shadows. This had been the riskiest part, but she had probably counted on our host to be tipsy, his attention focused on the party and his phone call.

When Saul left, she had simply replaced his glass with a clean one laced with Scotch she had brought with her. She had stolen the discs (the desk remaining unlocked because the study door was), slipped out the exterior French doors, taking her strip of tape with her, replaced the smock and gone home.

Saul hadn't looked closely, but he had noticed there were ten pipers. He had preferred Robin's nine. That's probably why he had frowned as he left the study.

"What did you do with those books?" I asked.

Mom retrieved *We, the Jury* from her bookshelf, and we poured over the pictures in the middle.

"Here she is," Mom pointed to the grainy picture of a five-year-old Cassie or Sandy as the picture identified her, crying in her grandmother's arms as her dad was led off to jail.

"Look who else was on the case, Judge Stone." I flipped to another page, one that showed the Judge in his chambers. "Out of shape even back then. You want to say, lay off the cheesecake, Bernie. Get some exercise. That pacemaker thing isn't going to work for you."

"Was it really less than a month ago that he passed away?" Mom asked, as I continued to flip pages. "I'm ashamed to admit that, with all that's happened, I've completely forgotten to check on Ellie. She sent me a card thanking us for…"

I looked up, to see why she had gone so quiet.

"You don't think?" she asked.

"Think what?"

"Surely not."

"Not, what?" I demanded. Could the woman milk a moment or what?

Mom's eyes were huge. "I sent the judge a funeral arrangement. Cassie delivered it. Remember what she said? That she didn't do poinsettias because he had gotten so many while he was in the hospital. She was there."

I stared at my mother, unable to take in much more.

"We need to find your father. This is unbelievable."

Mom dialed frantically while I flipped through the book, looking for more pictures, but all she reached was Dad's voice mail.

She turned back to me. "Should I leave a message?

I flipped another page, and this time I was the one who received a shock. "Mom, it's worse than we thought." She clicked off the phone. "It can't be."

I held the book out to her, my finger on another picture. "What was the name of that officer McGowan was telling us about? The woman who was hit by a car?"

Mom looked down at the picture of the young cop who had testified against Cassie's father. Margaret-Anne Margulies.

I jumped to my feet and started pacing. "Okay, let's think about this. We have to tell McGowan, right?"

"If we're wrong, we'll look even more foolish to him than we already do."

Not an appealing option.

"What about Margaret-Anne? If she saw the car that hit her and it matches the description of whatever Cassie drives, that's one more tie back to her."

Mom nodded. "I like that. Plus she's a cop, she can tell us if we have enough information to convince Detective McGowan."

I looked up Margaret-Anne's phone number on the Internet. The address popped up too, not too far from where we sat.

"Think we should drop by in person?" I asked, completely absorbed by our find.

"I'm game if you are." Mom stood.

Minutes later, I was sure we would be stopped by a cop before we reached Margaret-Anne's house, the way Mom was lead-footing the Escalade, but no one gave her cheerful disregard of speed limits or stop signs a second glance.

"I have a feeling about this one." Mom gave Margaret-Anne's doorbell a nervously triumphant push. The house was a modest ranch-style home in an older neighborhood on Birmingham's south side.

"Me, too. There's no way we're off base this time. McGowan will be so happy that he'll throw a parade in our honor."

"I wouldn't go that far, but a bottle of Champagne wouldn't be out of line."

No one answered our ring. Mom tried the knob and found the door locked.

"Want me to check around back?" I asked, not wanting to know the answer.

"I think you had better."

Margaret-Anne kept a tidy back yard with a covered brick patio and a chiminea that had seen lots of use.

A back window was cracked.

I peered in and saw a tiny bathroom with honeycomb tile and a pedestal sink, as I pictured a few scenarios, none of them good, in which I slid open the window and crawled in. Each scenario ended with me in a great deal of pain or humiliation - my being shot by Margaret-Anne, mauled by an as-yet-unseen pit-bull, or having to be freed by the jaws of life for underestimating my hip size.

These thoughts didn't stop me from dragging over a patio chair and sliding the window up further, though. Might as well add B&E to the other felonies I was racking up, I decided. Having climbed through without incident, I opened the front door for Mom.

"What are you doing?" she demanded.

"Shouldn't we make sure Margaret-Anne is alright?"

"Well, yes, but…"

"Then come on."

Sometimes a house tells you it's empty. There's a heavy quality to the silence, a somber feel to the way dust motes swim in the light. Margaret-Anne might have been a reserved, quiet woman, but the red walls, brightly patterned furniture and festive Christmas decorations, in which feather boas and martini glasses played an important role, hinted otherwise. A woman who uses that much tinsel has to be lively and energetic. The house felt empty of her presence. Either she wasn't home or something was terribly wrong.

"Let's check the bedroom," Mom said. "She might be staying with friends or relatives during her recovery, but we need to be sure."

As we moved to the back of the house, I felt unnerved by the silence. Amanda marched on without a second thought. I followed so closely that when she opened the back bedroom door and stopped abruptly, I walked into her.

"Watch it," she hissed.

"Why did you stop?" I looked over her head.

She took a tentative step into the room, so I could see better, not that I wanted to.

Just as the silence of the house had made us uneasy, so did Margaret-Anne's unnatural stillness. A small woman with curly blond hair and dark brows, she didn't flinch, twitch or start as we made our unceremonious entrance. She lay serenely in bed, a burgundy-and-navy double wedding ring quilt tucked gently around her.

"Is she...?" I whispered.

"I can't tell." Mom whispered back

"Should we...?" I didn't know how to finish.

"One of us should check her pulse," Mom stated.

"I'm not doing it." I knew where this was headed.

"You have to. I'm not very good at these things."

"What things?"

"Touching people who might be..." She waved vaguely.

"If we think she's...," " I waved vaguely, "then there's no need to touch her."

"Except that if she's not...," vague wave, "and we call somebody on a false alarm, we'll look like fools. Again. And after the disc episode, we need to be surer of our facts before we call in the cavalry."

I saw her point, but didn't budge. "Bridget. We could call Brige. She does this stuff all the time."

"Chloe, there's no time. Now get over there and check. Right now."

She used her mom voice, and God help me, I actually took a step before catching myself. "Nice try."

"It was worth a shot," she said. "So what do you think? Dead?"

"Let me check," a voice from behind us suggested.

Mom and I clutched at each other, startled. One of us may have yelped. I'm pretty sure it was me.

Cassie moved past us, silent in her size-seven Reeboks and touched Margaret-Anne's throat.

"Not dead," she said matter-of-factly. "Resting peacefully for now."

It wasn't until she turned that we noticed the revolver.

CHAPTER 39

Mom eased me behind her. Not that she and her Ann Taylor sweater offered much protection as a human shield.

"What the hell?" I addressed Cassie in what I hoped was bewildered surprise. "What's with the gun?"

"Don't give me that innocent look," she replied. "I heard Margie talking to you on the phone when she thought I was gone. I knew you two would figure it out eventually, but hoped I'd be finished with everyone on my list before then."

I had to smile at that, truly touched by her confidence. Such a nice girl. As homicidal maniacs go.

"Where's Margie?" I was suddenly worried about our favorite florist.

"At the shop, of course, arranging flowers the same as always. You don't think I would hurt her?"

"Well, you have been on something of a killing spree these last couple of weeks." I stepped from behind Mom. These boots were made for kicking. All I needed was an opportunity.

Cassie nodded sheepishly, conceding the point.

"I'm surprised you would try anything against Margaret-Anne so soon after your last attack," Mom said.

"I'm not here for her, not yet at least. Guns can be so loud and messy. No, I'll be delivering some flowers here tonight. A nice officer called and said you recommended Flower Fantasy. I can't thank you enough."

I shot Mom a look she ignored. "At the time, I didn't know you were out to avenge the death of your father."

"My dad was innocent, Mrs. Carstairs. Framed by Oscar Browley with a little help from Margaret-Anne here and a few others who shall remain nameless."

"Judge Stone, for instance?" I asked.

"Ah, you girls have been busy. When I heard Chloe on the phone pumping Margie for information, I thought it best to follow you around for a while. When you headed over here, I knew you were putting it all together, not that it'll do you any good."

"Why do you say that? The police know everything we do," Mom said.

"Now why don't I believe you?" Cassie asked with a slight smile. "No matter. I'm almost finished with everyone on my Christmas list."

Margaret-Anne murmured in her sleep.

"We'd better go," Cassie said.

"Go?" Mom met her gaze. "We're not going anywhere with you."

"I'm not going to kill you. I give you my word. You're not part of this. I only want revenge on the people who killed my father. Till that's done, I'm taking you somewhere, tying you up and giving myself a head start."

"Tie us up here," Mom suggested. "Margaret-Anne probably has rope.

"Or handcuffs," I added. "Handcuffs would work."

Obviously, Mom and I were on the same page. Never get in the car with a homicidal maniac.

"Right. Leave you at a cop's house with all her cop buddies dropping in - not likely. Now come on."

We looked at her skeptically.

"Or I could kill you right here." Cassie leveled the revolver at me. "It would be messy, noisy and blow my plan all to hell, but if that's what you want."

"I'll drive," Mom capitulated.

Cassie pointed at me. "She can drive. Now move!"

We did.

In the Cadillac, Cassie placed Mom in the back and me behind the wheel, then settled in the passenger seat, facing sideways, so she could keep an eye on both of us.

"Does this thing have child safety locks?" Cassie asked. "I wouldn't want your mom jumping out."

"They're already on," I assured her.

"And let's store your purses in the way-back. That way there'll be no cell phones spoiling our fun."

She was good. I had to give her that. We did as we were told, and I backed The Tank out of the drive.

"This car's huge. My feet don't even touch the floor. How does a little thing like you maneuver?" Cassie asked Mom.

"I manage."

Cassie laughed. "I don't doubt that for a second."

"Where to?" I paused at a stop sign.

"I'm thinking Saul's house, how does that sound? Margie sent me out there to pick up some stuff yesterday, and what do you know? Meagan was headed back to Berkeley. Shame I forgot to give back her key."

With a thirty-minute drive ahead of us in holiday traffic, I decided to get answers to the rest of my questions. Plus, it would keep Cassie talking while I thought of a way out of this mess.

"Aren't you curious about how we figured it all out?" I asked as I got us onto Highway 31 heading south.

"Sure. We have time to kill, if you'll pardon the expression."

"It was really quite simple when you knew where to look. I was watching *It's a Wonderful Life* when I noticed striking similarities to your description of your father."

"My father was better than the main character. Everybody loved him. Everybody turned to him for help," Cassie stated defiantly, "but nobody helped him when he needed it."

I let that one pass.

"Then when we were watching a DVD of Saul's party," Mom threw in, "we caught your little trick with the pipers."

"Pretty smart, huh? I had planned to tamper with Saul's medications - maybe frame Robin, maybe not, but when I saw how many people hated Saul, I figured why not go for a two-for-one deal and get Oscar in on the action? Two deaths at two parties - same suspects at both? It'd be weeks before anyone sorted it all out, if they ever did. Meanwhile, I could take care of the rest of my Christmas list."

"So Judge Stone was a lucky break?" Mom asked. "His being in the hospital and your delivering flowers to him."

"I like to think you make your own luck in this world, but yes, his being in the hospital did make things easier. Last year, I saw an article about your Christmas houses, and knew that was the in I had been looking for. It was like a sign, you know?"

"You had planned this for a while." I stated.

"Practically my whole life. When I was five, it wasn't an obsession - more a childish whim - you hurt me, I'll hurt you back."

Still is, I thought. Only there was nothing childish about her methods.

"But then I got older, life got harder and I got madder. I realized how much had been taken from me. I didn't know what I could do about it, but I had to do something, right? Luckily, in tenth grade, Janie-Lee Jensen gave me an idea."

"Who's Janie-Lee Jensen?" I took the exit onto Highway 280.

"Girl I went to school with. Nasty little thing. Not one of the popular girls, nothing cliché like that. Just one of those spiteful, careless girls who dish out random cruelties, fascinated by their power to do so." Cassie glanced at my side of the dashboard. "Slow down. We don't want a ticket."

I hadn't meant to let the speedometer sneak above sixty, but her talk of mean girls had gotten to me. Had I been the Janie-Lee Jensen of Angela's life? Thoughtless? Vicious? I felt a slow burn of guilt remembering how my friends and I had laughed at her journal. In my recollections, my laughter had been the loudest and most cruel.

"One time," Cassie continued, "Janie-Lee pointed out that a girl's shirt was on inside out. It didn't have a pattern or anything, just a plain T-shirt, but Janie-Lee noticed and said it was because the girl and her brother had been having sex at the bus stop before school. Everyone laughed and laughed."

Mom and I remained quiet, probably both wondering where this was going.

"They laughed at me, too, but the joke's on them now, because what she did turned out to be a good thing."

"What did she do?" I asked.

"Put a copy of *We, the Jury* in my locker, wrapped up like a real pretty Christmas present you would be excited to get, especially if Christmas was a hard time around your house. This after she had read selected parts to her friends. And, yeah, it was hateful, but it put a name to my pain - a bunch of names. I made my Christmas list that year, and I've kept it with me ever since."

Nobody said much for a few miles as we inched through holiday traffic, stoplights blinking a bright red and green, shoppers rushing home with their presents. "So, you saw the article and got a job with Margie," I broke the silence.

Cassie nodded, a little subdued. "I've always been passionate about flowers, so working at a florist shop was a natural. I asked around and discovered that Margie was the florist you guys always used. When I saw that delivery slip for flowers to Judge Stone, you can imagine how excited I was."

"And you gave him a shot of something, or tampered with his IV?" I asked.

"Digitalis, the same as Saul. It's a derivative of foxglove leaves. A few clicks on the Internet, and making your own is a cinch. Since Stone already had heart issues, it didn't set off any alarms, which was important. The deaths couldn't be suspicious, or I couldn't continue."

I met my mother's gaze in the rear view mirror. Unbelievable!

"Then I took those discs. The way Saul had guarded them, I figured they contained something important, and I had heard him tell Angela they referred to old cases. Oscar's cases as it turned out, but I didn't know that. I hoped there might be something about my dad."

"And the passwords?"

"That part was easy. I followed Saul for days, figuring out the best way to kill him. When I first started tracking him, I sent him an email with an embedded spyware program and retrieved lots of information about his password, which was his date of birth. He used the same one for everything - online banking, email accounts. Know thy enemy."

"And when you opened the discs, you read about Oscar fixing cases," Mom prompted.

"Something clicked then. In my heart, I'd always known my dad had been framed and something was screwy with the case. Sure enough, there it was."

"Saul didn't have anything on the discs about your dad, though," Mom pointed out.

"Not specifically, but it showed a precedent, a long-term pattern of abuse."

This definitely wasn't the time to tell her that before his execution, her father had sent a note apologizing to the widow of the security guard he had slain. Something else occurred to me. "That's why you changed your MO. No more poisons or deaths that didn't arouse much suspicion."

"It wasn't a conscious decision." Her voice hardened. "But then I saw Oscar sitting there all dressed up, so smug with his bag of gifts. It didn't seem fair that he should enjoy another Christmas, when he had ruined mine for twenty years. I mean, a Santa Claus? That bastard."

"Why did you send us the discs?" Mom changed the subject, lightening the mood.

Cassie shrugged. "My plan was still a good one, and more important than ever now that a full-blown murder investigation is underway. I knew you wouldn't turn the discs over to the cops right away. An anonymous phone call to the DA's office - they don't record their calls the way the cops do - would buy me the time I needed to finish my list. You would get caught with the discs and stop investigating. Suspicion would turn to you, or the cops would figure you were protecting Angela. Either way, I stayed off the radar. It was nice of Jack Lassiter to take the bait and be my fall guy, but it didn't buy me as much time as I had hoped."

Cassie's matter-of-fact avenging angel tone was chilling. Still that petulant child who had been denied what she wanted for Christmas, she was killing anyone she blamed for her displeasure. Did that include us?

"You left something out." Mom said.

"What? Oh, you mean the hand. That didn't turn out the way I had planned."

"You meant it to scare Saul." Mom stated.

"I wanted him to feel powerless, to have people look at him with suspicion and to feel things happening to him that he couldn't control."

"But he didn't play along," I pointed out.

"He turned the whole thing into a joke that helped him sell more of his vile books."

"How did you get the hand in the first place?"

"How'd you get the hand in the first place?"

"Like I said, I'd been following Saul to figure out the best way to kill him. I wanted to know his routine, his Achilles heel. I was there, hidden at the warehouse, when he talked to two friends of Trianos's. They were sweating this guy about some missing money, not because they thought he took it, but because they thought he knew who did. The guy starts blubbering, admits to everything. Saul must've figured out was about to happen and got the hell out of there. I didn't think I could leave without getting caught so I stayed put."

"They shot the guy?"

"It was quick. The cutting up part, not so much. They left to find a place to dump him and I took the hand. That guy wasn't using it."

"That's disgusting," I said.

"That's disgusting," I said.

Cassie shrugged.

"Then there's the matter of the Godiva chocolates," I reminded her. "Not cool."

"I'm sorry about that. I am. Margie came back to the store saying something about a DVD she overheard y'all talking about at Monica Dupree's house, and I panicked. You were probably the only people who could've put two and two together."

"I could've died!"

"But you didn't. The nitrobenzene was in insecticide we use in the shop, and I didn't use too much."

"I was sick for three days." Give or take.

"Who knew you would eat so much chocolate in one sitting? I thought a little scare would deter you, but you couldn't stay out of it, could you?"

"Like I'm going to give up after someone tried to kill me. That only strengthened my resolve."

"Most people, when they see death coming their way, turn and head in the other direction."

"I'm not most people. Must have more guts."

"Yeah? How's that working for you?" Cassie's voice was still pleasant, but her grip tightened on the gun in her lap.

"Drop it, Chloe," Mom said as we turned into Arbor Farms. "She's just pushing your buttons like you and your sister, Lily, always push mine."

That got my attention. Had the old girl lost her mind, or was she telling me something?

As we passed the Madison's house, I spotted Lady Chablis in the front yard. Get help boy, I telegraphed. LC trotted over to the crèche and sniffed one of the wise men. I turned away.

We pulled into Saul's portico. I was saddened by the neglected state of the decorations we had installed around the eaves and in the trees. Had it been only three weeks ago when Mom had assured Robin we had enough lights to be seen from the moon?

At that point, Judge Stone had been dead, and Saul and Oscar weren't long for this world. Three murders with more to come, and Cassie stood to get away with them all. We had to stop her, and we had to time things just right.

"Slide over behind me," Cassie ordered Mom, "and I'll let you out." To me, she added, "Don't try any funny stuff, or your mom gets it."

Think, I ordered myself. What was Mom telling me? Something about Lily and buttons.

I put my hands up. "I'll keep my hands where you can see them."

Cassie let Mom out the back and closed the door. Mom stumbled on the flagstone walkway, and Cassie prodded her with the gun. I scrambled out and slammed the door. Cassie tossed me the house key.

Inside, the air was chilly and stale. Cassie pointed to stairs off the kitchen that led down to a simply furnished game room with a bar, a big screen TV and sliding glass doors to the back patio.

"You'll be comfortable down there. I'll even put in a DVD if you see anything you like."

We preceded her down the stairs with Mom in the lead. My heart was pounding, knowing we only had her word that she wouldn't kill us. Would she shoot me first, or would I watch my mother die, knowing I was next? How long would our bodies molder before they found us? How long would Jacob sit at the restaurant before he decided he had been stood up and should, therefore, sleep with the waitress?

I felt light-headed, but fought to control my emotions. Life couldn't end in this way.

Cassie reached into her satchel and removed a jumbo roll of duct tape.

"Amanda, you do Chloe. Tight. I'll be checking." With her gun she pointed to two heavy steel, ladder-back armchairs.

"Put those in front of the television and think about what movie you want to watch. Saul has a pretty good collection, and y'all may be here a long time."

Mom began taping my ankles to the legs of the chair. "Don't ever let me catch you sitting like this in public," she said. "That skirt leaves little to the imagination."

"You crack me up." Cassie waved Mom into a chair. "Do your own ankles."

Mom did as she was told.

"Now your left wrist as best as you can," Cassie ordered.

It was awkward, but Mom managed and tossed Cassie the tape. Cassie tore off a long piece and taped Mom's right wrist. Not that there was any point struggling. She had proven herself only too willing to take a life, and I didn't think, in a pinch, she would be all that picky.

Once Mom was taped, Cassie added more tape to each of our extremities. We weren't going anywhere.

"Movie?" she asked, the good little hostess.

"Not really in the mood," I declined.

"Suit yourself."

Cassie tucked the roll of tape into her satchel, then held up Mom's key ring. "Which one's your front door key?"

"Why would you need to know that?" Mom asked.

Cassie looked disappointed. "You mean you haven't guessed? There are still a few names on my Christmas list. The bastard who testified against my father died two years ago of a brain aneurism, but the lawyer who defended him is still very much alive."

"Dear God, no!" Mom cried.

"Ah, the light dawns," Cassie said and calmly walked out of the house.

CHAPTER 40

"Did you do it?" Mom demanded in a whisper as soon as we were alone.

"She's going after Dad!" I said at the same time.

"Did you do it?"

"Of course!"

"We have to escape and warn your father."

I strained against the tape hoping for give. There was none. "We can't panic. I pushed the button. We've got that going for us."

It had been close, but I'd figured out what Mom had wanted me to do in the nick of time - push the OnStar emergency button the way Lily had when we first got the Caddy. Mission accomplished.

Mom tested the tightness of her own tape. "The police should be here soon, don't you think? What if the OnStar thing didn't work? Alex doesn't know to be wary of Cassie."

"How could it not work? I heard the chime just as I was getting out. That's why I slammed the door so fast. When the operator didn't get a response, she would've called the police and Dad, right?"

"Then why aren't they here?"

"Maybe they're tracking the car."

"Maybe you didn't push the button right."

I gaped at her. "It's a button. I pushed it. I heard the chime."

"We need to get out of here." Mom scanned the room. "Is there anything behind the bar we could use?"

"I could use a martini, but I don't know how we'd open the olive jar."

Clearly this was not the time for jokes.

"It would take us forever to get over there," I pointed out.

"We don't have forever. We have to get upstairs." Mom was obviously scared.

I couldn't see my watch for the duct tape, but I realized she was right. Why hadn't the police gotten here?

"Maybe if I just…" I pushed all my body weight forward until I was standing on my feet with the chair on my back. In this awkward position, the steel chair weighed a ton. My quads sang.

"Excellent." Mom spurred me on. "Can you walk?"

I staggered forward a step, then another.

"You're going the wrong way."

It was the most intense workout I'd ever done. My stomach muscles clenched, my legs shook and the tape pulled painfully at my skin. Somehow I managed to turn back around before having to sit down.

"Careful," Mom warned. "Don't fall over."

"I don't think I can make it," I gasped.

"You have to."

"No. I mean, physically, I don't think I can make it."

We heard the door at the top of the stairs open. We were saved!

"Thought I'd thank y'all for your OnStar trick - brilliant," Cassie called down. "The operator is sending Alex right over. Seems his daughter Chloe could use a little help. I said it before, and I'll say it again. You two crack me up."

She was still laughing when she shut the door.

"Chloe, I want you out of that chair now!"

I didn't even argue. I got back to my feet. The pain was worse this time, but I managed five more staggering steps before coming back down.

"Almost there!" Mom offered encouragement. "I hope you used a powerful antiperspirant. You sweat more than any girl I've ever seen."

I didn't have the energy for a biting retort. The front of the bar was a few steps away, and my next attempt brought me right to the edge of it.

"What do you see? Anything sharp?"

I ignored Mom because I saw something at the perfect height, mounted to the bar, its tiny silver point jutting forward.

"There's a bottle opener. If I can snag the tape on it, maybe I can loosen it," I said.

"Try!"

I rose on my shaking, sweating legs and angled the chair, so that the tape would snag on the point. My first two attempts failed, but three times is the charm. I dragged the blade dully across the silver surface.

"Anything?" Mom asked.

"I can't get it under the edge of the tape."

"You're doing great," she encouraged. "Keep at it."

On my next tries, I pressed the opener against my skin, snagged the tape and pulled as hard as I could. The point didn't cut, but it did stretch the tape from my skin, similar to pulling a bandage off over and over again. If I kept at it, I might stretch the tape away enough to wriggle my hand out. That was the plan anyway.

After what seemed like an eternity, using copious amounts of sweat as a lubricant, I was able to slide my right hand free. I grabbed the bar to keep from tumbling over backward.

"Thank you, God," Mom said. "Now your other one."

"It'll take too long. I'm finding a knife or something."

"Hurry! Cassie could come back down here any second to check on us."

That got me going. I reached down and felt the inside of one of my boots. The zipper wasn't covered by tape. What if I unzipped it and squeezed my foot out. Then the other. I stood and dragged the chair, still bound to me by one wrist, around to the bar where I found a pair of kitchen shears. Two seconds later, sore and drenched, I was free. I cut one of Mom's hands free, and handed her the shears.

"Go," she urged. "I'm right behind you."

I didn't risk going back up the stairs in case Cassie could see us from her vantage point. Instead I slipped through the doorway onto the back patio. Bare feet cold on the flagstones, I climbed up the steps of the tiered backyard to the back door where we had discovered the severed hand.

Here I crouched beneath the door's window and took a breath. Was Cassie standing on the other side waiting for me to take a peek? I had to chance it.

Edging my way up, I looked through the glass. Cassie was in the kitchen with her back to me, calmly reading the paper spread out on the counter. Not a care in the world.

Quietly, I tried the knob. Unlocked. Was this her escape route? Not if I could help it.

I would wait for Mom to run with me over to Monica's house and call the cops. But then I heard the one thing I didn't want to hear - the front door bell.

Cassie smiled and picked up her gun. "Come in," she called, in a voice that sounded uncannily like mine.

I revised my plan to something more swift and direct - running around the side of the house screaming "Daddy, no!"

I hadn't drawn breath, before I saw a uniformed cop creeping in my direction. The cavalry had arrived. I waved to get the cop's attention, pointing inside to where Cassie was heading toward the front door.

"Freeze!" He stood and aimed yet another gun at me.

What was with these people?

Cassie turned and looked out the window, immediately figuring out what was going on. She headed for the front of the house.

"Freeze!" the cop yelled again.

Like hell I would. I still had two parents unaccounted for.

I pushed through the side door and reflexively locked it behind me, as I headed after Cassie.

The house was too quiet. All adrenaline and courage drained out of me as I ran crouched over to the kitchen counter and waited, listening for any sound.

Had Dad come inside? Was Cassie holding him at gunpoint? Through the window I could see the cop radioing in, probably telling his cohorts to shoot me on sight.

I scooted over to the kitchen doorway and peered into the butler's pantry, then crawled to the next doorway. I could see Cassie in the foyer, peering unhappily through one of the entryway windows.

I pulled back into the butler's pantry, weak with relief that Dad wasn't visible.

"The house is surrounded. It's all over." I called to Cassie.

The ticking of Saul's grandfather clock was the only response.

Now what? Scary silence hadn't been in the script.

I sat with my back against the wall and took another breath. Was Cassie waiting for me to peek so she could blow my head off?

"Cassie?" My voice came out a whisper.

I chanced a quick peek at the foyer window.

She was gone.

Damn it.

Had she gone into Saul's study, up the stairs or into the living room? Crawling after her held no appeal. The cop had radioed in, so surely Dad was nowhere near the house.

I reversed my direction back to the kitchen. I'd go down the basement steps, make sure Mom was out of the house and run like hell to safety. Piece of cake.

Except that Cassie had circled back to the kitchen through the living room and now stood between the basement door and me.

"If I can't kill your father, I can kill someone he loves," she said to me. "Maybe there's justice in that."

I couldn't take my eyes off the gun. "Justice? You said yourself, this doesn't involve me."

"You got involved. I warned you to stay out of it."

"I couldn't. I care about my father as much as you cared about yours."

"Maybe we should see how much he cares about you - his life for yours."

My eyes filled with tears. "Why are you doing this? Why hurt another daughter the way you were hurt?"

Cassie started explaining her miserable childhood again, but I wasn't listening, my attention riveted to a shadow of movement under the basement door. Someone was standing right behind it. Mom?

I got to my feet. I wasn't going to die on my knees. "You can still get away, Cassie. You're standing in front of the basement door. Make a run for it."

"I don't care about me. I have to finish my list."

Was the doorknob turning? Please, please. Let the doorknob be turning.

"Run, Cassie. You'll never get to the names on your list now, but those folks won't have a moment's peace knowing you're still out there."

"I want it over."

"Safety is right there." I pointed over her shoulder. "You're so close."

I was overplaying my hand, making her suspicious, but it didn't matter.

The basement door flung open, knocking Cassie to one side, and I was on her. At the same time, the cop from outside kicked open the side door and yelled, "Freeze!" Obviously, the only cop skill he had mastered.

As the cop and Mom watched, Cassie and I grappled for the gun. Physically, we were matched, but she was a practiced killer with nothing to lose and I was a natural born 'fraidy cat. Cowardice trumped craziness, and I flung her toward the steps. She teetered on the top edge, reaching toward Mom.

With no hesitation, I closed my eyes and dove, hitting Cassie squarely in the chest and riding her downstairs like a toboggan. We slammed onto the basement floor, the gun went off and my world went black.

In the distance, I heard Mom scream and then many voices, other shouts and footsteps on the stairs.

The world came back into focus just in time for me to see Jacob leaning over me and to hear McGowan's sing-songy rendition of, "I see London, I see France, I see Chloe's underpants."

CHAPTER 41

The next day was Christmas Eve. Amidst the chaos of opening packages, trying on new clothes and exchanging heartfelt thanks for such thoughtful gifts, the horrors of the day before seemed like a bad dream.

Bridget and I had spent the night at Mom and Dad's house, so we could all watch Lily open her presents before she left to spend Christmas with her father. Now we were sitting down at brunch, everybody tired and happy, even me.

It had been hours since I'd had my last post-traumatic stress flashback, triggered not by having been poisoned, assaulted, tied up or shot at, but by the humiliation of having flashed my father, my boyfriend and eight members of the Birmingham police department. Jacob, who had arrived that morning, bearing bagels and croissants, was playing an important role in my recovery.

Last night, Mom and I had filled everyone in about our ordeal. This morning we were hearing the story from Dad and Jacob's perspective.

"The first call I got from the OnStar people said the emergency button had been activated, but they couldn't get a response from the Escalade or Amanda's cell phone." Dad buttered a cinnamon raisin bagel. "The air bags hadn't been deployed, so they didn't think there'd been an accident. We wondered if it was a button malfunction or Lily up to her old tricks, so we held off notifying the police and traced the car."

"Better safe than sorry, right?" I interjected.

My father ignored my sarcasm, but really, a more prompt arrival on their part might've saved a lot of effort and exposed flesh on mine.

Dad topped off my mimosa with more juice. Subtle. "About ten minutes later I received another call from the OnStar folks," he continued. "This time saying that Chloe had lost her purse and her keys and wants me to bring a second set. Still no word from Amanda."

He passed the cream to Jacob. "I couldn't figure out why Chloe was driving the Cadillac, and when I heard the address and realized it was Saul's house, I knew something was off. I remembered you two had a date so I called Jacob."

"I told Alex you hadn't shown up," Jacob said, stirring his coffee. "We called the cops and headed over to Saul's."

I tried to look nonchalant, but had a feeling my eyes were telegraphing, "My hero."

"Detective McGowan didn't think we were just causing trouble again?" Mom admired the diamond tennis bracelet Dad had given her that morning.

Dad shook his head. "He wasn't taking any chances. He met us in front of the house, sent cops around back, and then he and I rang the front doorbell."

"Which is when I met up with Mr. Loud Mouth Rookie Cop," I pointed out.

"When a cop says freeze," Bridget said, "you freeze."

"I thought Cassie was going to kill Dad, and Mom was nowhere to be found."

Turned out I had cut the tape on Mom's left hand instead of her right. As she had tried to cut the tape from her right hand, the shears had dropped and bounced just out of reach. She had tipped the chair over and scooted to the shears. None of us could picture the scene.

Inevitably the conversation turned to Cassie.

"Part of me thinks it'd be better if she never woke up," Bridget said, and the room fell silent.

Cassie had been rushed to the hospital, having sustained a massive head trauma from our ride down the stairs. She hadn't yet regained consciousness only to end up like her father, and like Bridget, I almost hoped she wouldn't, unable to reconcile with the fact that such a cute, likeable young woman was a multiple murderer.

"She seemed so sweet, like a really down-to-earth girl," I said. "I don't remember one malicious thing about her. Yet all along..." I thought I'd cried out all my tears during the previous night, but apparently not.

"She's obviously ill, seeing herself as a good person, but something inside her, some fundamental problem with her wiring, turned her into a monster," Mom soothed. "Chilling, isn't it, how one long-ago crime can leave so much damage in its wake."

"Or how much damage parents can do on their kids." I wiped my eyes.

"What happened when you heard the gun shot?" Bridget asked Dad.

Cassie's gun hand had hit the floor, the weapon had gone off and decimated Saul's plasma screen TV.

"Everyone went crazy," Dad exchanged an odd look with Jacob.

Just how shaken up had my hero been, I wondered. Shaken up enough to shake some sense into him? The idea bore further investigation when I got Dad alone.

"McGowan kicked the door in," Dad continued, "and we all rushed in after him."

"You, too?" I asked Jacob.

"They had told me to wait in the car, but I'm not any better at following orders than you are."

"We heard the commotion on the stairs and headed for the basement," Dad finished.

"And got there just in time to catch Chloe's floor show," Jacob teased.

"Watch it. I have lots of friends in the Birmingham police department, and they won't stand for your harassing me."

"Not that they could pick your face out of a line up," Bridget chuckled. "Polka dot panties maybe, but not your face."

I glared at Mom, equal parts blame-the-mother and spare-me-the-lecture.

"Don't give me that look," Mom responded. "It wasn't my fault you ended up in such a position, and what do I care if you choose underwear no bigger than a pirate's eye patch? You're a grown woman."

Bridget took pity on me and switched the topic to our parents' gift to us - a family trip to San Francisco in the spring, during which we would hit the shops on Fisherman's Wharf and drive up the coast.

The doorbell rang and I jumped up to get it, blueberry bagel in hand.

Mom shot me her "a lady doesn't walk and chew at the same time" frown to which I responded by opening up and showing her a mouthful of masticated bread, jelly and cream cheese. Her raised eyebrow said it all, "Thirty and still not married? Hard to believe."

I had invited Angela to share the holiday with us, and she had been only slightly put out by the suggestion. It was a start, but that's not who was at the door. A deliveryman handed me a beautifully wrapped box with a tag addressed to my mother.

"What on earth?" Mom exclaimed, admiring the lovely cobalt and silver wrapping encased in a huge organza bow. She opened the box, looking stunned by what was inside and downright shocked by the enclosed card.

"Who sent it?" I demanded.

Mom was speechless.

Bridget yanked the box from her hand. "Your Waterford Hope for Healing ornament. The one you've been looking for." Then she read the card aloud, "Heard you cracked the case. Beauty and brains, a delightful combination. Hope you'll join me for some more spanakopita soon."

My sister didn't bother to read the signature. She didn't have to.

"Nice going, Mom," I said. "Now Dad will have to join the witness protection program, all because some gangster has the hots for you."

"The hots?" Mom sent me a withering glance. "What kind of talk is that?"

Dad only laughed. "I'm not going anywhere. Tony Trianos can send all the gifts he wants. I've got a pretty big head start on wooing your mother."

Mom gave him a kiss. "No competition."

I snuck a peek at Jacob, hoping my parents' affection might be contagious. I couldn't have explained why, but I had a feeling we'd turned a corner in our relationship.

He had given me an iPod for Christmas, preloaded with all of my favorite songs, and it wasn't the Mini either, which hinted at deeper love and lasting commitment. Jacob gave me a little smile as if he could read my thoughts, and I smiled back.

Oh, yeah. His days were numbered.

From now on, I'd be relentless. I'd be fearless. I'd be...Mom. It was the one thing I hadn't tried. I'd grown up complaining about my mother's brand of sugar-coated manipulation, but now that I was grown up I had to admit that it worked.

I would just have to be patient and let my natural charm do its work, but Jacob needed to say some things and I needed to hear some things besides the voices in my head.

We cleaned up the breakfast dishes and were making plans for seeing a movie before church when the doorbell rang a second time.

"It's Grand Central around here," I said, going to answer it.

"Merry Christmas Eve," said McGowan.

I smiled. "Back atcha."

"I don't want to interrupt the festivities, but I thought maybe you guys could use this." He handed me a bottle of champagne - the good stuff.

"Thanks. And if you've got any more cases you'd like us to work on..."

"Not likely." But he smiled back at me.

"Tell Jacob to give me a call about that scrimmage." Given my luck with men, I hadn't been surprised to learn that my boyfriend and McGowan played soccer in the same league. I'd have to start going to the games again. You know me and soccer players.

"I'll do that."

Suddenly McGowan leaned in and kissed me. Very innocently. On the cheek.

"Mistletoe." He pointed at the greenery over the door.

"Actually, that's holly, but close enough."

"Merry Christmas, Chloe."

"You, too." Yankee.

Later, when my mother and I were alone, packing away the silver in the dining room, I gave her a hug. "We did it."

"Of course, we did. Was there ever any doubt?"

We laughed, knowing there had been. Lots of them. But there had been lots of surprises, too. Like how well our differences worked for us, for a change.

I hadn't felt threatened by the poised and pragmatic side of my mother that was so unlike me, and she hadn't despaired at the emotional, impulsive streak she saw in me. We now appreciated and respected our differences.

Respected them. For the first time, I felt the beginnings of a friendship with her - the kind adult women have. The kind she and Bridget have had as long as I can remember.

Apparently, her thoughts had been running along the same lines.

"You know." Mom smiled. "I'm not sure this retirement thing is working out so well. I've enjoyed being busy the past couple of months and might want to return to work - not full time, but select projects here and there."

"I think you should." I rubbed a silver knife and placed it back in its case. "Your clients would be thrilled."

"I'd need a partner. Someone with a good eye and loads of talent. Someone I would enjoy working with." She saw my blank look. "A daughter, perhaps."

I frowned, wondering where Bridget would find time to do interior design with her crazy nursing schedule and Lily.

"You, Chloe. I mean you." With some effort, she fixed a patient look on her face.

I was surprised by her offer and strangely flattered.

But…

"I don't know. Would you be the boss?" Negotiating curtains wouldn't be any easier than negotiating curfews.

"Partner. You would have your projects, and I'd have mine. Occasionally, we would collaborate if you think that we could."

"I think this last month proves we can. Pretty well, in fact. So, yeah. Partners."

She picked up a silver fork I had placed in the box and gave it another polish. "Now, Chloe, about those panties."

OTHER TITLES AVAILABLE FROM ANNIE ACORN PUBLISHING LLC

By Annie Acorn

Chocolate Can Kill

Murder With My Darling

A Stranger Comes to Town

The Young Executive

When to Remain Silent

On the Road

The Magic Sand Dollar

One More Christmas Past

One Last Gift To Go

A Haunting Christmas

Too Busy for Christmas

An Afghan of Many Colors

A Tired Older Woman: Loses Weight and Keeps It Off!

How to Survive Your New Home Purchase

How to Survive Your 203K Mortgage

By Beverly J. Crawford

A B-17 Christmas

The Christmas Child

The Best Homemade Christmas

While Shepherds Watched

Towards the Sun

By Peggy Teel writing as denise hays

Niki Knows the Dirt – A Niki Edgar Mystery

Merry Christmas Minus One

Walking for Weight Loss

By Peggy Teel

God and Grandma

Christmas in Tartan Glen

The Best Worst Christmas

A Merry Mary Christmas

By Juliette Hill

Pink Lemonade Diary

Two Beaux for Christmas

Christmas Shoppe Magic

The Christmas Spirit of Starlight Cove

By Angel Nichols

Christmas in the Mojave

By Sheila Lawrence

The More the Merrier

A Silent Night

Ho Ho Ho and a Bottle of Rum

All titles also available for NOOK!

Billie Thomas

Billie Thomas is the pseudonym of a Birmingham-based author. After the real Billie passed away unexpectedly at the end of 2011, getting *Murder on the First Day of Christmas,* the first of a series, revised and published was her daughter's top priority as a way to honor the mom who had given her a lifelong love of books.

In her real life, Ms. Thomas writes within the advertising industry and is a founding member of the writing collective, IndieVisible. Other publications include *Bar Code: Your Personal Pocket Decoder to the Modern Dating Scene.*

The author enjoys combining her interests in decorating and gourmet cooking with her writing. She is still trying to solve the mystery of her own love life.

Ms. Thomas welcomes your contacts at chloe@chloegetsaclue.com. You are welcome to friend her on Facebook as chloe.carstairs.73 and to tweet with her as @ChloeGetsAClue.

CPSIA information can be obtained at www.ICGtesting.com
Printed in the USA
LVOW01s0256071213

364292LV00024B/464/P